WHEN *the*
RIVER CALLS

With warm regards,

[signature]

Crossings of Promise
Historical fiction with a touch of romance

Dianne Christner
Keeper of Hearts

Janice L. Dick
Calm Before the Storm
Eye of the Storm

Hugh Alan Smith
When Lightning Strikes
When the River Calls

Heather Tekavac
Cost of Passage

WHEN *the* RIVER CALLS

HUGH ALAN SMITH

Herald
Press

Waterloo, Ontario
Scottdale, Pennsylvania

National Library of Canada Cataloguing in Publication
Smith, Hugh Alan, 1954-
    When the river calls / Hugh Alan Smith.
(Crossings of promise)
ISBN 0-8361-9268-0
    1. Hutterite Brethren—History—Fiction.
I. Title. II. Series.
PS8587.M5383W47 2004   C813'.6   C2003-906467-0

Scripture is from the Holy Bible, *New International Version* © 1973, 1978, 1984 by the International Bible Society. Used by permission of Zondervan Publishing House. All rights reserved.

The preacher's quote on page 13 is from John A. Hostetler, *Hutterite Society* (Baltimore: The Johns Hopkins University Press, 1974).

WHEN THE RIVER CALLS
Copyright © 2004 by Herald Press, Waterloo, Ont. N2L 6H7.
    Published simultaneously in USA by Herald Press,
    Scottdale, Pa. 15683. All rights reserved
Canadiana Entry Number: C2003-906467-0
Library of Congress Control Number: 2003114341
International Standard Book Number: 0-8361-9268-0
Printed in the United States of America
Cover art by Barbara Kiwak
Cover design by Sans Serif Design Inc.

10 09 08 07 06 05 04 10 9 8 7 6 5 4 3 2 1

To order or request information, please call
1-800-759-4447 (individuals); 1-800-245-7894 (trade).
Website: www.heraldpress.org

*To Beth, my wife
for the love we share*

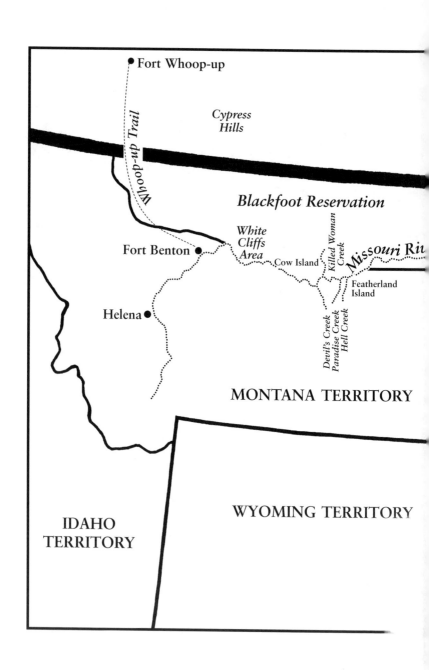

Acknowledgments

Where does my help come from? As Hannah might affirm, it comes from the Lord, for which I am eternally grateful.

Just as Hannah might not have reached the end of her personal journey without an occasional helping hand, I could not have written this book without the timely help of others. I would like to thank the following people: my wife, Beth, and my daughters for their love and encouragement; my friends and students at Springview and Armada Colonies for their interest and willingness to answer my many questions; and the readers of *When Lightning Strikes* who have encouraged me to keep writing.

I am grateful to Mark Bettis, author of *For Wood and Water: Steamboating on the Missouri River*, for the e-mail correspondence about steamboat travel; John Lepley, author of *Birthplace of Montana: A History of Fort Benton* and *Packets to Paradise: Steamboating to Fort Benton*, for taking the time to visit and share his expertise; Hank Armstrong, archivist at the Overholser Historical Research Center in Fort Benton, for staying after hours to help me dig through the center's myriad historical maps and documents; Rowena (www.steamboatrowena.com), who was named after the steamboat *Rowena*, and Captain Donald J. Sanders, a modern-day steamboat captain, for sharing their knowledge.

I appreciate the Reverend David Waldner and his family for showing my wife and me around Bon Homme Colony, and inviting us to stay in their home; Joe Tschetter (for the tour of Old Elm Spring, New Elm Springs, and Milltown Colonies) and his family (for the hospitality); Tony Waldner (for sharing from the wealth of his knowledge on Hutterite history) and his family (for so warmly accommodating Beth and me in their home); and Arnold Hofer, Hutterite historian, for the encouragement and invaluable discussions of Hutterite life.

Thanks, too, to David Berry, for helping me access some much-needed library resources; and the folks at the Gem Jubilee Library, for their unending patience and understanding about overdue books.

Finally, I would like to thank T. Davis Bunn for the continued friendship and guidance; and Sarah Kehrberg, my editor, and the others at Herald Press for seeing the value in bringing *When the River Calls* to publication and doing so much to make it the best novel it can be.

SPLIT ROCK
HUTTERITE COLONY,

SOUTH DAKOTA TERRITORY,

1880

Chapter 1

I crossed the trowelled straw-and-cow-dung entryway floor and entered the worship room. Andreas Wurz, at the front, happened to look up. His face was grim. I nodded respectfully, then found a seat by my Mueter—my mother—on the women's side of the church. It was hot already.

"Hannah, where have your been?" Mueter whispered. "The singing is almost over."

"Little Barbara hit her head on the walk. She needed help." The children were playing on their own in the yard.

The preacher's shrill voice sang out, and the congregation followed him, line for line, through another funeral song. I felt the sadness rise in my breast, but found comfort in the mournful singing. Then it was over, and the preacher picked up the sermon book and began to read. Like all of our sermons, it was old, almost as old as our 350 years of Hutterite tradition.

"Today we are fresh, healthy, and strong," the preacher read. "Tomorrow the body withers and health and strength are gone. When God takes to himself again what belongs to him, what is left but a dead corpse—a stinking abode for worms, which you cannot preserve, be it ever so dear to you. We must soon rush to the grave, else we must guard the nose from its stench."

How horrid, I thought, but that is how it is with us. An earthly body is just a body, and not the most important thing. The spirit, off to heaven, is what counts.

I heard crying in the family row by the coffin—Paul's four older stepsisters. Heaven or no, it isn't easy to say good-bye.

I looked across the coffin at Andreas on the men's side. Paul should have been beside him. Why was he gone?

Sometimes life hardly seemed fair. Was it only six years ago that I had sat watching Paul at the funeral in Hutterdorf Village in the Russian Ukraine? How awful it had been for Paul to see his parents struck down by lightning. My heart had gone out to him, but in his bitterness he had been hard to befriend. He blamed God and, even more, he blamed himself for what had happened.

And how he had hated his Sannah *Basel*—his Aunt Sannah —who had been so hard and so tormented herself. Thank God they had made their peace. It was a miracle the way so much misunderstanding and dislike had turned to love. But now Sannah was dead, and Paul had disappeared. Where was he, the best friend I had ever known?

Everyone filed out of the building. Booted feet boomed on the plank flooring of the church, then scuffled across the entryway floor, which I noticed was getting rough. Soon the men would have to resurface it with another batch of cow dung and straw. Such flooring would never do for a fancy New York hotel, but it was hard and smooth—and cheap. Good enough for us in these frugal times.

The pallbearers slid the coffin into the wagon and the driver flicked the reins. We all followed to the cemetery at the colony's western edge.

"I'm going to miss old Sannah." It was Checkela, my thirteen-year-old brother, falling into step beside me. His real name was Jacob, but he'd been called Checkela, or Little Jakey, ever since our mother married Jacob Stahl, our step-father. Our own father had been killed in a sawmill accident.

"She was a wonderful woman, Check—at least since coming here. Remember how awful she was to Paul when he first came to the colony in Russia?"

"She was a terror, for sure," Checkela agreed.

I remembered how Paul could do nothing right in Sannah's eyes after she and Andreas first adopted him. Sannah's youngest and favorite son, Daniel, had died of pneumonia, and it seemed that all of the love and goodness in Sannah's heart had gone to the grave with him. Paul could not measure up to Sannah's memories of her perfect lost son.

"What do you suppose changed her?" Checkela wondered.

"The epidemic, I guess." That had been the worst part of our trip to America. Thirty-four children and one old man dead to dysentery during our stay in Lincoln, Nebraska. "Maybe all that dying woke Sannah up to the beauty of living," I said.

Checkela smiled at that. "Pretty flowery, Hannah. What do you think you are? A poet?"

"As if you could tell," I retorted. "You wouldn't know a poem if it kissed you on the lips." I knew that would please him. He fancied himself a straight-thinking practical man.

"Kissed by a poem? Come off it," he muttered. "You're thinking about kissing because Paul isn't here."

I stopped dead. "That is a stupid thing to say! And you can go walk with somebody else." As if he knew my feelings! Or my worries. Not that I hadn't been worrying for over a year. But something about Sannah's passing filled me with a new dread for Paul. He should have been here.

Checkela was instantly contrite. "I'm sorry, Hannah. I shouldn't have said that. I know how you feel about him."

I bristled. "Check, I worry about Paul the same as everybody else. He is a member of our community, and a friend. Now I don't want to hear any more about it."

"I know exactly what you mean," Checkela said. "Just like everybody else." I walked the rest of the way to the cemetery in silence, chafing at the knowing smugness in Checkela's voice. Sometimes I thought the world would be a better place without younger brothers.

We watched the pallbearers lower Sannah into the grave. Shovels flashed in the sun, dirt flew into the hole, and Sannah Wurz was gone forever.

Oh, how this sight would have hurt Paul. When he found out, would he forgive himself for not being here? And where was he anyway? Not gone forever. *Please, God*, I prayed, *not gone forever, too.*

As if in sympathy with my feelings, the mournful lament of a steamboat whistle echoed across the muddy Missouri River, which flowed not fifty yards from the colony.

Chapter 2

"*F*ater—Father—all I'm saying is why can we not just look a little?"

My stepfather's face tightened in exasperation. "Hannah, nobody but the good Lord himself even knows where we could look."

"The steamboat levee in Yankton or Running Water. You read the note."

"There are dozens of steamboats on the Missouri. Besides, he could be at the other end of the Mississippi by now, in . . . whatever it is down there—Louisiana."

"But we cannot just abandon him. What if he needs our help?"

My father sighed, and massaged his black beard with his fingers. "You know what the colony elders said."

"I can't help it if the elders don't care about Paul," I retorted.

"Hannah, you are too headstrong. They say only that Paul has the right to make up his own mind, which is more than you seem willing to allow. We cannot go chasing after him as if he were a criminal running from the law. Is one not free to leave the colony as he wishes?"

"But what if he is in trouble? He would have explained where he was going if he could. You know Paul."

"Jon, Hannah, yes, I know Paul. The question of his leaving has always been open. Now he has gone. It is out of our hands."

"He was going to come back," I said stubbornly.

17

"Until he does, he has chosen not to be a part of the colony. Even Andreas agrees."

"Andreas is befuddled by grief." Poor Andreas. Paul's adoptive father. It had been hard on him to lose Paul. Now he had lost his dear Sannah as well, the wife of thirty-six years. "Besides, I told you how worried Sannah was," I added.

"Sannah was dying, daughter. It was natural that she wanted Paul by her side."

"Listen to your father, Hannah. You know he would love for Paul to come back. But Paul is eighteen years old, more than old enough to make his own decisions." My mother gently touched my shoulder and looked at me with her deep brown eyes. Eyes like my own, though mine, I'm told, are larger. Paul says I have the biggest, most amazing eyes he knows. He once said it was my eyes that saved him. The idiot. What would save him now? Or maybe I was the idiot. Maybe everyone else was right. What could he possibly need saving from? But still, I had my intuition.

"*Ma Lieba*—my love," Mueter was saying, "if you are lonesome, why not give some thought to the other young men who admire you?"

Lonesome? What was she thinking? "Mueter," I bristled indignantly, "it is not for being lonesome that I want to find Paul. There is something not right, and I am worried for a friend. That is all!"

She glanced at Fater, who had suddenly taken a great interest in fixing a loose foot on the potbellied stove in the middle of the room. She raised an eyebrow and added, "Well, anyway, this is a good time to meet friends with so many here for the funeral."

Friends indeed! I knew what she meant. It was one of our Hutterite ways. With travel so limited, funerals and weddings were two of the best times for young people to get to know prospective marriage partners.

"Lorenz Hofer is here," Mueter continued. "He would trip over his own feet just to be near you."

"Goodness, Mueter! Lorenz Hofer would trip over his own feet sitting at the dinner table."

"So visit with someone else!" she snapped. Then she softened again. "I'm only thinking of you, *Lieba*. Let Paul be Paul. Perhaps it is time for you to start thinking with whom you might spend your life. You have eighteen years already yourself."

I looked squarely at my mother, feeling a mixture of sadness and resolve. "Yes, Mueter, I suppose you are right." Yet if Paul was in trouble, shouldn't someone try to find him?

What else had Mueter said? *Eighteen is more than enough to make one's own decisions.* Paul wasn't the only eighteen-year-old. Perhaps it was time for me to make a decision of my own.

Chapter 3

Sitting on my bed in the attic, I once again examined Sannah's envelope marked with the single word, "Paul." I had climbed the stairs and closed the trap door to keep my sisters from surprising me. Our family lived on the top floor of what we called the high house, a huge two-story building made from great chalkstone blocks that the men had quarried from the yellow bluffs across the river. The apartments, twelve on the top and twelve on the ground floor, were 12 by 15 feet each. It was cramped, but since the cooking and dining were done in the communal kitchen, we didn't need much space. Our family was large enough to get attic space for extra beds.

I looked at the contents of the envelope. How strange that this should come to me after so many years, and stranger yet to have it come from Sannah. It had been only five days ago, yet it seemed like a lifetime. For Sannah, it was.

I thought back to how it had started for Sannah, with the terrible pain in her abdomen that had doubled her over and made her vomit and cry. Then suddenly, the pain had eased. Everyone breathed a sigh of relief, but by the next day her belly was swollen and she was nearly out of her head with fever. I sat with her while Andreas, worn out from the vigil, rested. "There, there, Sannah," I murmured, stroking her face with a damp cloth. "You must be strong. They have gone to Yankton for the doctor." Yankton was an eighteen-mile wagon ride to the east. I hoped they were driving hard. "He will have you better in no time." I sounded more convincing than I felt.

"Paul, tell us where you are." Sannah was mumbling. "No one will look for you. Who will look after you?"

"It's all right, Sannah *Basel*." Sometimes I called her aunt, just out of love. "Paul is a man now. He needs no more looking after." That too was easier for me to say than believe.

Suddenly, Sannah's eyes popped open and she clutched my arm. The blue of her irises sparkled, as if a lamp had been lit behind them. "Hannah? Hannah, is it you?"

"Yes, Sannah. Are you feeling better?"

"My chest. Take it from my chest." The urgency in her voice was frightening.

"Take what, Sannah? Does your chest hurt badly?"

"No, Hannah. My red clothes chest. From my clothes chest." I looked at her stupidly. "Open it," she said.

Her red wooden chest, the kind that every Hutterite woman owned for clothes and personal effects, was against the wall. I crossed the room and lifted the lid. "I'm opening it, Sannah. What do you need?"

"In the bottom. With the letters." I dug to the bottom of the chest until I found a large folded brown paper.

"Here they are. Would you like me to read some to you?"

"Perhaps for such a time as this, I have kept it safe. Use it to find Paul, if no one will go."

"Use what? A letter?" But she was lying back, eyes closed again. And then I realized, *Yes, a letter. Paul must have sent a letter telling where he is. But why hadn't she told anyone?* I leafed through the envelopes. Some were from Russia, some from Tripp Colony where Sannah and Andreas's son and two daughters lived. Some were from their other daughters at Wolf Creek Colony. But one, tucked right in the middle, was marked with the single word, "Paul." Quickly, but as carefully as I could, I broke open the wax seal. "Paul, oh Paul,"

I could not help but murmur. "Tell me where you've gone."

But to my surprise, instead of a letter there were four neatly folded, but worn, fifty-dollar bills. I remembered: they were worn from being inside Paul's shoe. I leaned close to Sannah's ear, and whispered, "Sannah, I cannot take this. It is Paul's."

She opened her eyes again, and reached for my hand, more feebly now. "He would not take it, Hannah. For pride or providence, I know not which. Use it as you see fit, for your sake and Paul's."

"But Sannah, I . . . It's not really that way," I stammered.

She smiled weakly. "I think Paul needs you, Hannah."

I said nothing. How could I argue with one so sick?

The doctor had arrived just in time to poke and prod and tell us that Sannah was infected inside. "Probably a burst appendix," he pronounced, shaking his head. "I am afraid she is apt to perish." And twelve hours later, she did. Without returning, the doctor did the paperwork in Yankton. The final chapter of Sannah's life ended with two cold words on a death certificate: *cholera morbus*.

~

I smoothed the fifty-dollar bills and laid them on the goose-down duvet on my bed. I remembered when Paul and I had found his mother's little treasure box back in Russia. It contained 500 rubles that would have been used for farm machinery had Paul's parents not been killed. Paul had hidden the money from Sannah, and changed it to American dollars at the Castle Garden immigration station. When he gave up his plans to run away, he presented the money to Sannah to turn over to the colony. But Sannah had softened, and told him she would keep it until he was old enough to decide, once and for all, whether communal life was for him. Now I had the money, and an assignment from Sannah. What was I to do?

Chapter 4

Maybe Paul could help me decide. I went to my own red-painted chest and found the letter. It was dated Tuesday, April 13, 1880. I unfolded the paper and scanned the lines, disappointed as usual. It didn't say much.

> Dear Hannah,
>   Sometimes opportunity knocks suddenly. Feel I ought to take new job, strange as it is. You may wonder at this, but I will write more when leisure allows. Have barely enough time to get to post before steamboat leaves. Remember me to Sannah and Andreas, and tell all not to worry. One last adventure.
>> Ever your friend,
> > Paul

How annoying he was, being so cryptic. Where was he, and what had happened that he did not write to explain himself? Two months went by, and not another word.

So he had caught a steamboat. As passenger or crew? I remembered how he had run away in Lincoln, Nebraska, when we first arrived in America. He had worked as a cabin boy on a gambling boat, of all things, until he got sick in the dysentery epidemic. Between sickness and seeing a cowboy shot by a gambler, I thought he'd had enough of riverboat travel. Yet he was gone again.

The long booming whistle of another steamboat sounded on the Missouri. Perhaps he was on that very boat. How often I had stood on the banks watching them go by—the *Far West*, *Key West*, and *Nellie Peck*, the *Red Cloud*, *Benton*, and *Rosebud*, the *General Sherman*, *General Terry*, *Josephine*, and more—wondering whether Paul might be standing on the deck looking toward home, almost within reach, yet a world away. Yet, if that were so, why hadn't he written?

I shuddered to think what might have happened. The river bottom was littered with the hulks of wrecked steamboats. Everyone knew that snags in the river, boiler explosions, fires, and a host of other mishaps had sunk hundreds of them. Few boats lasted longer than eight or nine years.

I thought regretfully about the letter I had sent to Paul just a few weeks before receiving his. I had only been teasing, I think. Or maybe, underneath, I had been trying to manipulate him. Maybe I thought that by telling him how Lorenz Hofer liked me so much, how steady, boring men sometimes made the best husbands, I would bring Paul home. That was a problem with colony life: men had the power, the opportunity to take action. Women had to wait on their decisions, which made it tempting to be manipulative. I had given in and written a very stupid letter. Maybe it had set Paul free.

He had never quite given up on the idea that he might homestead with the *Prairieleut* and become a non-communal Hutterite as his father had been in Russia. So he had taken a job with Joseph Wallman, up the James River. "I will go for a year," he had said, "and then I will know for sure. I'll either be back to stay, or gone for good." I had certainly expected him to come home. After all, the year was up. But he hadn't come back. Then came our exchange of letters.

I wished I could have my letter back to do over, to tell him how I really felt. But how did I feel? I wanted to look into his gray-blue eyes, run my fingers through his sandy brown hair.

Or punch him in the nose! He always did make me crazy.

I put the letter away, and opened the attic door. Normally, I'd have been over at the kitchen helping prepare supper, but after an early lunch for the visiting funeral crowd, there was no formal evening meal. Still, I felt hungry. I headed for the garden to sneak a few peas.

≈

The shrillness of my own scream surprised me. Scratchy legs kicked and rubbed on my stomach, and I scrambled wildly to get away. Yanking my blouse loose, I hopped up and down, shaking like an Arabian belly dancer I once read about in a newspaper.

Finally, it leaped away, probably glad to be out of my blouse as I was to see it go. I felt the heat in my face, and knew I was blushing. I glanced quickly side-to-side and was grateful to see no one watching.

Paul would have laughed and called me ridiculous, but I have hated grasshoppers since our arrival in South Dakota. I remembered that first summer—1874. It had been a beautiful day when the plague began. The sky was hot and bright until a huge cloud blotted the sun, so thick that it cooled the air. The whole colony had stared in wonder as it came, black except for small gleams of silver that flickered like winking stars. And the buzzing, faint at first, built to the roar of a shrieking sawmill. Grasshoppers! Millions of them descended in a seething mass that piled up until the ground began to writhe.

They were everywhere, crawling on top of one another, squirming into sleeves, pant legs, and skirts, spitting their filthy brown tobacco juice over everything. They crawled over the buildings and into them. And they ate! Crops, grass, the garden, tree leaves, bark, and even straw hats and leather harnesses. They chewed at the windowsills and boardwalks, and then they began to eat each other.

No one had ever seen anything like it. Only the geese were happy, gobbling them down as if they were manna from heaven. But it was no manna. More like the plagues of Egypt. I remember old Christoph Walter falling to his knees and crying, "*Der Jüngste Tag*!—Judgment Day!" He was embarrassed by it later, but many of our people wondered whether God had not wanted us to come to this country.

Finally, when the hoppers had eaten everything there was to eat, they laid millions of eggs in the ground, and flew off to wreak devastation somewhere else. The following summer the eggs hatched, and it started again. It had been only the last three years that they had not threatened to destroy everything we have. I did not like grasshoppers.

Now I looked a sight. Trying to get tucked back into my skirts, I turned around and almost bumped smack into Lorenz Hofer, who stood as if affixed to the ground, his jaw going up and down like a pump trying to catch its prime.

Chapter 5

"Hannah, I . . . I just needed to see you for a minute."

"Well, I'd say you managed it," I snapped, my face beet red. "You almost saw more than you ought to." I'd had my blouse lifted over my belly button.

Lorenz blushed and apologized. "I didn't mean to."

"Then what were you doing sneaking up on me like you were after my scalp?"

"I wasn't sneaking," he said, making an effort to stand up to me. "Anyway, how . . . how was I to know you come here to dance like a heathen, or whatever you were doing?"

"It was a grasshopper. I may have overreacted a little," I said, feeling more foolish all the time. This was the boy Mueter wanted me to see, though I don't think she had meant for me to meet him in the garden with my clothes hanging out of my skirts. And Lorenz wasn't exactly a boy. He was twenty-four-years old. He had not had much luck with females, and was still single. He was all right, really, and good looking enough, for all his ineptitude. And I couldn't blame him for his timing. He was probably more surprised than I was about the grasshopper episode.

"Well, Lorenz," I said, "what did you need to see me about?" As if I didn't know. Like Mueter had said, he would fall over his feet just to be near me.

"I've heard you are worried, not knowing where Paul has gone and all."

What? Was the whole country talking about me? "Who isn't worried?" I said defensively.

"Well, most say he is just out adventuring."

I remembered the letter. *One last adventure.* How could I argue?

"But I know you worry."

And you would like to comfort me, I thought, cringing at my own cynicism.

He fidgeted uncomfortably, as if working up the courage to speak his mind. "I thought you should know about my cousin Alex Glanzer. He lives out in the world, you see, and he was down at Running Water to buy a cow." He paused as if he had said something interesting.

I looked to see if his eyes were in focus. "You thought I should know your cousin bought a cow?"

"No, no, I'm just saying I was talking to him, and he mentioned seeing someone who looked like Paul get off a steamboat a couple of months ago at the Running Water levee."

My heart kicked like a baby in the womb. "He recognized Paul?" I repeated. "How did he know him?"

"Well, you know, Alex met Paul once. When his mother was sick, he came here to stay for—"

"Lorenz! I know how he met him. I mean how did he look—this fellow he saw?" *Was he stupid or just trying to irritate me?* I wondered.

"Oh, well, I don't know. He said he looked like Paul, that's all. He had light hair. And he was—you know—wiry, like Paul."

"And?"

"And nothing. He knows what Paul looks like, and it looked like Paul."

"Well, how old was he? Did he look Paul's age."

"No, Hannah, he looked fifty." Lorenz was exasperated. "Of course he looked Paul's age. Do you think he saw a middle-aged man and said, 'There goes Paul'?"

"Okay, okay, but what else?" I caught his arm. "Where did he go? Is he working for someone in Running Water?" I could not keep the quaver out of my voice.

"I don't know. He got off for a few minutes when the steamboat stopped, and then he got on again. It came from down river."

"He got on again? Going where? What steamboat was it?"

"I asked Alex, Hannah, but he didn't notice. He didn't think too much of it, except he was surprised to see Paul on the river. He didn't even talk to him."

It wasn't much, but it was worlds more than I had known a moment before. I tried to be gracious. "Well, thank you Lorenz, for telling me. I do admit that I've been curious about what might have become of him."

"The other thing Alex mentioned," Lorenz continued, "is that he seemed to be with a rancher kind of man—a cowboy—so he probably wasn't part of the boat crew."

"A cowboy! Goodness, what next?"

"He was on crutches, and Paul was helping."

I couldn't help but smile. *Always willing to help a lame dog.* That sounded like Paul.

"And also with a girl."

"A . . . a girl?" I stammered stupidly. "What kind of a girl?"

Lorenz looked at me with blank eyes. "Why, uh, just a girl. A female girl, I guess."

"*Ach, Himble*—heaven's—Lorenz!" It was my turn to be exasperated. "Of course a female girl. Hutterite or *Englisch*?" To us, living in English-speaking America, anyone who was not Hutterite was automatically labeled *Englisch*.

"*Englisch*, of course, like maybe the cowboy's daughter."

"Wonderful! And is there anything else cousin Alex had to tell you?"

Lorenz shuffled uneasily, and replied, "If you must know, he said she was pretty, and it looked like they had money, by their clothes. That is all I know." He said it with finality to end the conversation.

"Helping lame dogs, indeed!" I scowled.

"Lame dogs?"

"Never mind, Lorenz."

Lorenz looked at me with a lame dog look of his own, and I felt as though I ought to pat his head and scratch his chin. Instead I thanked him very kindly and left him standing by the peas.

Behind me, he called. "Hannah, I'm sorry if I shouldn't have brought it up. I wanted to tell you first. I . . ." But I kept my back straight, and walked stiffly out of the garden. To think I had been worried about Paul being in trouble. Hah! This wasn't the kind of trouble I'd had in mind.

Chapter 6

I left the garden and walked through the colony to the big riverbank hill on the northeast side. I needed to get away. To move. To think.

A small piece of chalkstone on the path caught my eye. I bent without stopping and picked it up, fingering the soft rock. Somebody in Yankton said this whole area used to be under water and the chalk is really limestone made from shellfish. I didn't know whether to believe it, but the stuff was everywhere. It was so soft our builders sometimes marked boards with it, and we had even used it with our slates in school.

On the hilltop, I sat down on a large rock, scribbling on it absently with my chalk. From here you could see the forested hills rising to misty heights in the east, the flat benchland stretching toward Bon Homme town site to the west, and the colony nestled next to the mighty Missouri.

Below me were the yellow chalkstone houses, and the original owner's wooden corrals and barns among spreading cotton-wood trees. More stone houses, barns, and shops would go up as the men quarried building blocks from across the valley in winter. I could see the ninety-foot chalk bluffs rising majestically across two-and-a-half miles of river and fertile bottomland.

Surrounded by water, our corn crops added their shade of yellow-green to Bon Homme Island, a little bit of mystery on our doorstep. Years ago, someone had discovered an old grave on the island with a wooden cross marked *Bon Homme*—French for *Good Man*. No one knew who he was or how he had died, but the island and a town just upriver were named for this long-lost and nameless good man.

My thoughts returned to Paul. Was he still the good man I had known? Many people in the colony believed he had lost his soul by leaving. I hoped he would not be lost forever.

What was I to do now? I felt like a fool for even thinking about going off to rescue Paul. "I think Paul needs you," Sannah had said. Hah! He needs me all right. For what? To save him from a pretty *Englisch* girl? Was I supposed to tie him up and drag him back to the colony?

Maybe Fater was right. Paul had made his choice. I shouldn't have been surprised. He hadn't wanted to join the colony in the first place. When he ran away to work on the gambling boat, we thought we had lost him to the world that time, too. Then came the disaster that saved him—the dysentery epidemic in Nebraska. It had hit him while he was away, and Andreas had brought him home. I caught it too, and had perched with Paul on the precipice of death. But when the epidemic passed, God's inner healing came. Sannah had opened her heart to Paul, and Paul had learned the meaning of love. It's strange how disaster can help us learn the important things in life.

But this time, there was no epidemic. If Paul had made his choice he needed no rescuing, from either Andreas or me. It was that simple.

I started back. A horse and rider were loping my way. I stared and hoped it wasn't anyone who felt like talking. Checkela again. He was on old *Homercupf*—Hammerhead— the colony's bay horse, zeroing in on me like a pony express rider to a relay station. "What mission are *you* on?" I asked sourly as he approached.

He reined tightly around me, as if I were a gatepost, and

walked the horse beside me. Checkela helped with the cows and was a good rider. "I've been thinking, Hannah. Fater—"

"Did it hurt?" I interrupted.

"What?"

"Thinking. Did it hurt? You're not used to it."

"What makes you so nasty? I just want to talk."

He was right. I was being nasty. "I'm sorry. What do you want?"

"I hear you want someone to go after Paul."

"Who said that?"

"I heard Mueter and Fater talking."

"Then I guess you didn't hear right."

"Yes, I did. They think you're pretty strong on it."

"Well, if I was, I've changed my mind."

Checkela's stare bored into me like an auger. "Why? Because of the *Englisch* girl?"

I bristled. "How do you know about that?"

"Lorenz. He said Paul has taken up with an *Englisch* girl."

Naturally, Lorenz had told everyone already. On a colony there was nothing so hard to keep in one's pocket as news. I looked at my brother, and sighed. "Checkela, that isn't why. I just think Paul is old enough to look after himself. That's all. He's a man, for goodness sake. I think he knows what he is doing."

"Well I don't."

"*Joh*, but you're young. Someday you'll learn."

"Learn what?"

"To know what you're doing." I shouldn't have jabbed at him again, but I wanted him to go away.

"Hannah, don't try so hard to be funny. You'll crack your face. Anyway, I'm thinking of going after Paul myself. He might need me."

One thing about Checkela, he was loyal. On the ship from Europe, Paul had saved him from being washed overboard in a storm. Checkela was only seven then, and Paul had been his hero ever since. He would jump at the chance to be a hero for Paul.

"Paul doesn't need anyone. I'm sure he's *well* looked after." I heard the unintended sarcasm in my voice.

Checkela heard it, too. "You're just *naidish*."

"I am not jealous! And if you say that again, I'll smack you so hard your head will come off."

"Hah!" he scoffed. "You're too proud to do what you know is right."

"I don't know what's right. Okay, Check? Now, just stay out of it, and leave me alone."

Checkela stopped the horse, letting me go on. Then he called, "What's the matter with you, Hannah? Yesterday you were worried about your friend. Why not today?" I ignored him. He called again. "Sannah was worried. Don't you think the dying can sense these things? Don't you think Sannah knew what's right?"

Chapter 7

The lanterns were out. I had said the long bed-time prayer with Maria and Barbara, my younger sisters. They were asleep already, but I couldn't get settled. Too many thoughts leaped about in my head.

Checkela had his nerve, calling me *naidish*. Jealousy had nothing to do with it. Nobody understood, including old Christoph Walter with his assessment of the ones who leave—the *vecchclufnan*—the runaways. *Out for fun, soon gone to the devil.* For all the rebellion Paul had when I first knew him, he had come to love the Lord. How strange, though, that he had taken up with an *Englisch* girl.

Stranger still that he hadn't written. Even if he had decided to stay away, even if he had gone astray, he would have written to let Sannah and Andreas know he was all right. So why hadn't he?

Maybe Checkela was right about Sannah's fears. Did those who were dying have special insight, or had Sannah only wanted Paul's comfort, as my father suggested.

I tried to pray, to ask God for peace, or maybe wisdom, or a revelation, but my busy mind kept pushing prayer thoughts aside. Who was right? Sannah, Fater, Checkela, Mueter, old Christoph? How could Paul take up with a girl from out in the world? Wasn't that enough in itself to suggest trouble? On the other hand, if an *Englisch* girl was what made him happy, what was that to me? As Fater had said, it was his life, his choice.

~

In bed, I heard it. Cooooom—low and far off. Cooooom. A voice calling deep and long across a great distance. In the beginning, I thought the voice was with Paul; then I realized the voice was Paul. It was coming from the Missouri River, down and down across the water from wherever it was that Paul had gone. Right to where I lay in my room it came. Cooooom. It stirred my spirit, tugged at my heart, and in the pristine clarity of the moment I knew what I must do. My eyes opened and the rafters above me were pillars of black night. But already a murky suggestion of light filtered in through the attic window, worrying the darkness as the sun hooked a tentative fingernail over the edge of the horizon.

Then, even as I awakened, I heard it again—*Cooooom*— and I realized it was not Paul's voice, but the deep-throated steam whistle of a riverboat starting out with the pre-dawn light. Only a steam whistle, yet my heart quickened with a certainty I had not known since our journey from Russia. There was no sleep in my eyes. It was as if I had been awake the whole time. The call of a riverboat; it felt like more. I knew what I was going to do.

We Hutterites believe that God will sometimes guide our thoughts through dreams. In fact, it was because of the dreams—or visions—of our preacher Michael Waldner that we were once again living together in colonies. He said an angel told him that we must live together and share everything in common, as Hutterites had always done, before giving in to the desire for private ownership.

Whether my dream was coincidence or confirmation I could not be sure, but somebody needed to find out about Paul. It looked as if that someone would be me.

I slipped out from under the covers as quietly as I could and opened the red chest by my bed. I removed two each of underskirts, *Tiechl* kerchiefs, blouses, dark skirts and aprons. I dressed in one set of clothes, putting my light jacket on last, and tied the other clothes in a bundle in the extra apron. I tied my shoes together and hung them around my neck. I groped at the bottom of the chest until my fingers found the pencil stub I knew would be there. I put it in my pocket and descended the steep stairs to the room where Mueter, Fater, Checkela, three-year-old Joseph, and baby Dora slept.

I took a deep, silent breath. I'd need a miracle not to wake anyone. The shadowy form of the big clock from Russia clung to the wall. The regular tick-tock of its swinging pendulum measured the night. Its hands were hidden in darkness, but I knew it must be about four o'clock. I would have to hurry. Checkela would soon be up to fetch the cows for morning milking.

I crept to the wood box by the stove, where I knew there was an old newspaper, used for getting the fire started. I pulled it out, cringing as it crinkled noisily. A piece of firewood clunked. I froze as Fater snorted and Mueter stirred in her sleep behind the curtain that served as a nighttime room divider. I glided across the floor to the table, licked the end of my lead pencil, and wrote a note in bold letters across the newsprint. In the dimness of the room I could not see my own writing, so I hoped it would be readable. Then, feeling like a robber, I helped myself to half a dozen funeral buns from under the checked tea towel, and gently lifted the latch on the door.

Our apartment was on the second floor. A hallway ran the length of the building, and our door was only a few feet from the south exit. Fresh, cool air bathed my face as I stepped onto the stairway that angled down the outside wall to the ground. I hurried to the bottom and sat down to put on my shoes. I hoped no one would choose this moment for an early visit to the outhouse, which reminded me that I could use such a visit myself. But the darkness was weakening, and I needed to hurry. I'd find my own outhouse later in the bushes.

I skirted the old chalkstone Burleigh House, named after the wealthy rancher who had built it before we bought his land. It was a large house, and we had divided it into apartments for several families, with room left over to serve as the community kitchen and dining hall.

Leaving the colony yard, on the benchland road to the west, I passed the graveyard. A shiver ran up my spine. There was Sannah's grave, a dark mound of dirt among the cottonwood shadows that snaked in from the edge of the road. A lonesome doubt crept into my heart at the barren sight. Did I really know what I was doing? Had Sannah been right to worry? Did Paul really need my help? One thing was certain: if Paul did not need help, then I did. The outside world was no place for a female alone. Hearkening to the voice of a steamboat whistle! I must have been crazy!

I looked at the graveyard again, hoping not to see any life. On the colony, all kinds of stories were circulating about the omens of Sannah's death. Old John claimed to have seen someone walking in the cemetery the night before Sannah took sick. But when he approached the figure—or spirit, as many suspected—it disappeared. Susanne claimed to have dreamed about stepping on a black mouse, and Ruhanna had dreamed of seeing two black beetles in the house. Many Hutterites believed in such signs, and without fail, the stories surfaced after a death. Someone had always seen shadows in the graveyard or dreamed an ominous dream. I told myself it was nonsense, and smiled bravely.

When I finally passed the graveyard, I breathed a sigh of relief and glanced over my shoulder. What I saw stopped me dead in my tracks. A ghostly figure glided past the shadowy graves on the far side of the cemetery. I would have screamed had fear not choked me. Then it stopped and turned toward me—

staring! It leaned forward, peering so intently in my direction that I was sure it was about to deliver a message from the dead—but it remained as silent as the graves that lay between us. Then it raised an arm, pointing at me like the specter of doom, and my insides turned cold. I had not yet paid my visit to the bushes, and at that moment, I almost wet my skirts.

Chapter 8

If I'd had control of my legs, I would have run, probably hollering all the way back to the colony yard. But they say fear can give you roots, and I stood, planted like a garden scarecrow, staring in terror as the being came at me, first walking, then breaking into a run. It had an awkward gait, arms and legs pumping as if the bones were out of joint.

That did it! I tore my feet from the ground and ran as if the road were paved with fire. Then it struck me: I knew that run—and the spirit wore a *Katus*, a Hutterite boy's black cap.

I stopped as suddenly as I had bolted. Now I was the one giving the ominous look. "What's the idea, sneaking around like a ghost?" I hissed as my brother approached.

"What? I wasn't—"

"And hiding in the graveyard yet!"

"Hannah, I wasn't hiding," Checkela whispered noisily. "I was trying to find which way you went, and I ran through it, that's all."

"And I suppose that's why you were pointing at me like the angel of death."

"The angel of death? Are you out of your mind? I was waving to get your attention. I didn't want to shout and wake the whole colony. Sheesh, I'm sorry if I scared you."

"You didn't scare me," I retorted dishonestly, feeling like a silly fool as I recovered from my fright. And now a worried silly fool. How would I get rid of Checkela?

"You weren't scared?" he asked innocently.

"Of course not!" I replied. I had almost quit shaking.

"You thought I was a ghost!"

"Don't be ridiculous. I don't even believe in such things!"

"Then you sure must be in a hurry," he chuckled. "You took off like a sinner with the devil on his tail."

"Checkela, just go bring the cows in. Isn't that what you're supposed to be doing?"

"Not yet. You woke me up early. Are we going to find Paul?"

So he knew what I was doing. "Not *we*, Checkela. *You* are going to fetch the cows, and I am going to do what I need to do."

"No, Hannah. You are not going out there by yourself. If I don't go, you don't go, and that's it."

It's funny how life sometimes goes in cycles. I was reminded of an earlier time in Russia when Paul had stolen away to Hutterdorf to look for his mother's diary. That time, it had been him trying to get rid of me. Now I was in Paul's position, and from my brother I was getting the same treatment I had given Paul. Checkela's tone of voice suggested that nothing I could say or do would change his mind. In a way, I was relieved. It was not right—or safe—for a woman to travel alone. All the same, I couldn't give in too easily.

"Mueter and Fater would be worried sick. They won't know where you've gone."

"'Don't worry. Gone to protect her,'" Checkela said, sounding self-important.

"What's that supposed to mean?"

"It means I left a note to say I'm protecting you."

"Protecting me!" I snorted. "That's a good one. Protected by Little Jakey."

"I'm fourteen years old. On the colony that makes me a man."

"Your birthday isn't for three more weeks."

"Three weeks is nothing."

I laughed. "It will take a lot more than three weeks to make a man of you, little brother. Mind you, I've babysat you for over half my life, so why stop now? Come if you want, but I can't tuck you into any nice comfy bed when you start to get tired."

I laughed again at the thought of babysitting Checkela. More than four years younger than me, he was raw boned and gangly and didn't shave yet. Still, at five foot nine he already had me beaten by an inch.

He bristled at my laughter, but instead of arguing he crooked his arms like sticks over my head, and said, "Whoooo! Run, Hannah. Here comes a ghost!"

How annoying brothers could be! I started walking. "If you're coming, come! You've slowed me down enough."

We walked quickly down the lane between the planted trees, then followed it to the bottomland trail by the river. "Where are your extra things?" I asked.

"Got none."

"I can see you'll be a lot of help," I said sarcastically.

"That's your fault. You took off in such a hurry, I had just enough time to write a note and get going."

"I hope you didn't write over the top of my note in the dark."

"Nope. I wrote on the floor."

I jumped in front of him so I could see his face. "On Mueter's floor? Whatever possessed you?"

"All I could find was a piece of chalkstone Barbara had played with. I had to hurry, and there was nothing else to write on."

"That settles it then. You have to come. If you go back, Mueter will get a rope and hang you."

"I know. I'll be safer out in the world with all the thieves and murderers," he chuckled. "By the way, where did you tell them you are going? I would like to know myself now that we are on our way."

"That, dear brother, is the question of the day. I really don't know—which is probably best, because if I knew I would have put it in my note, and Fater might come to get me." Although I was the same age as Paul and easily an adult by Hutterite standards, and even though Fater insisted that Paul had to make up his own mind, he would probably have a different opinion when it came to his daughter. "I wrote that I was going to ask around about Paul, and I would keep them informed. They'll probably think I've gone to look up Alex Glanzer. They won't worry too much."

By now, the sun was clawing its way over the hills behind us. The morning light was wild-rose pink. Checkela nodded and said, "But we are not going to Alex's?"

"No. He told Lorenz all he knew. We'll go to the Bon Homme steamboat levee."

"But we don't know which way Paul was going."

"Check, how many directions can you go on a river? Upstream or down, and we know that Paul went up."

Checkela looked doubtful. "But we don't know how far."

"True, but he went with a rancher," I said, deliberately not mentioning the so-called pretty girl. "And what better place to ask where ranchers go on steamboats than at a place where the steamboats stop? Now, if you will excuse me for just a moment, I need to go and look at something behind those bushes over there."

He stopped, and looked stupid. "What do we want to look at in the bushes?"

"Not *we*, Checkela," I said to him for the second time that morning. "*You* are going to wait on the road, and I am going to do what I need to do."

Chapter 9

Checkela dutifully turned his back as I darted behind the bushes. I sighed at the nuisance of having a brother along, but smiled, remembering his birthday. I couldn't resist calling, "Don't worry. In another three weeks, you'll probably understand."

"Hannah, I know what you're doing," he replied indignantly. "I wasn't thinking, that's all."

"I've noticed you have that problem," I laughed, straightening my skirt and emerging from the foliage. Checkela had already started down the road again, so I hurried to catch up.

Bon Homme was only four miles from the colony, so it wouldn't take long to get there. Meanwhile, it was a beautiful morning for a walk. Checkela had not asked me about food, accommodations, steamboat fares, or anything practical. I wondered whether it hadn't occurred to him, or if he simply trusted that I had it all figured out. I had no idea how much we would have to spend but hoped it would not be too much. While we walked, I told him how Sannah had insisted I take Paul's money. I also told him how Paul and I had found the money, and the crazy time we'd had when Paul changed it to American dollars at Castle Garden, the immigration station.

A big woman had been shrieking bloody murder at Paul because she thought he was stealing her blanket. Both Paul and I had been afraid we'd be thrown out of America before we even got in. It seemed like a long time ago now, but I remembered trying to talk Paul out of changing the money.

"Why is it," I had said, "that every time I go somewhere with you, it means trouble? Next time I hear you say, 'Come on,' I'm staying put."

But he'd had a twinkle in his eye and answered, "Come on," and, as usual, I had followed. Now I was doing it again. Because of a dream and a steamboat whistle that sounded like, *COME*, here I was chasing after Paul. How wonderful if, just for a change, it wouldn't mean trouble.

About halfway to Bon Homme a creek ran down to the Missouri. Here, Checkela and I shared the buns for breakfast. Then we knelt down to drink at a spot where the water pooled. It was clean and refreshing. There was a little wooden bridge, and then the road angled up from the creek to the level plateau above the river. We were puffing by the time we reached the top, but it gave us a fine view beyond the waist-high prairie grass and into the misty valley, filled yellow by the morning sun.

At Bon Homme we could see the steamboat landing far down in the flat below. The bluffs were of crumbly clay; the river was sixty feet straight down. The main road veered away to meet the stagecoach road on the north end of town. Ahead of us, a trail followed the bank.

Checkela peered over the edge to the landing, then along the trail. "It's a lot farther that way," he complained. "It would be quicker to climb down the bluffs."

I rolled my eyes. That was my brother talking. A thirteen-year-old boy who thought he was invincible. "Forget it. I'm not in a mood to be killed."

"You won't get killed. I'm here to look after you. Remember?"

"Well, you can look after me now by staying away from that cliff. I don't want to have to drag your dead body home if you fall. Come on. We'll follow the trail and go into town. There's no steamboat down there anyway, and we have to ask around and find some food."

His eyes lit up at the mention of food. "Okay," he said, "but when we get to town, stay away from strange men. I don't want anything happening to you."

"Thank you for that advice, Mr. Man of the World. I'll try to remember." As if he knew anything about strange men. He hadn't been off the colony any more than I had. "How will I know which ones are strange?" I asked sarcastically. "Exactly what should I be looking out for?"

Checkela frowned. "Strange, Hannah, just strange." Then he laughed and admitted. "How do I know? I've never met anyone stranger than old Christoph Walter, and he isn't exactly dangerous."

"No," I smiled, "but he does have a habit of spilling soup in his beard."

"Well, there you are," Checkela said wisely. "When we get to town, stay away from men with soup in their beards!"

We were still laughing as we entered the town, but if I'd been honest with myself I'd have been whimpering. I had no idea who to ask or what to say. For a moment it occurred to me to pray, but I was too busy thinking about what to do next.

Glancing at the sun, I guessed the time to be about 5:30 a.m. Who in an *Englisch* town would be up at this hour? Just a few miles away, the colony would be coming to life. The women would be taking their pails and three-legged stools and going to milk the cows. I flexed my fingers. All that squeezing had made them strong. "I imagine there will be an uproar when they see you haven't brought the cows in this morning, Check."

"And when you're not there to milk. I can just hear Gloria Walter now. 'Where are they when there is work to be done? Brother and sister, and one as lazy as the other!' I'm glad I'm not there to listen."

"Well, there are others who will soon think worse," I

replied. "They will think the devil has twisted our hearts with desire for the world's evils. Especially mine." It was one thing for a male to leave the colony for a time. Everyone understood a young man's restlessness, but a woman who abandoned the colony for the immoral world outside—she had to be a bad one. My heart sank as I thought of poor Mueter this morning. For her sake, I was almost tempted to return. *Why,* I wondered, *was it so important to find Paul?* Other young men had left the colony. As for the girl, Paul wouldn't be the only runaway to fall in love with a pretty *Englischer*. Still, other men weren't Paul, and no one had ever mysteriously disappeared on a riverboat. *Ach,* my head was spinning. There was nothing to do but keep on.

Bon Homme was deserted. We entered the dusty town at the bottom of Main Street, where it turned and sloped down to the steamboat levee. We walked the other way toward the false-fronted buildings of the business section. We passed the blacksmith shop, wagon shop, shoe shop, two stores, and a post office. None of them were open.

"Goodness, it's quieter than the cemetery back home," I remarked, striding down the boardwalk beside a rough one-story tavern-house.

"Makes you wonder if there's anyone alive," Checkela agreed. He started to chuckle.

"Now what?" I asked impatiently.

"Oh, nothing, except you and that cemetery thing." He laughed some more, and raised his arms like a ghost. "Whoooo! Run, Hannah! The Bon Homme ghost is going to get you."

"Check, you're wearing that one out. I—Hey!" I turned toward the tavern door. "I think I hear something in—" Suddenly, the door burst open, and the scariest man I had ever seen came charging straight at me. All I saw was a filthy brown shirt and a disheveled bushy face. Then he was on me,

his hands clutching at my shoulders. I screamed and staggered back under the assault, my face pressed against his
shirt. I couldn't see, and the stink of liquor, smoke, sweat, and
goodness knows what else, choked the breath out of me.
Instinctively, I reached up, scratching at his neck and face to
get free, but my legs gave way and I fell backward. Then, just
at the height of my panic, something smacked into him and
he spun away sideways. I stumbled and fell, rolled once, and
was running almost before I was off the ground. I shouted for
Checkela to get going, when a flurry at the corner of my
vision stopped me short. Checkela! It was he who had
knocked the man away. He had come to my rescue! As I
watched, he tumbled with the man in a tangle of arms and
legs. And now he was going down with the wild man on top!

Chapter 10

Never in my life had I been so glad to have a brother. I instantly regretted making fun of his desire to protect me. Lord, don't let that terrible man hurt my brother, I thought. He was not large, but Checkela was no fighter. I had to do something. If only I had a big metal skillet like the one in the colony kitchen. Then I remembered I was a pacifist. A Hutterite never lifts a hand against another, I could hear the preacher say. How could I fight? But didn't Christ also say there was no greater love than to lay down your life for another? Checkela had come to my aid. How could I live with my conscience if he died trying to save me? I cringed, remembering how my father had been killed saving me from my own foolishness in the sawmill when I was little. I could not stand by and let it happen to my brother.

These thoughts were little more than a flash of awareness, and with barely a hesitation I scanned the empty street for something—anything—I could use as a weapon. Then another man emerged—this time a big one, with sleeves rolled up over bulging muscles. He came straight at me out of the tavern.

From of the corner of my eye I could see Checkela flailing to get free. The bushy-faced man had him down, but there was something strange about the way he fought. He hardly seemed to move.

The second man reached toward me. What could I do? Help Checkela? Run? I could never fight this man. He came closer. Then he did the last thing I expected. He said, "My word, ma'am, I'm sorry. Awfully sorry. I didn't even see you!"

Now Checkela had almost rolled free. "Don't worry, Hannah. I got him now," he called.

With one quick movement, the second man stepped over and kicked the first one off my brother. "Filthy varmint," he said disgustedly. The bushy faced fighter rolled over and tried to sit.

"Thank you," Checkela said, looking from the big man to his adversary. "I must have hit him pretty hard. I haven't had a fight like that since Peter Dekker threw my hat in the river." The man struggled to his feet, stumbled, and fell down again. I didn't know whether to be proud of Checkela or appalled.

My brother rambled on, a maniacle grin stretched across his face. "You see what a bad one he is, Hannah? He's the kind I warned you about. Ten to one the man has soup in his beard. I sure hope he's okay."

"What did you say?" the other man asked.

Just then bushy face rolled over and vomited into the dirt. "Man," Checkela said in a worried tone. "I hope I didn't damage him inside. I don't want trouble with the sheriff or anybody. He was attacking my sister, and I had to hit him hard."

Something was happening to the bigger man. His face was twisting up. His eyes opened wide until I was afraid he was about to have some kind of fit. Then out burst a booming laugh I was sure would wake the entire town. "Son," he said, finally, "you're the funniest thing I've seen all night. That fella is barely conscious."

"I know," Checkela said, "that's what I—"

"I mean, he's been in my tavern all night long and he's nigh-on drunk himself into a coma. When he finally fell out of his chair and threw up on the floor, I picked him up and fired him straight out the door." He looked back at me. "And I truly am sorry, ma'am. I'm not laughin' at what happened to you. The last thing I intended was to throw a varmint like that in a lady's face."

I looked at the so-called varmint, and saw the sticky vomit glistening in his beard. Now I knew what the other awful smell had been when he first attacked . . . or rather, landed on me. And I'd had my face buried in his shirt! I almost threw up myself.

The big man caught his side and laughed again. "I'm sorry. I just can't get over the young sport, here, thinking he'd been in a real knock down, drag 'em out. How in thunder did you manage to get under that fella anyway?"

"I—He—" Checkela was red faced and stammering. "He was hanging on to me. He woke up and started to fight. . . . He . . ." The big man laughed again, and Checkela gave up.

The man slapped him on the back, and said, "I'll give you one thing. It must have been an awful surprise, and you jumped in there quicker'n a spider on a fly. By the way," he said, sticking out his hand, "my name's Ben Crane. Why don't you two come in for a little something to get you going this morning?"

"Sir," I said, "we thank you kindly, but we do not need alcohol to get us going in the morning, or at any other time of the day."

"Good gravy, I don't mean that! This is a stage-stop tavern, and my wife is the best cook in the country. She'll be getting the food on right smartly now to prepare for the morning trade. This breakfast is for eating, not drinking."

As if to prove him right, food smells were beginning to emerge from somewhere in the building. I was sure I could smell bacon, and my stomach was beginning to growl.

As we sat down in a clean, but roughly finished barroom that doubled as a dining area, the muscular man called to the kitchen. "Beatrice, we need two breakfasts, on the house, for a couple of youngsters. I owe the girl something for scaring her, and the sprout here needs a little building up. He just had a fight with an unconscious man and came out on the bottom." Two other men entered at that moment and stared curiously at my brother.

Checkela stuck his chin in the air and tried to look defiant. "Let's just go find a steamboat, Hannah. We don't need free food from this great comedian here."

"Stay put, Check. I'm hungry as a baby bird, and it seems to me that this river town tavern man is bound to know a few things that we need to find out."

Chapter 11

The afternoon sun poured heat into the river valley like milk into a bowl. Humidity rose to meet it, sucking the sweat from our bodies.

We clumped down to the deserted levee, and Checkela set his wooden box heavily on the bank. "My, Hannah," he complained, sitting on the box. "Do you think we're going to feed everyone on the boat? We need a mule to carry all this."

"You *are* a mule, Check. Now quit your braying." I set my box—the lighter of the two—beside his, and pulled out one of the heavy woolen blankets. It was filthy.

"Phew," Checkela groused. "Did you have to get the most disgusting blankets in all the Dakota Territories? It wouldn't surprise me if they're what the guy died in."

"Why do you think we got such a good deal? Here, fill this spider with water," I said, yanking a cast iron cooking pot from my box. These pots were called spiders because they had three long spider-like legs to hold them up from a fire.

Then I took the blankets and our new cake of soap, and walked barefoot to the bank just down from the levee. The levee was really nothing more than a raised embankment beside water deep enough to float a steamboat. I tied up my skirts and waded in. The Missouri was as muddy as ever, *And about to get a lot muddier*, I muttered, plunging the blankets under, watching the filth from the cloth mingle with the murky river flow.

Nervous energy powered my arms as I scrubbed. I looked

upstream, feeling small and alone in the big water. More than sixteen hundred miles farther west it twisted like a gigantic serpent. I hadn't been more than twenty miles from the colony since arriving from Russia, and here I was, a *Vecchclufner*—a runaway, waiting for a steamboat to take me through the wildest country left in the United States! All to look for someone I did not know was there or even wanted to be found. I scrubbed harder. It was too late to change my mind now.

The run-in with the scary drunkard had turned out to be a blessing. Mind you, Checkela would have disagreed. At breakfast, every time someone at another table laughed or looked our way, Checkela's ears burned red and he chewed on his bacon like a wolf ripping the head off a chicken. I was afraid he would go over and start a real fight with someone awake and sober.

But if not for the drunkard, we might not have met Ben Crane. "Where do you suppose such a man would be going?" I had asked the tavern owner, explaining about the well-dressed rancher and his daughter.

"Fort Benton," he replied confidently. "If he was only going to Bismarck, he would have taken the train. And between Bismarck and Benton it's mostly Indian land north of the river, and unsettled sagebrush to the south. There's ranches starting up in Benton, and beyond it to the southern foothills, if you have to go farther. But Benton is as far as the steamers go and you've got to go there first."

Just like that, I had a destination. But when he told me that a single steamboat cabin-fare was over a hundred dollars each, I almost fainted. Until he added, "Mind you, deck fare is somewhere between forty and sixty these days, if that suits your budget better."

It did, which explained the spider pot and blanket washing. Deck fare meant preparing your own food and sleeping on deck with the cargo. Ben Crane had sent us to a grocer who also had a back shed full of secondhand goods. A farmer had died, and his wife sold all their possessions to the merchant and moved back east. After an hour's shopping, we had utensils and provisions that I hoped would last the three- to four-week trip upriver.

I swished the last of the soap out of the blankets. They were so heavy with water I could barely lift them out of the river. I yelled at Checkela to help, and together we wrung them out. "They look good," Checkela said, with some surprise. "I didn't think they'd come clean in that water."

"That's nothing," I replied. "I've seen wash water twice that dirty after bathing you, baby brother."

"Hannah, your baby brother is going to throw you into the river and drown you if you don't quit already."

"Okay, okay. Here," I said, "hold the blankets while I wash off the other supplies. I don't want to catch whatever killed the farmer." I pulled a hunting knife from the box. It was a nice one with a leather sheath and a deer antler handle. I'd had to spend seventy-five cents to get it, but I hoped it would be worth it. I used it to scrape flakes from my soap cake into the spider pot.

"What do you think, Check? Did I spend too much, or did I do all right?" On the colony, almost all the purchasing was left to the householder and his wife. The rest of us never saw the prices, and didn't know much about them.

"Well, Hannah, I'd say the way you bargained and bartered with the poor guy, he was probably glad he still had his shirt and a little money in his hand by the time you got out of there."

"Well, we have to be frugal. This isn't even our money we're using." I shuddered to imagine what Paul would think if Sannah had been wrong. What if he was counting on using the money to marry the rancher girl and start a home? *Ach*, I couldn't stand the embarrassment. I tossed the other items into the water and washed them. Besides the blankets, cooking pot, and knife, we had two old spoons, two five-pound lard pails for bowls, and three different-sized baking powder tins for cups. I was especially pleased with these. They fit one inside the other and each one had a lid. Finally, there were three fish-hooks and some string. All for $3.15.

And then there were the groceries. For another $4.85 I had gotten five pounds of dried beef, ten pounds of flour, twenty pounds of cornmeal, forty pounds of potatoes, two pounds of dried apples, a five-pound pail of lard, half a gallon of syrup, some baking powder, salt, and coffee, and a soap cake. That was the box-full Checkela had complained about.

"My, Hannah," Checkela griped, "what am I supposed to do with these blankets? Do you think I'm a clothesline that I should stand here holding them all day?"

"Why don't you quit grousing for two minutes and try using your brain?" I said, pointing to a cluster of wooden barrels standing on the levee. "Drape them over those kegs, for goodness' sake."

Checkela stomped off with the blankets, and I went back to washing our makeshift dishes. *Poor Checkela*, I thought. He was probably still chafing from the so-called fight. I shook my head and smiled. But it was over now, and if we were lucky, we'd never have to see that soupy-bearded old drinker again.

You should never trust your fate to luck. I had just dried the spoons on my apron and tossed them into one of the lard tins, when the long booming cry of a steam whistle echoed up the valley. I leaped to my feet and scanned the river. A steamboat was coming! "Forget hanging the blankets!" I shouted. "We'll soon be on our—" I turned around as I yelled, and there he was—Bushy Beard, on the levee road. Fear caught in my throat as he reeled on unsteady legs. His eyes were fixed on my body, pulling him straight toward me. And this time, he was wearing a gun!

Chapter 12

"Now, what is this?" bushy beard said, coming close. "I've been told you want to leave town." It was the first time I had heard him speak. He had an accent that I realized must be from England, though his words, like his walk, were still unsteady from the all-night binge.

"We're waiting for a steamboat," I mumbled.

"Like the one over there?" he said, nodding toward the river.

"That one would be fine." *And the quicker the better*, I thought.

"Then I have caught you just in time." He took a step closer, and the smell of him fouled the air. "I've been told about a little skirmish we were involved in, which appears to be a big joke in this town. I have come to settle the matter."

"Then you'll have to settle with me first," Checkela said, stepping between us. He had the blankets in a bundle in front of him. I wondered if two wet woolen blankets were thick enough to stop a bullet.

"Checkela, don't cause trouble," I whispered. I didn't want him getting us both killed. *Lord, show me what to say, and show me now*! I breathed. "Sir," I said, "it's too late for this. That steamboat will be here any moment."

"I don't think it's stopping, ma'am." I glanced to the river. He was right. The boat was going by. We'd be alone with this crazy man!

His hand dropped to his side, and the revolver seemed to

leap up from the holster to meet it. He held the gun easily, as if his hand were independent, untouched by his general decrepitude. "Young lad," he said swinging the barrel casually toward Checkela, "put your hands up over my ears."

"Wha . . . What?" Checkela sputtered. "Don't you mean over my . . . "

"Just do it. Quickly!" the man demanded.

Checkela dropped the blankets and put his hands in the air. "Just don't hurt my sister."

"What are you doing?" bushy beard asked, glowering at Checkela. "I said put your hands over my ears, not up in the air. I'm not too chipper, and my head can't stand the noise of this gun."

Trembling, I edged closer to the two of them. This was ridiculous! Whoever heard of holding a man's ears so he could shoot you? I made up my mind to leap for the gun the moment he pointed it. If I was lucky, maybe Checkela and I could get it away from him together.

"Just don't hurt my sister," Checkela repeated, putting his hands over the man's ears.

"Nobody's hurting anyone," he said. Then, before I could move, he hoisted the gun and fired. The boom reverberated through the valley, answering itself with a series of fading echoes. But Checkela was okay. He had shot into the air. "Now wave a blanket or something," he commanded.

"Wha—?"

"So they see you," he added impatiently.

As quickly as I could, I untied my apron, and waved it like a flag at the steamboat. "You shot to stop the boat?" I said in amazement.

"Of course," the man said. "I told you it was passing by."

"But I thought . . . Never mind," I said, feeling sillier by the moment.

The steam whistle blew again. "Good. She's turning," the

man said. "And now, before it gets here, let it never be said that Harry Orman does not apologize when the necessity arises. It appears that a bit of, ahh, overindulgence on my part resulted in an unpleasant experience for the two of you. I want you to know I am sorry for my part in the event. And I am glad for the opportunity to help out by stopping your steamboat. They don't stop at every little landing, you know."

Checkela and I looked at one another in amazement. This was the second time in one morning we thought this Harry Orman fellow was trying to kill us. And, instead, the result both times was exactly the kind of help we needed. Maybe the Lord *did* want us to succeed. "Well," I said, reluctantly extending my hand, "We are very, uh, glad you came along. Thank you, sir, for all you've done."

"That's quite all right, ma'am. When Harry Orman sees a lady in need, he likes to be of service." He leaned close to me, taking my hand. "It is a pity I'll be on the stagecoach to Yankton tomorrow. Otherwise, I would happily stay by your side to watch over you on your travels."

"Oh . . . yes, what a pity you can't," I agreed, holding his hand and wanting to hold my nose. "But I will be fine. I have my brother to protect me." Checkela's face lit up, and I could hardly believe I'd said that. But I didn't want our Mr. Orman feeling obliged to stick around.

Chapter 13

It was late afternoon of the first day, and already I felt as if I had been away for a year. "Wave good-bye to Scary Harry," Checkela had chuckled as the steamboat *Silver Mist* pulled away from the Bon Homme levee several hours earlier.

What a relief it had been to see the big boat glide up to the levee with its crowd of passengers lining the decks. But, oh, how strange to walk up that gangplank, knowing how far those few steps would take us. The front of the boat had no rail, and the heavy reinforcing wood around its edge stuck out like the ribbed and pouty lip of a Missouri River walleye. I felt like Jonah entering the fish's mouth, but whether it was according to God's will or my own whim, I could not be sure.

"Yes, good-bye Scary Harry," I had muttered, waving, almost ducking for cover as the diminishing man fired a one-gun salute into the air. *And good-bye to the Gemein*, I had thought wistfully.

I leaned on the woodpile near the front of the main deck, glad to have my thick blanket, now clean and dry, between me and the rough deck planking. The big paddle wheel at the back noisily and steadily slapped the water, propelling us forward. The boat vibrated to its rhythm. A man emerged from the little cookhouse behind the boilers. I caught the aroma of burned food, and he strode to the edge and dumped a big pot of some black looking mess into the river. I wondered if even the fish would eat it.

A twisted tree branch floated by, and I thought it strange that it would soon drift past my home while I traveled away in the opposite direction. Had it been only twelve hours since I had caught my fate by the throat and abandoned the safety and isolation of Split Rock Colony?

I sighed with fatigue. Never had I faced so many challenges as on this one day. At least, not since my adventures with Paul on the trip from Russia. Paul. Sometimes I thought I'd have been better off not knowing him. At least my life would have been normal. Boring maybe, but normal.

I sighed again, not looking forward to the night. Up above on the boiler deck, the passengers were comfortable in their private cabins. Down here we had to compete with buffalo hunters, gold seekers, and whiskey traders for a place to flop down among the stacks of firewood and freight that crammed the deck.

I watched six rough-looking men playing poker around a crate they used for a table. I shuddered. Those men had to be more dangerous than the roosters we had been warned about. When I paid the clerk our fare of forty-five dollars each, he had looked me over and announced, "Ma'am, you are an attractive-looking young woman. I would advise you to keep a sharp eye out for the roosters, especially at night."

"Roosters?" I had repeated with disbelief.

"Roosters," he affirmed. "A bad lot, too."

"Sir," Checkela had said loftily, "my sister is not afraid of roosters. We raise them on the colony farm."

The clerk choked on something and coughed. "In that case," he said, walking away, "I shall tell Captain Anders, in case he wants to buy a few. He sometimes has trouble finding good roosters for a trip."

"What was that all about?" I had asked. "There are a few cows tied up at the back, but I haven't seen any roosters."

"He's an idiot," Checkela replied. "Trying to scare us

about roosters! He's a worse comedian than your tavern keeper friend."

"He's not my friend."

"Whatever. I'm going to look around some more. If you have any trouble," he had added, nodding toward the poker game, "call me."

"Of course, of course," I assured him. "Just don't fall in the river. The pilot said a man drowned not long ago."

Yawning, I leaned back on the woodpile and gazed up at the structure of the boat. Because the Upper Missouri was so shallow, these mountain boats, as they were called, were smaller than the kind Paul had worked on when we arrived in America. Still, it was towering and beautiful. Overhead on the boiler deck, a woman in a fancy dress sat with a child by the promenade rail outside her stateroom. Higher yet, on the roof of the staterooms and big central salon, more people stood talking or lounging about. That was the hurricane deck, and on top of it stood the little pilothouse from which the pilot commanded the boat. On the pilothouse were printed the words, *Silver Mist*.

The whole superstructure was stacked up in layers like an *Englisch* style wedding cake. I had seen a picture of one with a little bride and groom standing on top. I was soon wondering what it would be like to stand up on the pilothouse roof with Paul. *Wouldn't that be a dream?* I mused, wearily closing my eyes, letting my imagination go. Standing on our own steamboat wedding cake, holding hands with the beauty of the river and the sky and the chalkstone bluffs drifting lazily by. Facing a fresh clean breeze, gazing into the future together, crossing a land of promise on the great and wonderful Missouri River, steaming toward Fort Benton. Fort Benton and . . . and what? At the end of the river all I could imagine was the face of the rancher's pretty daughter. She rose up in front of me, tall and seductively beautiful, one of those worldly-women—

Jezebels—the preacher had so often warned the young men about in church. I clenched my fists in irritation, and at that moment, as if the Lord himself were reprimanding me for such foolish thoughts, a tremendous thud shook the boat. For a moment I thought I was tumbling from the pilothouse roof, and I flailed my arms to catch myself. I heard shouts, and something smacked me on the head.

I must have been in that dreamy halfway place between sleep and imagination. I snapped awake to find sticks of firewood falling on my head from the pile behind me. My eyes opened just in time to see the six card players tumble from their chairs. Two pant legs and a pair of feet were disappearing over the edge of the boat. I recognized the shoes as Checkela's —gone overboard with my brother still in them!

Chapter 14

I leapt to my feet. The boat shuddered and groaned. People were shouting. The gamblers cursed, picking themselves and their cards up from the deck. What was happening? Was the boat going down? Had a snag ripped it open? I had to help Checkela! He could swim, but the Missouri was full of dangerous undertows. And then a worse thought came to me. He had fallen off the front. What if he got sucked under the hull? He'd be dragged to the back and the paddle wheel would tear him apart!

There was no alarm, no rescue. No one seemed to notice that Checkela was gone. Somebody had to save him. I dashed for the front of the boat, shouting, "Help! My brother fell in!" Coils of heavy rope lay beside the capstans. I struggled to lift one. If I threw it in, maybe Checkela could catch hold.

One of the gamblers, a big mountain man in a buckskin shirt, casually looked over the edge and laughed. The cold-hearted clod! I swung the bundle of rope back for momentum, and threw with all my strength—just as Checkela's head and shoulders appeared in front of me. I shrieked as if a ghost had risen from the water.

Checkela's eyes went wide. "*Ach*! What?" Then the rope hit him square in the chest, and he disappeared again into the muddy water. Now, all six gamblers were laughing so hard, I was surprised they didn't fall in, too. Only then did I realize the boat was not moving. Finally, Checkela emerged again, sputtering and mad—and standing in only three feet of water.

I figured it out just as the big bell in front of the pilothouse rang, calling the deckhands to action. The steamboat was stuck on a sandbar.

"Hannah, *du Nookela Cupf*," he shouted at me in German. "You are a dumpling head for sure. You almost drowned me."

It is strange how feeling foolish can make you angry. I shouted back, "What do you mean, I almost drowned you? I told you not to fall off the boat, and you went and did it anyway!"

He climbed out of the water, and we stood there arguing, while an amused crowd gathered at the bow, some to listen, some to peer into the dirty water to see what had stopped the boat.

"That's one spicy gal you got there, boy," the buckskin man chuckled. "Do you think you're man enough to handle her?"

"She's not my gal. I'm just here to protec—"

"Oh, shut up, Check," I snapped. That got more laughter. "And the lot of you can clam up and mind your own business," I added, then stomped off toward the rear of the boat—aft, as the boatmen said. Even more laughter followed. I squared my shoulders and pretended not to hear.

"Hey, come back." It was the buckskin man's voice. "I think I'm in love." *The brute. I ought to go and slap him*, I thought. But I didn't dare look back. Already the anger was wearing off and I felt like crying. The day had been too much. I was tired and hungry, and growing more sure by the minute that I had lost my sanity that morning when I awoke to the sound of a steamboat whistle. I rubbed my sore head and looked up at the pilothouse. A wedding cake! Hah! I had deserved getting klonked with the firewood. Maybe God was trying to knock some sense into me.

"Yes, sir," someone guffawed behind me, "that's a spunky

one. Boy," the voice said to Checkela, "you oughta let a real man tame her down a bit for yuh. You're too young for such a wildcat."

"She is not a wildcat, and she is not my girl," I heard Checkela correcting. "She's my sister, and if anyone tries anything, he'll have to go through me."

Oh no, I cringed. Can't he just keep his mouth shut? I stopped to listen. More laughter. And then a splash.

I had to look. Checkela—in the water again! And the man in buckskin grinning at me with crooked, tobacco-stained teeth.

The signal bell stopped ringing commands as deckhands hustled to the bow. Mostly, they were hard, rough-looking men. They made me uneasy.

"Get out the way, lad," a big red-headed deckhand shouted to Checkela, "or we'll grasshopper ye into the mud."

Once more, Checkela heaved his dripping body onto the deck. He cast a dark look at the buckskin man, but walked away to sit on a crate. A miniature flow of Missouri River water marked his passage across the deck. I went to him, and put my hand on his shoulder. "Thanks, Check. But can't you try to be more of a pacifist?" I hoped I might keep him out of trouble by reminding him that Hutterites don't believe in fighting. I knew it wouldn't do any good to warn him against getting killed. I don't know what it is with some young men— you warn them from danger and they charge headlong into it just to prove it doesn't scare them.

"Hannah, I told you. I am here to keep men like that *Sholch* from causing you trouble."

I sighed. "Just don't let scoundrels be your excuse to act like an outlaw."

"Do I look like an outlaw?" he replied, righteously. "Besides, I don't have any weapons."

"Okay, Check, okay." But I had to smile. He was right about the weapons part. I had seen him trying to fight.

On both sides of the boat, deckhands swung the towering, jointed sparring poles out into the river. Steam winches lifted the boat on the poles and struggled to drag us over the bar as the paddle wheel beat the water from behind.

"No wonder they call it grasshoppering," I said to Checkela, looking at the jointed poles. "They look like big grasshopper legs."

"*Joh*—they do," Checkela replied, "but they don't have much hop in them, do they?"

~

"I can't believe we didn't buy matches," I grumbled to myself, blowing on the glowing ember I had borrowed from a squat little man who was cooking a piece of meat on a stick nearby.

When it became obvious that the *Silver Mist* would be stuck for hours, the captain had allowed passengers to row ashore in the yawl. He said he would tie up at the bank for the night when the boat came free. Earlier, because there were no woodhawks in the area, some of the crew and deck passengers, including Checkela, had been put to work cutting wood to fuel the boat. Woodhawks were men who lived by the river cutting cottonwood and cedar for the steamboat market. I knew that Indians had killed many of them. We had come to the enormous Sioux reservation which bordered the opposite side of the river, and I felt my scalp tingle in spite of being told the danger had diminished recently.

Most of the cabin passengers had remained on board because the cook was preparing supper. Since morning, I had eaten nothing but a bit of dried beef, and the cooking smells had been driving me mad.

After loading wood, Checkela had gone upstream to fish, but now the closing darkness would force him to quit. I hoped he would show up with a catch. I had potatoes for a stew, but I wanted to save the dried beef as long as I could. We couldn't afford to spend any more of Paul's money if we wanted to pay our way back down the river. Besides, what if we needed the cash to help Paul? I snorted. What did I think I would do—buy him from the rancher girl?

Overhanging cottonwood trees became flickery shadows as my fire caught and flared. I heard the grass rustle. Footsteps approaching. Good, Checkela was back. I hated to admit it, but the night had an eerie feel, and I was glad to have him nearby. I felt a surge of sisterly affection.

"*Cum, Bruder,*" I said in German, "and let's see what you caught." I'd hug that brother if he had a fish. Then I heard a horse nicker. And when I heard the voice that answered my words, I almost fell into the fire.

"Miss, if you speak with me, it will have to be in English."

Chapter 15

"What do you want?" I stammered, dreading the answer. Had the buckskin man come to find me? I clutched the antler-handled knife I was using to peel potatoes.

"I thought you might be lonely," the figure replied.

"I'm not. So you can leave."

"I say, I don't mean anything that way." The voice was familiar, but not the buckskin man's. It sounded like our bushy-bearded acquaintance from Bon Homme. But when he entered the firelight, leading a horse, I saw that he was beardless, and much younger looking than the man who had stumbled from the tavern. He was, perhaps, in his mid-twenties. This man wore clean clothes and a round-topped, black bowler hat. A pair of dead birds dangled from the fingers of one hand.

"Harry Orman?" I asked, staring as if I had just seen a worm turn into a peacock.

"At your service," he said, flashing a weary smile.

"What in the world are you doing here?"

"It looks as if you're about to prepare a meal," he replied. "I am wondering if I might join you in exchange for these prairie chickens. I've had a day of it, I can tell you. I don't feel like cooking, and my guess is you could use some fresh meat."

I had to admit, he was right about the fresh meat, and my mouth watered as I thought about how those birds would improve a stew that otherwise might be nothing more than potatoes boiled in Missouri River water with the mud settled out. Still, my hand tightened on the knife, and I replied, "I thought we got rid . . . that is, I thought you said you were taking a stagecoach to Yankton. How did you get here?"

Harry Orman grimaced. "Ma'am, I admit that I must have made a rather unfavorable impression in Bon Homme and I can understand why you may not be overjoyed to see me. However, I assure you I mean no harm. This morning I realized I didn't even know why I wanted to go to Yankton. When I saw you heading upstream so full of purpose, I thought I might clean up and go back to Fort Benton myself, perhaps try to improve my fortunes. I shall see the captain tonight about getting on the boat. Meanwhile, I'd like to make up for a deplorable first impression."

"I still don't see how you got here. We've been steaming upriver all day."

Harry chuckled. "Yes, but the boat doesn't go upstream very quickly, does it? A good rider can make better time, at least for a day or so. Fortunately, you got stuck on a sandbar. Now, I've been suffering all day, so what do you say about sharing a supper?"

"Your suffering serves you right after the shape you were in this morning." I did not like the notion of traveling all the way to Fort Benton with Harry Orman.

"Ma'am, you are quite right, as I have already said. But supper?"

Finally, I shrugged. "Oh, why not? If you clean those birds and cut them up, I'll make a big pot of the best stew you've had all day." Maybe I was crazy, but he didn't look very threatening, and Checkela would soon be back. Which reminded me—"There's just one thing," I added. "If my brotl tries to run you off, you must let me talk to him, and promise not to hurt him."

"Ma'am, you may consider that a bargain."

∾

The steamboat had finally gotten off the bar. Because of the danger of river snags the boats did not often run at night, and the captain had ordered the *Silver Mist* anchored until daylight.

Glad that the day had finally ended, I lay between a stack of boxes and a big crate marked *River Press*. Apparently it was a printing press for a new newspaper in Fort Benton. The deck was hard, and I had nothing but my blanket for cushioning. I was so stuffed with prairie chicken stew I had to lie on my side. What a meal it had been. I had boiled water in the spider pot and browned the chickens over the fire. Then I boiled the meat and potatoes, and added flour for thickening, and salt. It was delicious. And there was enough left over for tomorrow.

Harry Orman had enjoyed it, too. He was true to his word about not hurting Checkela, who had returned empty-handed from fishing. After warning Harry about minding his place, Checkela settled down and stopped inviting disaster. It was probably the aroma of those prairie chickens cooking in the stew that turned the tables in Harry's favor.

I recalled our after-supper conversation by the fire. "Ma'am, that was the best supper I've had in ages. My lord, my lord, you have a gift for cooking."

"Don't call me Lord. It wasn't that good," I replied.

He grinned, showing white teeth in the firelight. "Ah, a sense of humor to accompany your loveliness."

"Don't you think you'd do better to seek the loveliness of God? There is a *true* Lord to call upon, you know."

Had he rolled his eyes any farther, they'd have flipped right around in his head. "Ease up. It was only an expression."

I let it go. "Well, it's better than the expressions the men on the boat use. Their language belongs in a *Shvainhok*."

"A what? Speak English, girl. Speak English."

I sighed in exasperation. "A pigpen. Do you have any idea how hard it is to speak English all the time? I haven't had much practice."

"In that case, I'd be delighted to help you," he replied, the firelight winking off the white of his teeth. "Where should we start?" He leaned a little closer.

I leaned away, but asked, "I don't suppose you do any ranching around Fort Benton?"

He hesitated. "No ma'am. I was there for business purposes."

"Oh." I was disappointed. "What kind of business?"

"I had big plans for a store." A note of bitterness crept into his voice. "My father is in England—rather wealthy, you know. I invested his money. Thought I might offer some competition to I. G. Baker and T. C. Powers in Fort Benton, so I bought a small mountain of goods and loaded them onto a steamboat.

"That must have been exciting."

"Very. Until the boat sank. The steamboat *Sundown*. Good name for a boat, isn't it?" he said ruefully. "When it sank, the sun went down on my dreams."

"No store?" I asked.

"No store. All lost."

"All your father's money, too?"

"Oh, he has lots more where that came from, but he won't risk it on me again."

"But it wasn't your fault."

"Business does not forgive failure."

"Your father must be a hard man."

He smiled and shrugged. "I've been told he had a hard son to raise."

"What will you do now?"

"Don't worry about me. They're pulling gold out of the Yogo mine field near Benton. I think I'll see if there is some with my name on it." He seemed fidgety, uneasy. He kicked the end of a burning branch farther into the campfire. "That's enough about me," he said. "What's a nice girl like you doing on a steamboat with just a little brother."

Checkela stirred. "Not a—"

"Yes, I know," Harry corrected himself, "accompanied by this young ball of fire."

I told him my story, and asked again if he knew a rancher and daughter matching my information.

"I wish I could help you," he said. "It sounds like you think rather highly of the lad she's stealing from you."

"Don't be ridiculous. I'm just wondering if he's safe. It's a dangerous world."

"Especially for a young lady like yourself." Harry leaned close again, resting a gentle hand on my shoulder. "I want you to know, if you have need of protection, or even companionship, I am at your service."

I pushed his hand away. "That, sir, is another dream you may consider permanently underwater."

"And you'd better not be having dreams about my sis—"

"Checkela, shut up," I snapped.

~

I rolled over on the hard deck, hard thoughts rolling in my mind. Why had Mr. Orman assumed I was on some romantic crusade? And him wanting to comfort me. That was so irritating.

Something else disturbed me. I was losing my peace in God. His love had sustained me through so many hardships. Yet, lately I felt as if I were living in a godless vacuum. I had known God's peace ever since accepting him as Savior, since accepting forgiveness . . . since recovering from my father's death. But what was happening to me now? I couldn't even pray with conviction. Was I feeling guilty for leaving the colony, for becoming the *Vecchclufner*?

Was I embarrassed about chasing after Paul? Or was it the girl? That should not have bothered me. Paul and I had been friends for years, but it had never been more than that. Maybe it was because she was an *Englisch* girl, probably some god-less heathen leading Paul away from his intended path. Still, if I believed Paul was free to live his own life, then it shouldn't have bothered me. I trusted him to know what was best.

So why did I feel so empty? I was going to the aid of my friend. Should I feel guilty for that? All I wanted was to do the right thing.

~

I awoke to the sound of the bell ringing on the kitchen roof. *Himble! I'll be late for milking!* I thought, sitting up quickly, swinging my legs over the edge of the bed—and kicking a black iron monstrosity! What? *Ach!* I remembered—the printing press. The steamboat bell was summoning deck-hands to work. I hadn't realized during the day how much it sounded like the colony bell.

I yawned. The sun was barely up. Checkela rolled over between his boxes. We had lain foot-to-foot, our bodies forming an *L*. I kicked him. "How did you sleep?" I asked.

"Good, until I heard the bell. I thought I'd slept in and forgot the cows."

"Me, too." I grimaced, rubbing my hip. "I feel like I slept on a rock."

"I didn't find it too bad," Checkela replied.

"Sure, but you're lucky."

"Why?"

"No hips." I looked at him lying there comfortably. "Your body's so straight, it probably thinks it's just another plank in the deck."

Checkela sat up and crawled over to my side. "I don't know what you're complaining about. Look what you had to sleep on." He plucked something from my skirt. A feather.

"Well," I said. "It's a good thing there weren't any more."

"Why?"

I grinned. "If one prairie chicken feather was that hard, can you imagine how uncomfortable a whole mattress full would have been?"

For a change, my brother and I laughed together. We hadn't done much of that lately. Then he said, "Speaking of feathers, have you seen any roosters around yet?"

"No."

"Me either. I told you that clerk was a joker."

Chapter 16

We chatted as the sun came up. Again, I was surprised how much I enjoyed Checkela's company, though I had always liked him when he wasn't being a high-strung little pest. We recited our Hutterite morning prayers and dug out our lard-pail dishes. Congealed fat lay on top of the stew.

"I don't know, Hannah. Cold stew is not my idea of breakfast."

"I know, but it's better than being hungry. Tonight I'll cook some cornmeal." When we had finished eating, I handed Checkela my pail. "Here, you can wash the dishes. You've got the whole river for a sink."

"Wait a minute," he protested, "I didn't come along to be your housemaid."

"I know; you're here to save me. So you can wash out those tins and save me from having to tan your hide. I'm going up to the toilet. If Harry Orman comes along, give him some stew." I said it, though I doubted I would be cooking for Harry again this trip. He had bought first class passage, which included a stateroom on the boiler deck and all his meals. I paused before leaving, and looked at my brother. "Checkela, when you're doing those dishes—don't fall into the water!"

I made my way to the narrow stairway next to the engine room at the stern. The boiler deck was supposed to be off limits to deck passengers, except for one necessity. The flimsy looking toilets hung over the back edge of the deck above the paddle wheel. A crooked pipe ran from underneath it down to the water. The whole contraption looked as if it were about to fall into the river, and inside I found myself hanging on for dear life as the paddle wheel, slapping away just under the seat, shook the room. I thought of the time the toilet blew over with little Eli Wurz inside. He had easily climbed out through one of the holes, but I didn't like the idea of trying it in the river.

Fortunately, the thing stayed put and I scrambled out and stopped to admire the scenery, breathing deeply by the rail above the cookhouse. Whiffs of bacon wafted up, but there was that faint burned aroma again. *Must be something wrong with that stove*, I thought.

The view was certainly better from the boiler deck, if you could afford it. But even the main deck wasn't so bad. Better than the crowded trains we had traveled on from Russia. I yawned. Maybe I could catch a snooze in the afternoon. I was about to go down when someone on the bow yelled, "Rooster fight!" I hustled forward along the promenade to get a look.

Below me, a group of passengers and crew had gathered on the bow, forming a circle around two shirtless men. One was tall and lean, the other barrel-chested and hairy. I flinched as a blue sleeve appeared at the rail beside me.

"Captain Anders, you startled me." I had not spoken with the boat's commander, though I had seen him in the wheelhouse. Sharp-eyed and handsome, he exhibited the serenity of a man comfortably in control. He smiled warmly.

"So the roosters are finally having it out," he said matter-of-factly.

"What roosters?" I asked, just as the tall man punched the hairy one in the mouth.

The captain raised a quizzical brow. "The deckhands."

"The deckhands are the roosters?"

"First trip, ma'am?"

I nodded.

"They're roustabouts—rousters. Sounds like roosters, you see?"

I felt a pink blush creep up my cheeks. "So that's who the clerk said to watch out for? Not real . . ."

The captain allowed himself another smile. "Do you mean you've been looking out for roosters of the chicken type?"

I nodded again, and he smiled more broadly. "You would be better advised to watch out for the featherless variety. They are a rough lot, I'm afraid."

By that time, the hairy man had pummeled the tall one, who left a trail of blood as he crawled out of the circle. The winner waved his hand in challenge, and another man stepped in.

"I've never seen such savagery," I said in disgust. "What in the world are they fighting about?"

"They're a new crew. You might say this is their way of getting to know one another, to see who gets the respect."

"Well, I'm surprised you allow it," I said.

"Good for morale," replied the captain. "In fact, some captains, like the legendary Joseph La Barge, even organize such fights to initiate a new crew. Once the pecking order is sorted out, they work better together."

"Men!" I shook my head and wondered why so many of them were not happy unless they thought they could bash in the other fellow's head. Which is exactly what the hairy fighter was doing to his latest challenger.

"Well, I must get back to the wheelhouse," Captain Anders said. "Would you like to come up and see how a steamboat is commanded?"

"Why not?" I said. "I'm sure it's better than watching a *rooster* fight."

In the little house on top of the boat, Captain Anders motioned to a younger man in a uniform similar to his own.

"I'll take it, Henry," he said. "You can watch the fights if you like. I'm afraid it doesn't please the young lady."

"Thank you, sir," the younger man replied, glancing eagerly toward the stairway as a cheer sounded from the lower deck.

"How is the channel?"

"True as a fair maid's heart," Henry said with a grin.

"He's young, but has the making of a fine pilot," the captain said as Henry disappeared on the stairs. Scanning the river, he turned the big wheel and the steamboat angled to the left. "You see that little swell on the surface?" he asked. "It's an underwater snag. There are lots of water-logged trees hung up on the river bottom, and it's so shallow they stick up enough to rip the hull right out of a boat." He pulled a rope that he said rang a bell way down in the engine room. "That tells the engineer and the fireman that I want more steam. The water gets deeper on the next stretch. We'll make up some time." Then he moved the lever on the gleaming brass control pedestal to *full ahead*. I felt a quickening in the rhythm of the boat's vibration, and the slapping of the big paddle wheel increased its tempo. It was marvelous the way the machine responded to the boat master's hand. I wished I could control my own life half so well as the captain controlled this big boat. I envied the simplicity of the boat's purpose: up the river, down the river—no questions, no doubting. I wondered again what I was doing, chasing Paul up a river with a boatload of buffalo hunters and fortune seekers. Maybe this whole adventure was simply a snag in the river of my life, and I was about to be shipwrecked. I should have been home baking bread.

The captain had just stuffed his pipe with tobacco and was sucking a match flame into the bowl when a shout rose up from somewhere over the forward deck. "Perhaps they have established a champion," Captain Anders said, "but what the devil are they doing with the derrick pole?" I could see the top half of the tall poles the crew had used for grasshoppering over the sandbar. One of them swayed, and a rope was sliding through its pulley.

Henry, the young pilot, reappeared, flushed from a run up the stairs. He poked his head into the wheelhouse. "Sir," he panted, "I think you should have a look below. The crew is hanging a passenger from the portside derrick.

That was when a pair of feet, attached to a derrick-pole rope, rose into view. The derrick swung out over the water and I gasped. "*Himble*! It's my brother!" Then the rope reversed direction, and Checkela disappeared, plummeting headfirst toward the water.

Chapter 17

Behind me, the calm voice of the captain said, "Take the wheel, Henry." I took the stairs two-at-a-time to the boiler deck, and raced to the main deck stairway in time to see two men let out the pulley rope, and Checkela's head go underwater for what must have been the second time. I choked a scream as his arms flailed and splashed. The deck was so crowded, I couldn't get to the bottom of the stairs. Finally, Checkela reached up and caught hold of his own pant legs, curling from the waist in a sort of upside-down sit-up. The crowd roared with laughter as he popped his head out of the water, sputtering and gasping for air. He had just enough time to shout, "Anybody who touches my sister will—" Then they dunked him again, dousing his fiery tirade in the river.

Good heavens; what's he saving me from now? I wondered. If Checkela kept protecting me this way, he would never live to see me get into any real trouble.

The men holding the rope stood only three feet from the stairway. They hoisted the rope again and he came up coughing. This time he was not crowing, which wasn't as much fun for the crowd. Someone shouted, "Dunk the little rooster again!"

Before they could drop him, I yelled, "For crying out loud, you'll drown him!" and I jumped. Crashing into one of the men, I scrambled over his back and grabbed the rope, just as they both let go. I held on, and would have kept Checkela above water, except for one problem. He outweighed me. I went up like a flag as Checkela dropped like an anchor. Hanging from the rope, I looked in horror as Checkela's head and shoulders disappeared, and for the first time in my life I wished I were fat. I willed my body to be heavier, but could not make the rope come down. If the rowdy crew and misfit deck passengers were delighted before, they howled with merriment now. No one lifted a finger to help.

Then, from behind, a pair of hands gripped my waist. A familiar voice said, "Here, little lady, let me help you save your brother." I held the rope with a death grip, dragging Checkela out of the water as the man pulled down on my hips. Then he spun me around and leaned toward my face. I smelled the stink of his breath. The buckskin man! "Now how about a little smooch because I'm such a hero?" he said with a rotten-toothed smile. I don't know if it was anger, indignation or plain terror, but in spite of my good intentions for Checkela, I let go of the rope, and slapped his face with all my strength. A brown gob of tobacco juice splashed out from his surprised lips, splotching the jacket of a man next to us.

Time seemed to stop. A stillness came over the people, who waited to see what would happen next. The only sounds were the wheezing chuff of the steam engine and the distant slap of the paddle wheel. The buckskin man's face twisted in anger, and his fingers dug like talons into my waist. My feet still dangled in air, and for a moment I thought he would break me in two. I could hardly breathe, but I gathered enough air to reply, "The day I kiss a brute like you is the day the Missouri River runs dry."

His face went rigid, and he pulled me toward him until we were nose to nose. "Missy," he snarled, "you don't know what trouble those words could buy you." The pale blue glaze of his stare made me realize how easy it is to die. I think he wanted to kill me, but with all those people watching he just stood there, leering and squeezing my waist. Yet the stupidity of my pride reared up. Because I wanted to win, I stared right back with all the fierceness I could muster. Which probably wasn't much, since I was turning blue and going cross-eyed for lack of air.

Finally, I heard the sound I had been waiting for. "Gentlemen, break it up!" Captain Anders! At last! He was still calmly puffing on his pipe. Did nothing get this man excited? "I don't know what this is all about, but the next man who raises a hand against one of my passengers will find himself ashore."

The buckskin man chuckled nastily and dropped me to my feet. "You'll soon be wishing that river *had* run dry. I think you just drowned your brother, little lady."

I gasped, looking frantically into the water. I had let go of the rope! The knotted end had caught in the pulley, and the rope stretched out like fishing line from the top of the derrick pole. My brother was nowhere to be seen.

Chapter 18

I had to get that rope, but I knew I couldn't climb the pole, and the crew and passengers stood gawking as if a drowning boy was part of a show for their entertainment.

"Can't someone help?" I cried. The captain himself shook off his gold-buttoned officer's coat, and made for the edge, but not before a deckhand brushed past him and leaped into the river. I watched as he floundered in the current, searching for the end of the rope. Then a yell and a blur caught my attention. A man had leaped from the boiler deck. His body was stretched horizontally over the water as if he were trying to fly.

It's funny how quickly thoughts flash. I had just enough time to muse, *He's an angel descending from the clouds—or an idiot about to kill himself.* Then his reaching fingers curled around the rope near the top of the derrick, stopping his flight and whipping his body in a short arc around the pole. It was Harry Orman! For a moment he swung wildly, his knees banging the pole. He almost knocked himself loose, but hung on and grimly pulled himself up the rope to the pulley. He reached, grabbed the knot on the other side, and swung himself across. Then he rode the rope to the water, his weight pulling Checkela, still hanging by the ankles, out of the muddy Missouri.

"Swing her in, boys!" someone shouted, and several men hauled the derrick back over the deck. Checkela dangled in the air, lifeless as a big swordfish I once saw in a newspaper, hanging by the tail from a fishing boat winch. Checkela did not so much as twitch.

I ran to him, and for the second time in three minutes I slapped someone's face. This time it was my upside down brother. "Wake up!" I commanded. "Checkela, wake up!" But he didn't move, and a wave of guilt swept over me. How could this happen? My little brother drowned. And why? Because I wouldn't listen to Fater's advice, or Mueter's, or Andreas's. I had to go off on my own, traveling up the river with a bunch of gamblers and drunks, dragging my brother along with me. What was I thinking?

They say time slows down in an emergency. Checkela probably hadn't been hanging over the deck more than a few seconds, but it seemed like an eternity. Most of the numbskulls on deck still did nothing.

A strong arm pushed me gently aside. "Excuse me, Miss," the captain said. "I think he's in as good a position as any." He stepped behind Checkela, wrapped his arms around his chest, and gave a sharp squeeze. I heard the most welcome sound I had heard in days—Checkela choking! He sputtered and coughed, and the captain commanded, "Okay, let him down."

Two men grabbed the pulley rope from Harry Orman, who was still half in the water at the edge of the boat. The captain cradled Checkela's body as they lowered him to the deck. Then he rolled him onto his side. "We don't want him choking on his own vomit if he happens to let fly," he said. But Checkela was already flopping like a fish, trying to get up. "Untie the lad's feet," the captain ordered.

As Checkela regained his senses, he stopped thrashing, and sat on his knees panting like the colony sheep dog.

I knelt down and threw my arms around him, squeezing until he beat his arms to get away. "*Ach*, Hannah, let go. I'm fine."

"Thank God! I thought you were dead."

He shook himself free. "You're worse than Mueter for choking a person." Our mother had always been expressive that way. Maybe it was something I had inherited from her that caused me to do what I could not have imagined only moments before. Harry Orman was dragging his dripping body onto the steamboat deck. As he climbed to his feet, I ran to him, grabbing him in a joyful hug. He stumbled backward, and caught the wooden spar to keep us both from falling into the river.

Until that moment, I hadn't truly noticed the appealing side of Harry Orman. First impressions die hard, especially the disheveled, bleary-eyed, and smelly first impression he had made. Now, I noticed an endearing up-curve at the edge of his smiling lips, and the light dancing in his bright blue eyes. "Thank you," I said. "*Du bist e Engala!*"

"I don't know what you said, but I hope it's good."

"I said you're an angel. You saved my brother."

His eyes sparkled as he looked at me. "Maybe dreams do come true."

"What?"

"Nothing. Happy to be of service, that's all." He met my eyes with his and said, "Did anyone ever tell you you're lovely?"

A cheer sounded on the deck, with calls of, "Hey, missy, I helped, too!" and, "Don't forget me!"

What was it with men? Did they all have think that way? I jumped back from Harry, as if I had just hugged a cactus. "Harry, that has nothing to do with this moment!"

A voice behind me croaked, "That has nothing to do with you, period!" It was Checkela, at it already.

"Checkela, shut up," I said. "The man just saved your life."

Checkela's jaw dropped. "He did?"

"*Joh*. He hauled you out of the water."

I turned back to Harry. "Thank you, again. Now I'm sure you'll want to get back to your cabin. You are wet to the core."

Harry shrugged. "As I said, happy to be of service."

The captain broke up the gathering, and offered his own cabin so Checkela would have a place to relax while his clothes dried. I accepted on Checkela's behalf, and we climbed the stairs to the boiler deck, trespassing once more on the domain of the wealthy.

Looking back, I noticed the buckskin man, leering, watching me go. A tingling chill crept up my spine.

Chapter 19

"Checkela, Checkela," I sighed. We were alone in the captain's cabin near the back of the boiler deck. My brother sat wrapped in a blanket on the small bed while his clothes dried outside on a makeshift line. I glanced around the cramped room, and sat on a chair at the captain's desk. "How in the world did you get yourself hung from a rope? Why do you do these things?"

"What? Do you think it was my idea? *Excuse me, I'm bored. Would you hang me upside down in the water?*"

"No doubt you asked for it somehow."

"I was protecting your honor."

"Why can't you leave my honor well enough alone?"

"Hannah, they said the prize for the best fighter should be a kiss from the pretty girl in the kerchief. Somebody had to stick up for you."

"So you got yourself stuck up on the derrick pole. Good going. Who started this kiss idea anyway?"

"That big ape in the buckskin jacket."

I shuddered at the memory of breathing just inches from his rotten-toothed mouth, and felt the skin crawl on my hips where I knew fingerprint bruises would be forming. "Don't tell me you tried to teach him a lesson."

"I just told him what I thought."

"Checkela, you are an idiot. He might have killed you. If our Mr. Orman hadn't been so quick, you might have drowned."

Checkela scowled. "Oh, so it's *our* Mr. Orman, is it Hannah? What's the matter? Have you already forgotten *our* Paul?"

My spine stiffened. "I would not even be here if I had forgotten Paul!"

"*Doss is recht*, Hannah—that's right. And he would not appreciate you clinging onto Harry Orman!"

"And I do not appreciate your stupid talk! Harry saved your life! And in case you've forgotten, Paul is a *Vecchclufner*—a runaway. Do you think he and his little rancher girl care what I think of Harry?" I glared at my brother. That wasn't quite what I had intended to say. "And if you even think the word *naidish*," I snapped, "I'll tear your ears off."

He looked at me with wide-eyed innocence. "Why would I think *naidish*? I'm just saying we have to keep thinking of Paul."

"Sure, sure," I answered. "Just like Paul has been thinking of us all this time, with so many letters and visits home." Why didn't I stop? I sounded petulant even to myself.

"Fine, Hannah. Throw your arms around whoever you like. Paul is nothing to us."

How had I ever let him come with me? I could have drowned him myself just then. Instead, I yanked open the promenade door, and stormed outside. Checkela's clothes hung from a rope a cabin boy had strung between two deck supports. The pants hung top down, just as they had when Checkela went into the water. I snatched them off the line, and called through the slatted door. "If you want your clothes, I'll have them hanging for you down on the main deck." I wanted to be alone.

"Hannah, you leave them be!" I heard him scrambling inside the cabin. The door opened a crack, and his head popped out. "Give me those clothes!"

"You can come and get them when they're dry."

"How am supposed to go down with nothing to wear?"

"I'm sure you'll figure something out."

"Hannah!"

"I'll bring them back later."

"I'll put them on now. They're dry enough."

"No, I think they won't be dry for a long time yet." Checkela's protests faded as I walked the promenade. I felt better already.

The crowd was cheering again at the front, so I took the aft stairway. Obviously, the fights had resumed.

I draped Checkela's clothes over a crate in the sun, and pinned them down with a box so they wouldn't blow away. After filling a tin with cold stew, I sat down to watch the river run. There wasn't much to do on a steamboat all day. No wonder the men drank and gambled and fought.

I breathed deeply. That brother could be so irritating— accusing me of jealousy one day and of being untrue to Paul the next. As if there was anything to be untrue about. Paul had left us. Sannah had been worried. I was trying to help. Why couldn't Checkela leave it at that?

At least he was loyal, I'd say that much. I just hoped he wouldn't find a way to get himself killed. Every time I turned around he was trying to fight somebody. Some pacifist.

That was when I had an unpleasant thought. I hadn't been much of a pacifist myself. It was I, not Checkela, who had slapped the buckskin man's face. And I had done it out of selfish anger and dropped my brother into the river besides.

I felt almost guilty enough to give his clothes back, but I wasn't quite ready to talk to him. I told myself I was doing Checkela a favor. The captain's cot was more comfortable than my perch among the boxes.

So I sat and let the day drift, its slow passage marked by the restless water swirling and worrying its way down the length of the steamboat's hull.

~

That night, the captain kept us pushing steadily upstream. The moon was bright, and he wanted to make time while he could. An occasional shout came from a group of gamblers and drinkers somewhere on the other side of the boat.

I drifted into a troubled sleep, dreaming of herding the colony sheep to safe pasture. They kept running away, leading me farther and farther from the colony until I was lost in a huge bare plain with night closing in like a shroud of black wool. Then the sheep were gone, and I was alone, except for a circle of yellow eyes, devilish in the dark, closing me in. I tried to run, but the woolen shroud encumbered my legs. I struggled against the stifling darkness and yanked at the fleece to free myself, but it was tangled too tightly. Then, finally, just as it was too much to bear, I tumbled out of sleep and felt the hard boat deck on my back.

I awoke with a gasp, fists clutching my woolen blanket. In my sleep it had twisted itself around my legs. I shook it off and sat up on my elbows. It must have been late. Except for the thrum and slap of the steam engine and paddle wheel, the night was still.

Moonlight splashed the water with cold silver, and beyond the overhang of the deck above, stars winked pinpoint designs in the sky. I shivered, glad to have escaped the dream, yet still tingling with unease. What was wrong? Then another pin-point of light winked in the dark. A red one. My heart caught in mid-beat. A man stood in the shadow by a deck support—perfectly positioned to see the spot where I lay. The red light moved, then glowed brightly, illuminating the man's face as he sucked on his cigarette. In the glow, I recognized the hard eyes of the buckskin man. Watching me.

Chapter 20

He edged closer, coming around the corner of the woodpile. The pungent smoke from his cigarette drifted over me like a thin, reeking blanket. My heart pounded.

"What do you want?" I whispered.

He sucked on the cigarette again, his eyes animal-like in the red light. "I thought you might need some company, so I come over to give yuh some. I like a feisty gal like you."

"Stay back."

"You know, it's fun to watch you sleep. Whose eyes were you scratching out, wrestling around like that?"

"Come any closer and I'll scratch *your* eyes out." I tried to cover my fear with bravado. It was sickening to have him watch me sleep. Being awake was worse.

He laughed. "Just what I mean. Feisty." Something rasped in his throat and he spat it on the deck. Checkela stirred. I didn't know whether to hope he woke up or stayed asleep for his own protection.

"On the other hand, maybe I don't like the way you slapped me today." He puffed the cigarette again. This time I could see that the left side of his face was swollen and bruised. Surely I hadn't slapped him that hard.

"Somebody ought to teach you some manners. I got half a mind to take you huntin' buffalo hides with me when we get to Benton—teach you a little respect along the way."

"I would not go with you across the deck of this boat."

"That's just fine. 'Cause, for now, I'm gonna stay right here with you. Maybe collect that little kiss you were so uppity about this mornin'. Turns out I'm the best man on this boat—better than all them roosters—and I kinda decided you're the prize." His rotten-toothed grin was an evil leer in the mask of his grisly and purpled face. I knew now where the bruises came from. The fighting. Had he beaten them all?

My blood went cold. I wanted to run, but there was nowhere to go. We were caught between the woodpile, the printing press, and stacks of boxes. The only way out was right through the buckskin man.

A Bible verse ran through my head. *Where does my help come from? My help comes from the Lord.* But where was the Lord?

"Get away from my sister!" It was Checkela—standing up in his blanket. Not quite the help I needed.

"So the squirt has woke up from his nap." The man spat again in Checkela's direction. "Why don't you take a swim in the river, kid? It's what you're good at."

If only the captain would come. If only Paul were here. But what could he do? The old ones in Russia were right when they said that America was fit only for people with their pockets full of guns—not for pacifists. How could a Hutterite survive in a place where you had to fight to stay alive? I promised myself that if I ever got home, I would never leave the colony again.

Checkela grabbed a two-foot length of firewood, brandishing it over his shoulder like a club. "If you try anything, I . . . I'll hit you."

"I said beat it, kid, before I eat you for a snack and use the stick you're holdin' to pick my teeth." He looked back at me. "And lady, if you scream, I promise you, I will break the kid's neck."

"Check, please go," I implored. I knew the man was telling the truth. I hoped Checkela would realize that if he *beat it*, as the brute said, then I could scream all I wanted, and he would be free to find the captain.

Checkela swung the firewood back and forth. It was too thick for him to get a good grip on. "I'm staying with my sister," he said. "You're the one who needs to get out of here." He swung the stick again, awkwardly. I doubted he could use it effectively against a mosquito, never mind this hulking barbarian. He was like David against Goliath. Which might have made me feel better, except this wasn't a Bible story, and God had not handpicked Checkela for greatness.

The buckskin man puffed smoke. He had the eyes of a demon, and he was going to murder my brother. Why didn't Checkela have the sense to leave? The brute took a half step forward. I tensed for action. I didn't know what to do, except jump in front and scream bloody murder. But before I could move, the man stopped and went rigid. He stood frozen, glaring at Checkela. Then, to my amazement, he backed away slowly, and vanished around the corner of the woodpile. Was I dreaming, or had something glinted behind him, a flash of reflected moon?

Checkela and I waited, looking at each other. Finally, Checkela banged his stick on the woodpile. "And stay away!" he called, in a shaky voice, more surprised than commanding.

He dropped the stick. "Whew, Hannah, I think I bluffed him pretty good," he whispered. "Now you see why you need me here?"

"I don't know, David. Maybe you're right."

"David?"

"Never mind." I crept around the woodpile. "*Where does my help come from*? Thank you, thank you," I muttered in prayer.

"You're welcome," Checkela answered. I heard him let out a deep breath. "To tell the truth, I didn't really think I could do it."

I peeked around the corner. Sure enough, I could just make

out two figures disappearing into the shadows at the rear of the boat. I didn't have the heart to tell Checkela that for all his bravery, the Lord had sent a more effective reinforcement.

We kept watch the rest of the night. By the time the sky lightened in the east, I was haggard with weariness and worry. We had gotten through another night, but how would I avoid the buckskin man for the rest of the journey?

Early morning brought savory aromas wafting from the cookhouse. "I'm hungry," Checkela said, rummaging through our food box. "What can we eat?"

"Dried apples. Or a piece of dried beef." The stew was gone and, since the boat had run all night, there had been no chance to cook anything else.

"That's it?"

"Unless you like raw flour." I sniffed the air. There was that burned smell again. *That must be some troublesome cookstove*, I thought.

As the sun climbed into the sky behind the boat, deck passengers appeared like pocket gophers from their holes. They folded blankets, dug into caches of food, and milled about. Some filled buckets from the river and splashed water over their faces. Already, little groups of men had gathered around the cards. The daily monotony was underway. Fortunately, the buckskin brute was nowhere in sight.

It was a little before noon when a half dozen men stomped down the boiler deck stairway and marched past our little nook. Their faces were angry, their jaws set. Then a commotion erupted behind the boiler at the cookhouse. We followed—to an uproar of box stacking, yelling, and smoke!

The men were piling freight in front of the closed door and shuttered window of the cookhouse. Inside, the cook yelled and pounded on the walls, while smoke curled out from every crack in the room. At first, I didn't know what was going on, nor did I suspect how it would impact the rest of our journey.

Chapter 21

What a hot little room it was. Already my face was damp with sweat, and no wonder, with the steamboat boiler just outside the wall, and the cookstove inside. I felt like going back into the hold, which I had just inspected for perishables. A trapdoor led to a space piled with sawdust-covered ice for cold storage.

I stood in the cookhouse, and wondered how the round little man they nearly asphyxiated had ever managed to get himself hired. Obviously, he wasn't much of a cook. So he must have talked a good bluff.

Then again, maybe I had, too. I adjusted the stove damper to keep the fire from getting too hot. That cook must have been inept. Operating a wood stove was an art, but an art this colony girl had mastered early. Cooking food that would satisfy those high-paying cabin passengers might be a different matter. I had spoken with more confidence than I felt.

The burning food I had smelled so often had spawned a rebellion.

Several men had locked the cook into the kitchen while someone else stuffed a sack into the stovepipe above the hurricane deck.

Checkela and I had watched with morbid curiosity as the angry men shouted into the billowing cookhouse. "Let's see how you like smoked meat!" someone shouted.

"You can roast in your own burnt juice," added another.

"We oughta set the place on fire!"

Soon the cook quit banging on the door. No sounds but coughing and choking came from within. Finally, they let him come crawling out, gasping like a rickety steam piston. His first words were, "I quit."

He ignored Captain Anders' attempt to get him to try another meal. "I would not boil a pot of coffee for this rabble," he said, to which someone replied, "You'd burn the water if you tried." And he had stalked off, hacking and muttering nasty imprecations.

The captain had shrugged and looked at the crowd of insurgents. "I hope you are happy with your results. He wasn't much, but we are now half way up the river and you've done me out of a cook."

"Captain Anders, perhaps I can be of service." I had spoken up so quickly I surprised even myself.

"Ah, the interesting Miss Stahl. You are good with a derrick rope," the captain said, winking. "But can you cook for thirty-five people?"

"Where I live, we cook for 140," I replied.

"Well, then" he said, "you might be the answer to our problem. I'll give you a try. If it works out, your payment will be your passage to Fort Benton."

"For me *and* my brother," I said. "He'll be my kitchen rooster."

Checkela's mouth dropped open. "Wait just a min—"

"Agreed," the captain interrupted. "Passage for you and your brother. Satisfy the passengers, and I will add a bonus in Fort Benton." And just like that, my brother and I were members of the crew.

A murmur of agreement ran through the crowd.

"Just one thing," I said to everyone present. "If you don't like the food, please just tell me. I would rather work in a kitchen than a smokehouse." Laughter sealed my agreement with passengers and captain alike.

Now, I wondered what I had got myself into. It was time to start, and I had no idea what to cook. I was panicking about how to live up to the expectation I had created with my confident speech, when Harry Orman walked in.

"Well, congratulations," he said. "I understand you are rescuing us from the ravages of our former cook."

"Mr. Orman, I'm afraid I don't know anything about the fancy foods rich people eat."

Harry snorted disdainfully. "My dear girl, I shouldn't worry about that. Most of these people would not know a tureen from a tournedos. They just happen to have a few dollars in their pockets. Put any hearty meal in the captain's silver dinnerware and you're already two steps ahead. They'll think they are dining at the height of culinary refinement."

"What are you talking about—two steps ahead? I've never even heard of tureens and tournedos myself. I certainly don't know how to cook them!"

Harry laughed.

"Is there something funny about that?" I snapped.

"A tureen, cooked or not," he said, "might be rather a tough chew. It's a serving bowl."

I felt the heat rise in my neck. What was I doing? The passengers had almost turned the last cook into a smoke-house delicacy because of his incompetence, and now I wanted to cook a serving bowl! I'd be lucky if I didn't get strung up on Checkela's derrick pole—by the neck. "You're not much help with your fancy words," I muttered. "Why can't you just call a bowl a bowl?"

Harry only looked at me, his lips curving like dove wings at the corners. Then his eyes softened. "Do you know you're beautiful when you blush?" Just for a moment he touched my cheek with his fingers, brushing from my eyes the hair that had escaped my *Tiechl*.

If I hadn't been so surprised I might have bitten his fingers.

I should have. Instead I reached up and touched his hand. Maybe it was the weakness of being alone and unsure, I don't know. But the tingle that fluttered my heart was warm and alive. I pushed his hand away. What was wrong with me? Was I that desperate for a friend already? Maybe I was simply shallow enough to enjoy Harry's flattery. At any rate, this handsome man now seemed nothing like the disgusting creature we had first met in Bon Homme.

"There are too many words in the English language," I grumbled. "You and your tureens."

Harry shrugged. "I was simply suggesting that any good meal would be welcomed. You can prepare a well-cooked meal, can you not?

I nodded doubtfully. Colony food was never very fancy. But it was hearty and wholesome. "Yes," I said, "I think I can do that."

"Good," Harry said cheerfully. "Just one word of caution."

"What would that be?"

That wingtip grin flashed again. "I would be extremely wary of burning it, if I were you."

For the first time we laughed together, his amusement easy, mine edged with worry. Still, there was something reassuring about having Harry nearby, something that made my problems seem a little less overwhelming. "I'll try to keep that in mind," I said. "Now, you'd better get out of here and let me get to work, or I'll have nothing ready to cook or to burn."

Harry walked to the door. "Let me know if you need anything else."

"Harry!" I called. I didn't want him to go. "Have you seen that big man in the buckskin clothes? The one who tried to drown Checkela yesterday?"

"Ah, the buffalo hunter. It seems that he decided to go ashore late last evening."

"He went ashore?"

Harry winked. "Apparently, he became weary of riding this particular boat."

I shouldn't have been surprised. Who else stepped in every time either Checkela or I needed help? "You're lucky he didn't kill you," I chided. " Don't you know he beat everybody in the big fight yesterday?"

"Yes, yes, but I had a little friend on my side and the mighty fighter didn't want to argue. Quiet as a pussy cat, he went."

I remembered the glint in the moonlight. Harry's gun. I looked at it hanging heavily in his brown holster. It reminded me of the time Sannah *Basel* caught Paul looking at a rancher's gun when we first arrived in America. What a fit she would have if she could see me now in the company of this man. She'd have thought him the devil's cousin for sure. I took his hand in mine. "Do you believe in angels?" I smiled ironically, unsure whether I was joking or not. After all, angels in the Bible often showed up looking like ordinary people.

"I believe you mentioned that before," he said. "I hate to disappoint, but angels are nothing to me, not one way or the other." He sighed, and for a moment I thought I smelled whiskey on his breath.

"No, Harry, I suppose you're no angel. Still, you have been a fairly decent stand-in." I wondered when it was that I had started calling him by his first name. I looked again at his face—handsome, confident, yet sallow and sad around the edges. I knew the love he needed. "There is a God who cares about you, Harry."

When I heard the crash, I jumped, letting go of Harry's hand.

"Hannah, *vos tuost du*?" It was Checkela, his armload of firewood scattered on the floor. "What are you doing?" he hollered again. "Is that how you cook dinner, flirting with this old drunk?"

Chapter 22

My brother could be irritating. It was a fact I had to accept. But his rude suggestion that there was something between Harry and me was too much. He had spoken in German, but Harry would have been dull not to guess at the meaning. I shouted right back. "Can you not mind your own business for two minutes? Can I not talk to another person for two seconds without you opening *daina Freisn* with a fat mouth insult?"

"Hannah, I'm only here to watch out for you. You know that."

"You are acting like a grouchy old preacher whose head is so stuffed with rules his hat fits too tight. This man saved your life twice already, and this is the thanks you give!"

That got Checkela's attention, but he said in a surly voice, "Only once."

"As if once isn't enough! But last night too—he got rid of the buckskin man."

Checkela squared his shoulders defensively. "No, I had a club. I—"

"Oh, don't be ridiculous. You couldn't see it, but Harry was there with a gun. Do you really think the man was afraid of you and your stick of firewood?"

"I could have hit him," Checkela answered lamely.

"Sure you could, Checkela. You could take over the world with a matchstick sword." I pointed at the floor. "If you're so good with firewood, stack up those sticks you dropped. Then get out of my kitchen!"

I shouldn't have belittled him, but at that moment I didn't care. He pumped his jaw a couple of times, but no words came out. He knew he was beaten. He picked up the wood, dropped it into the box by the stove, and stomped stiffly outside to the deck.

I stared awkwardly at Harry. Finally, he slapped an open palm on his thigh, breaking the silence. "Well," he said, "I'm not sure what all that German was about, but I think it may be wise for me to seek a safer location. I believe I'll go for a cigar in the salon."

"I'm sorry about my brother," I said, as he walked out the door. "We owe you too much."

"Think nothing of it," he said. "Just get busy and cook. I'm sure everyone will be grateful for a good meal."

"If you see Checkela, please tell him to come back. Chase him in with your gun if you have to. I have an awful lot to do."

Still churning with anger, guilty doubts, and misgivings, I threw more wood into the stove. Yellow flames embraced the wood, already transforming it to ashes and the purity of heat. If only the Lord would send a purifying spiritual fire to burn the dross from my life and clean out the confusion. But I had too much work to be worrying about that. For a second, I wished the whole stupid boat would catch fire and burn so I could quit and go home. I shuddered, thinking that this was how people turned into fire-crazy lunatics. I slammed the stove door.

When Checkela came in, I was dipping water from a barrel into a huge cooking pot on the stove. I pointed to the trapdoor. "Get down there and bring thirty-five eggs." Frantically I dumped flour into a big mixing bowl. "Then get bacon and salt pork. I'll make *Nookela* soup, but I'll have to use bacon instead of chicken." The cabin passengers were about to experience some Hutterite cuisine.

Checkela slouched toward the trapdoor. "You think you're the captain of the boat now or what? This sweat-room is a kitchen, not the wheelhouse."

"Yes, and I'm in charge of the kitchen. Hurry, Check, please. There's barely time. Those passengers want food, and I said we'd give it to them."

"Okay, okay," he relented, moving a little faster.

"And when you get back, start peeling potatoes!"

How we managed, I'll never know, but by the time the stewards came to take food up to the fancy tables in the boiler deck salon, it was ready. *Nookela* soup with bacon, followed by fried salt pork with potatoes and salt pork gravy. For dessert I found a supply of preserved cherries. It was simple, but well prepared. There would be time to get more elaborate later.

I mopped my sweaty brow. What a morning! At least Checkela and I had been too busy to fight, and the terrible heat of the little galley had the interesting effect of cooling our tempers. In fact, I began to wonder why I had been so angry with my brother. Maybe it was my own guilty feelings over enjoying Harry's company. But what was wrong with that? Paul had not claimed my affection, and no matter how charming Harry might be, it meant nothing. I was Hutterite, and a Hutterite did not get involved with an *Englischer*. It was strange, though, to think that Paul may have done just that.

I sent Checkela for more wood, and tried to think what else I knew how to cook with the supplies on hand. It would soon be time to prepare supper. I sighed. At least there were stewards to wash the dishes.

That night I felt I had never been so exhausted. I had cooked bigger meals at home on the colony, but not alone. Though Checkela was helpful, he was a poor substitute for a crew of Hutterite women.

I snuggled into the mattress. Captain Anders, announcing himself pleased with the first day's cooking, had given Checkela and me a room. It was a hot room right over the boilers, but it had a real bed. And sheets. And privacy, except for Checkela.

It was only eight o'clock, still light outside. Checkela was somewhere out on the decks, but I was completely done-in and I knew I'd have to be up at five to start breakfast. I had mouthed the words of my evening prayer and was drifting off, luxuriating in a sleepy comfort I was sure I had not experienced in years. My head nestled more deeply into the feather pillow, soft dreams drifting in through the open window. Sleep, precious sleep, reached down to fold me in its arms.

Then the first gunshot roared.

Chapter 23

I sat bolt upright. The buckskin man was coming to kill Checkela and me! More gunshots cleared all sleep from my mind. Shouting and running echoed on the decks. Surely all that could not be for one man. But for what? Indians?

Custer's massacre had been four years ago, and the Nez Percé battle only three. I vividly remembered the fear among the Hutterites and settlers on the Missouri when the Sioux gathered together in 1876. Could Sitting Bull have come back from Canada to fight, as the newspapers reported he would? I thrust my arms into my blouse and practically leaped into my skirt. Could Indians capture our boat? I had heard frightening stories about Indians kidnapping women, and as far as I knew, there were only two women onboard—me and the one I had seen with the child.

I peeked out the door just as a man in a suit ran past carrying a rifle. At first I saw nothing but smoke rising in little white clouds from the guns, and men jostling along the rails, shouting like children in a peanut scramble. Then I scanned the shore and caught sight of the *enemy*, at least five on the dead run, disappearing into the shoreline trees. One lay unmoving on the shore, head almost in the water. I could not believe what a pack of lunatics we had on board, and what poor shots. All that shouting and shooting, and only one killed.

I watched from the rail as several men rowed across in the yawl and towed the carcass back to the steamboat. The deckhands quickly hoisted it with a derrick pole and winch, and I guessed that it would soon be coming to me.

Once again, that blue sleeve rested on the rail beside me. "Captain Anders, good evening," I said. "I'm afraid I have never seen such an undisciplined rabble."

The captain smiled. "They appreciate the excitement. The passengers get bored doing nothing all day."

Men! I shook my head and wondered why they were not happy unless they were fighting one another or killing something. I said only, "I'm happy to say boredom is not a problem I have worried about since you hired me to cook."

The captain responded with a fatherly pat on my shoulder, and gestured toward the deck below. "I'm looking forward to what you do with that elk. The men will have it skinned and dressed in no time. Have you prepared elk meat before?"

"No," I replied, "but it can't be much different than beef. I believe we will have roast for dinner, and steaks for supper tomorrow."

"Ah, fine, fine," the captain smiled. He puckered his lips and walked off whistling.

I have heard that the way to a man's heart is through his stomach. I had no idea how popular a bit of good cooking could make me among a boat load of men with little else to do but look forward to the next meal.

～

Over the following days, the *Silver Mist* pressed north upriver through the Dakotas, grasshoppering over sandbars, stopping for wood, and slowing sometimes to pick up game the men had shot. The Missouri was a changeable river. The main channels—the only places deep enough to float a riverboat—were constantly filling with silt and shifting to new locations, which kept the captain guessing. A leadsman often stood at the bow sounding the channel with a long pole. Every five seconds, he sang out the depth so the captain could hear it in the pilothouse. In the trickiest spots, the captain himself sometimes went ahead in the yawl, searching for the channel.

The farther upstream we pushed, the more restless the passengers became. The pastimes of cards and drinking, from either a private stock or the bar in the main cabin, went on endlessly.

U.S. army posts perched on the banks reminded us that it could be a violent land. We crawled past Fort Randall, Fort Hale, Fort Sully, and Fort Bennett. Six miles south of the thriving town of Bismarck, at the edge of the unsettled frontier, we steamed past Fort Abraham Lincoln. What strength it suggested, surrounded by ravines and ragged bluffs, with a palisaded infantry post towering over the river on a hill. Captain Anders said it had been home to Colonel Custer and his wife, Libby, until Custer went to Montana to die at the hands of Crazy Horse, Sitting Bull, and Gall, leaders of a desperate Sioux nation.

Then the river gradually swung west, and we passed Fort Buford and finally entered Montana, with the enormous Blackfoot Reservation on both sides of the river. We often saw Indians along the bank or watching from the bluffs overhead. At first it scared me, but Captain Anders said the Indians' fighting spirit had mostly been broken, and they were more likely to hold up a blanket, the symbol of friendship, than a bow or gun.

The river was beautiful and unsettling at once. Hell Creek and Paradise Creek both spilled their waters into the valley. Featherland Island looked like an invitingly soft pillow in the river's brown quilted bed, but names like Devil's Creek and Killed Woman Creek sent shivers down my spine, even in the steaming heat of my kitchen.

Still, I was too busy preparing meals to worry much, and as Checkela ever reminded me, I had my protector. And there was Harry, our guardian angel, though lately his wings were drooping. He had taken to spending much of his time at the steamboat bar.

We passed Cow Island Landing, where the captain said a friend of his, Judge John Tattan from Fort Benton, had fought Chief Joseph's Nez Percé Indians only three years before. Tattan still had the dented belt buckle that stopped a bullet and saved his life.

Ever west we progressed, nestled in the wide valley from which a vast and naked land extended as far as the eye could see, and somehow it did not seem right that a colony-raised man like Paul should travel into such a remote part of the world alone. Or that a colony-raised girl should follow. I missed my family and the fellowship and routine of the Gemein. Though it seemed as if Sannah *Basel's* death had been years ago instead of mere days, my heart ached for her, and for the loss her death would be to Paul.

I missed the assurance of our religious tradition, too. Here, there were no daily church services reminding me that God was on my side. I had never been away from my people before, and prayer seemed different now. Here, it was just between me and God, with no community coming between. Somehow, I knew I had not been trusting as I should have. Maybe I had become too used to letting my assurance rest on being a member of the colony instead of my relationship with the Savior. It was a common Hutterite failing, though I should have known better after all I had gone through as a child. Yet, here I was, unable to find time, or humility, for personal prayer time with my Lord.

~

Leaving a gooseberry mousse to cool, I climbed out of the little ice room in the hull and shut the trapdoor. I knew the dessert would be a hit. When the captain stopped to repair a leaky steam pipe, we had tied up right beside a rich and ripe patch of gooseberries. I promised the cabin passengers that I would make a fresh gooseberry dessert if they would do the picking.

Now, with just enough time to catch an hour's nap before cooking supper, I headed for my room. Three steps onto the main stairway I glanced up just in time to see Harry Orman coming down—boot-heels in the air. Tumbling straight toward me.

Chapter 24

I almost managed to avoid him. A quick sideways leap would have been easy had my foot not come down on my skirt. The tough cloth tightened like a rope between my foot and hips, and I felt the waist-tie loosen. I grabbed frantically to hold it together, Harry momentarily forgotten. I could lose my balance, my footing, or almost anything else, but, good heavens, not my skirt.

Harry hit me like a runaway barrel, and we tumbled the rest of the way together. This was an all-too-familiar experience. Even before we landed I could smell the high-heaven reek of alcohol. I was already kicking and gouging as we hit the deck, this time not terrified, but mad.

"*Gea hinter! Gea vecch!*" I shouted. "Get back! Get away!"

We came to rest in a tangle, face-to-face on the deck. He looked at me stupidly and said, "Eshcuse me, Hannah, but wash that firsh step. Iss a tricky one."

"*Du bist sholcnoar!*"

He tried a charming grin, but only looked pathetic. "I'm shorry, but you muss abuse me in English, or I shall miss alluh benefit."

"I said you're a stupid idiot." I shoved Harry aside and stood up angrily, clutching my skirt. "And you stink!" I felt another tug, and something clattered onto the deck. My apron had tangled around the handle of Harry's gun, yanking it from the holster.

"Uh, oh, there goes my bess friend." Harry rolled over and

reached for the gun, but I snatched it away. It was surprisingly heavy.

"As if you need a gun in your condition. You'll kill yourself." It was all I could do to resist throwing it into the river.

"Hah! I could shoot a hole in the moon at a hunner yards." He laughed as if he had said something clever.

"More likely you'd shoot a hole in what's left of your lucky star. Which can't be much, the way you carry on."

By now, a crowd had gathered. We had just become the boat's best entertainment.

"Hey, the cook's got a gun on somebody."

"Got him down on the deck."

"Did she plug him?"

A couple of boiler deck passengers stood over Harry. "What in tarnation are you trying to do?"

"You cause a lick of trouble to our cook and we'll string you up from the jackstaff." They were scowling so fiercely, I was afraid they might hang him on the spot.

"Well, I'll be! It's the Englishman who saved the boy, and now the cook's got a gun on him."

I tried to explain. "It's not like that. It's—"

"*Himble*, Hannah! You didn't shoot him, did you?" Checkela, now.

"Of course not. I—"

"What are you doing with a gun, Hannah?"

Checkela's face was drop-jawed in astonishment. I looked at the gun in my hand. This was escalating too quickly. I disliked guns. Though I had to admit, the handle had a nice, form-fitted feel. I tried again to explain. "I'm not doing anything with it. I just took it away from Harry. He's—"

"Whooo-eeee, wrassled his gun away!" somebody shouted.

"Do we got a cook or a tiger?"

"Don't mess with *her* kitchen, boys!"

No one wanted to hear my explanation. It was more fun to

have a pistol-toting woman for a cook. If anyone had been doing portraits, I'm sure they would have drawn me with a frying pan in one hand and a pistol in the other. I wondered if any of the gunfighters the newspapers wrote about had gotten their reputations so easily.

Harry staggered to his feet. A deckhand picked up his bowler hat and shoved it so far down on his head it made his ears stick out. He looked like a prairie dog with a hat.

One of Captain Anders' blue-jacketed steamboat officers elbowed through the crowd and grabbed Harry by an elbow. "So you want to molest our cook, do you? You'll think better of it when you're locked in irons."

"Wait!" I said, and tried yet again to explain that the whole thing was an accident. "Couldn't you just throw him in his bunk to sleep it off? And this . . ." I held up the gun. "Please take it, before I end up shooting somebody."

The crowd laughed, and the officer took the gun. "Peacemaker .45," he said with admiration. "Beautiful." He unloaded it and put it in his pocket. "I don't think he'll need it today."

~

Early the next morning I stood in the doorway to Harry's cabin carrying a tray of coffee, bread, and preserves. Even with fresh air coming through the outside shutters, I could smell the disgusting reek emanating from his body. He lay on top of the bunk, his shirt hanging out of his pants, looking like a rumpled rag someone had used to mop the toilets. I couldn't believe the contrast between the sober Harry Orman and this pathetic excuse for a man. Even back on the colony some people liked alcohol too much, but I had never seen anyone let it control him so completely.

I kicked the bed and called until he finally stirred and emerged into what would have to pass for consciousness. His eyelids dragged open like two dirty blinds on the windows of a ruined house.

"Ah, our lovely cook," he mumbled. "With a tray. What did you bring? Hair of the dog?"

"Dog hair? Don't talk nonsense!" *Was he hallucinating?* "It's breakfast."

"I'm afraid I haven't an appetite."

"I know where your appetite leads," I replied sourly.

Instead of answering, he tried to sit up. His wrist pulled tight against a handcuff hooked to the bed frame. "What the—? Oh, the officer." He slumped back.

"He wanted to shackle you down in the hold. You got off easy."

"Hmpph. They lock you up for slipping on their shoddy stairs. There's justice for you."

"I think it was because of the gun," I said. "They thought you might be a danger—"

"My gun. Where is—"

"Don't worry. They'll give it back."

He pulled at the handcuff. "What a way to travel."

"Those aren't your only shackles, Harry. I think you're a slave to alcohol." He reminded me of someone else I had met—Vanya the Great, who had tried to steal Paul's money on our trip from Russia. A talented man, aging and alone, whose only comfort was his *samogon*, the drink of the Russian peasants. "Why don't you quit before it ruins you?" I said.

"I thought I had, Hannah, after I found you. I really thought I had." He grinned sardonically. "But I guess I am how I am."

"You could change."

"Some things, Hannah, simply require too much effort." He looked weary.

"What if I knew someone who could help you?"

He scrutinized me. "I sense a snake oil pitch coming."

I ignored his sarcasm. "Have you ever thought about letting God into your life?"

"Is that where *you* get your strength?"

A verse from my Bible lessons came to mind. *The Lord is my strength and my shield; my heart trusts in him, and I am helped.* "It is," I replied. But I had to wonder. *Was I trusting in God, or my own strength now?* "Giving in is not the easiest thing," I said, "but, truly, I don't know where I would be without my Lord."

"I would be happy enough just to get my gun back," Harry said. "It will be hard enough for me to hold my head up on this boat after being disarmed by a woman, without getting a reputation for religion, too. But thanks anyway. You're a good head, Hannah."

"And you are an idiot," I said, only half joking. What a strange man this was. When sober he was handsome and brave, when drinking he was a jackass. "Still, I want you to know how much I appreciate all you've done for my brother and me. We would not have gotten this far without you—even if we are on a wild goose chase."

"You're not."

"Thank you for your confidence, but that remains to be seen."

"No, I'm telling you that you're looking for Carson Tate, as miserable a man as you'll ever find. His ranch is on the Teton River near Fort Benton. If not for his daughter, I'm half convinced I would have shot him. You'll find your Paul with Carson and his daughter."

"What?" For a moment, the boat seemed to pitch and sway. The muscles in my body had suddenly gone weak.

Chapter 25

I stood planted like a flagpole, the forgotten breakfast tray at half-mast in my hand. "What do you mean he's with Carson Tate and his daughter? How do you know that?"

Harry groaned and sat up on the edge of the bed, his cuffed hand next to the rail. "Fort Benton is not exactly New York City. Do you know how many eligible females there are?" I did not answer, so he continued. "Not many. One notices the young ladies—and the men who keep them company."

"You told me you didn't know any rancher with a daughter."

"I said I wished I could help you."

"Well, obviously, you could have. Is Paul okay?"

"When I last saw him he was fine."

I sighed with relief. I wanted to hug Harry for providing the information, or slap him for being a liar. "What else do you know?"

"Last fall, Carson and Pearl—his daughter—went east. Apparently, he was arranging buyers for his cattle. They stayed for the winter. When they came back in May, your Paul fellow was with them. Carson was on crutches, and I suppose he hired him as a personal errand boy or something for the trip upriver. Paul stayed on at the ranch with Carson and the girl." Harry glared at me through puffy eyes. "Satisfied? Ranchers hire all the time. It's nothing special."

"Then why didn't you tell me before?"

"I don't know. Sometimes life is confusing, Hannah, and

115

no one said I needed to tell you my life story."

"Hmmph," I grunted. "All you had to say was, 'Yes, I think I saw them in Fort Benton.' Your life story has nothing to do with it."

"I had my reasons. Besides, you were on this boat. You couldn't very well go chasing off in the wrong direction, could you?"

"No, but it would have saved me from worrying." His evasiveness made me wonder what else he knew, or what he was trying to hide. "Why did you come after Checkela and me?"

Harry hunched uncomfortably. "As I said before, it was something about you. You looked so full of determination, maybe I thought I could catch something good from you. I don't know."

His face turned just a shade red, and it occurred to me that there was more to it than that. I rolled my eyes. The last thing I needed was Harry Orman as a suitor. Yet I had to admit, I had felt something. For all his faults, Harry was an attractive man. I liked him.

"I'm going to quit drinking," he said.

I met his blue gaze, which was a bleary-eyed excuse for resolve. Yes, except for the drinking, Harry was a likable man. But its effect on him was terrible to see. "I'm sure you will," I replied skeptically.

"I want to, Hannah. You make me want to, you know that?"

"Harry, you know what I think?"

"What?"

"You have no idea *what* you want."

He smiled wistfully. "That's another thing I like. Your tender compassion. Why don't you get out of here and tell the captain to let me go?"

I set the tray on the little stateroom table. "My job is food," I said, grabbing the door handle. "What the captain does about your handcuffs is his business, not mine."

"Cruel woman," he muttered. "Thank you for the coffee."

Outside, I breathed deeply, forgetting Harry and filling my mind instead with the beauty of the river. For several days we had been chugging up the long stretch known as the Missouri Breaks. We had struggled through the Missouri badlands, with its rocky rapids and were now into the White Cliffs area, which meant we were getting close to Fort Benton.

Once again, I caught my breath at the river-world vision before me. A wondrous array of cliffs and pinnacles soared 200 to 300 feet straight up. Towers of weather-carved rock overlooked the river and pointed toward the sky. White and golden sandstone formed the cliffs, and I was sure no fairy castle could be more elegant or majestic. Wisps of morning mist still lingered over the water. God had created all of this.

We parted the vapors as we passed, leaving our plume of wood smoke swirling and settling behind us. Tiny on the little boat on the valley bottom, I felt again how insignificant in size was a human being in the face of God's creation, and I couldn't help wondering whether God really had time to be in charge of the details of my life. In my head I knew he must. I had never doubted it. Not even as an insignificant speck in the middle of an Atlantic Ocean storm had I doubted it. So why was my heart perforated with misgiving now? I remembered the morning I started this journey. Why had I left? Because of Sannah's intuition? Because I was concerned for Paul? Because I was lonesome for Paul? Because the river had called?

I hunched my shoulders, feeling weak and alone.

But hadn't God looked after us so far? We had experienced our share of trouble, mainly because of my overprotective brother, yet Harry, our real protector, always seemed to be there at the right time. *God's angel?* I rolled my eyes. If Harry was an angel, things must be grim in heaven. Still, God could use anyone to serve his purpose. Even Harry, the drinker.

Harry, the charmer. Harry, the adventurer. The secretive Harry, who, I was sure, knew more about the girl and the rancher than he admitted.

I stared upriver, my thoughts racing ahead to Fort Benton. Soon, very soon, we would arrive at that thriving community of ranchers, miners, traders, wolfers, and buffalo-hide hunters. I wondered if Paul would be there. Maybe he would be on the steamboat levee. Maybe whatever had drawn me to this journey would draw Paul to the river when we arrived. Gazing across the water, I could almost see him standing there, waiting for me on the levee with the buildings rising behind him. "*Ach*, Hannah," I chided myself, "*Du bist sholc-noar*." I was a bigger idiot than Harry.

And then I really did see a building, barely visible on the water ahead. I stared hard. What in the world was a house doing in the middle of the river? The clang of the steamboat bell announced that the captain had seen it too.

Chapter 26

All along the boiler deck bleary-eyed passengers peeked through cabin doors to see what was happening so early. As we labored upriver, I recognized the wheelhouse of a steamboat—a sunken wreck, the hurricane deck just above water level. I could see the big paddle wheel facing into the current. River water swirled through he paddles and licked at the cabin walls. The entire structure had warped and buckled in waves like the pleats in a woman's dress.

The *Silver Mist*'s pajama-clad and half-dressed passengers crowded to the rails for a better view. A blue uniform stood out among them, and I recognized Henry, the young steamboat pilot. "There," he said, pointing to the wreck, "is the reason we watch so closely for snags."

"That boat's superstructure will soon collapse," he continued, "and the main deck will be completely buried in silt by the end of the season. It won't be long before you would never know it was here. No monument, no marker, but a decent burial for a steamboat."

Decent for a steamboat, maybe, but to me it sounded horrid and lonely to be lost in the river-bottom mud. Right now, it was the center of attraction to one little crowd witnessing its finish. Soon, however, it would disappear and be forgotten. That, I thought, was the way of all earthly things—even people. Known and loved by a mere handful of others in the vast world, and mourned briefly when we pass on. Then gone and forgotten, grave marker or no. I thought of Sannah *Basel*, so recently buried and departed—and my father, who had died saving me from the sawmill back in Russia. I would never forget them. But how many of my ancestors from even two generations ago did I know anything about? Not many. I shook my head as we closed on the ghostly wreck of the steamer. What strange thoughts this river gave me. I thanked God for the hope we have of the life beyond.

As we passed, I read the name of the steamer, clearly painted on the side of the wheelhouse. *Sundown*. The boat that had drowned Harry's dreams. Was that why he drowned himself in alcohol?

~

Two days later, we emerged from the Missouri Breaks. Then, on the evening of Friday, July ninth, Harry played river guide for me. "See those two hills on the right?" he said. I followed his pointing finger to a long spur of land that jutted into the belly of the river, forming a bend. Two rounded hills sat on the end as if to hold it in place. "What about them?" I asked.

"Fort Benton should be just on the other side."

"All I can say is it better be," Checkela added, excitement edging his voice. "I can hardly wait to get away from Hannah's kitchen."

"What is wrong with my kitchen?" I asked, playfully cuffing my brother on the head.

"It's a slave galley, is what. My birthday, and I get buried in potato peels. I hope I never see another potato in my life. Or mix another batch of dough."

I laughed. Here he was turning fourteen, and I had kept him jumping the whole day preparing an enormous end-of-journey feast for Captain Anders's cabin passengers. I felt as if we had cooked a lake of soup and mountains of potatoes, onions, and preserved greens. Not only that, but several buffalo had blundered into our path, so we ended up cooking a genuine delicacy of the plains—baked buffalo tongues. I told Checkela that all the fuss was just for his birthday.

"Sure, and I do all the work. A man now, and I have to do my own cooking."

For all his complaining, Checkela had responded wonderfully to the challenge, not just tonight but over the entire trip. "I'm glad you were with me, Check," I said. "You did fine, when you weren't getting in the way. And just think, you know more about cooking now than any Hutterite man in our history."

"As if that will do me any good."

"Of course it will. You can bake Tsucer pie for all your sweethearts. They'll be so impressed, they'll be lining up to marry you." Now that Checkela had turned fourteen he was, by Hutterite tradition, old enough to start courting.

"Hannah, if I have to bake sugar pie, or even go near an oven to find a girl I'd just as soon stay single."

"Your choice. Anyway, I think we turned out some lovely meals."

"That is a fact," Harry agreed. "At least, it certainly beat the charcoal we were eating before you took over." Harry was pleasant company again. He hadn't touched a drink since the handcuffs came off.

"I will second that," said another. I recognized Captain Anders's quiet voice. It seemed he was always coming up silently behind me. "Good food means satisfied passengers," he said, "and satisfied passengers make a satisfied captain. Did the clerk give you your money?"

"He certainly did. Thank you, captain. I can't tell you how grateful I am." Tucked safely into my deep skirt pocket, beneath my apron, was a wad of bills. The clerk had returned our fare, and added a forty-dollar bonus.

"You won't forget my offer for a return trip, will you? We'll be leaving as soon as I get my cargo lined up."

"Captain, my brother and I would love to cook for our return fare." I glanced at Checkela, who scowled. "But I'm afraid I don't know when we'll be leaving."

He put a hand on my shoulder. "Just keep it in mind. There are fewer passengers going down river at this time of year. I have a crew member who can handle it if need be, but I would be happier with you in the kitchen."

The boat rounded the bend, and the land on our right opened into a large flat-bottomed bowl scooped out of the bluffs. We skirted a small island, and watched a collection of low buildings nestled behind an adobe-walled fort materialize. From a mile away, Fort Benton looked lazy and peaceful. I soon learned that appearances can be deceiving.

Chapter 27

The fort, a great square structure with defensive bastions on two corners, stood like a heavy cornerstone to the rest of the town. Captain Anders said it had been a fur-trading fort from 1846 until 1869, when it was taken over by the army. The town would not be here had the fort not come first. Yet, as we drew nearer, I could see that it was filthy and falling apart, with not a soldier in sight. Inside the open main gate, raggedy children chased one another with sticks.

"How can the army live in such a slum?" I asked as the boat slid by.

Captain Anders laughed. "It doesn't. The place is so full of rats they abandoned it to squatters years ago. The men are quartered in town at the Chouteau Hotel."

With steam whistle blasting, we laid in at the levee. Our decks were crowded with passengers eager to go ashore. The levee was a jumble. Crates, barrels, and boards—scattered cargo off-loaded from previous boats—were piled everywhere waiting to be packed into stores and warehouses. Bundles of buffalo hides and sheep's wool lay in piles that I assumed were destined for downriver shipment.

Some of the townsfolk had gathered to watch us come in. A man in an elegant black suit stepped forward as the woman and her child crossed the gangplank. He took her hand as she stepped to the levee, then kissed her cheeks and caught the little girl, swinging her joyfully into his arms. Scanning the crowd for Paul, I envied their reunion. Paul was not there. *One fantasy down*, I sighed. *How many more to go?*

Now the rest of the passengers were noisily disembarking. I spied Checkela and Harry crowding toward the gangplank. "Captain, I think I'd better catch my brother before he wanders into trouble."

"The voice of wisdom," Captain Anders smiled, touching my shoulder again. "You stay aboard in your stateroom tonight. Then go about your business tomorrow."

"Thank you so much," I replied. "I will."

～

The streets of Fort Benton were little more than trampled ground separating the rows of buildings. Adobe structures and the typical false-fronted clapboard boxes of the West lined the streets. New brick buildings were going up everywhere. I gazed in astonishment at an imposing two-story edifice with a row of high round-topped windows on both floors. A sign across the top read, *T. C. Power & Bro.* I turned to Harry. "Where do all the bricks come from?"

"Benton's own brick factory," Harry replied. "People here are optimistic. They want the town to last."

We had accompanied Harry as he put his horse in a livery, and now our shoes kicked up little puffs of dust on Front Street, which ran the length of town along the river. "Where are you off to in such a hurry, anyway?" Harry asked, striding beside me.

"Where am *I* off too? I thought you were showing us the town."

"I'm just trying to keep up with you. You're nosing along like a hound on a fox hunt."

I slowed. Where was I going? Did I expect to see Paul waiting for me on a street corner?

"I am not nosing along," I said indignantly. "I'm . . . I'm trying to have a look at the town. And you're not much of a tour guide."

"Well, in that case," he said, "let's walk and talk." He turned to Checkela, so I couldn't see his face.

"And don't you dare smirk at my brother," I groused.

"I wouldn't dream of it. Now, please calm down and note the buildings on your right."

I looked, and saw a row of wooden false-fronted buildings jammed in beside one another, some with wooden awnings, some without, and most with a painted sign announcing what was offered inside.

"This," continued Harry, "was known a few years ago as the bloodiest block in the West. Fort Benton was the most dangerous town in America and this the most dangerous block in town."

I looked nervously at the buildings. There was a shoe shop and a saddler. But half of the rest were saloons or bars. Harry pointed to a hotel saloon boasting the name *Extradition*. "Why, the owner of that very hotel was part of the Cypress Hills massacre seven years ago."

"Cypress Hills massacre?"

"You've never heard of it?

"No."

"Fifteen men from Fort Benton went up to the Cypress Hills in Canada and opened fire one night on an Assiniboine Indian village. Killed somewhere between thirty and seventy-five Indians—nobody knows for sure."

"You mean that saloon, right now, is run by a murderer who did that?"

"If you put it that way, yes."

"Why isn't he in jail?"

"Have you heard of the North West Mounted Police in Canada?"

"With the red coats?"

"The very same. That massacre was why the troop was formed. That, and to stop the American whiskey trade with the Canadian Indians. The Mounties have a couple of forts up there now. They tried to get five of the men extradited to Canada for a murder trial."

"It failed, I take it?"

"Of course. There was an extradition hearing and a U.S. Commissioner set them free. Nobody cared about a few Indians in Canada."

"Except the Mounties?"

"Quite right. But in Fort Benton, the men were greeted as heroes. When they were acquitted at the extradition hearing, there was an all night celebration. There were bonfires in the streets and all the saloons were full."

"And the hero buys his own saloon and calls it the Extradition. Lord, help us, what a place."

"Well, don't worry," Harry added. "It's taming down now. I saw only two or three shootings here all last winter, except for Indians."

I shuddered, but saw Checkela looking with eager curiosity toward the open door of the Extradition. "Hannah, maybe you should buy me a gun for my birthday so I can protect us. It seems like a man needs one out here in Montana."

"Checkela, think like a Hutterite. The best protection is to stay away from trouble." I didn't care if he *was* a man now. The thought of a gun in Checkela's hands was more frightening than a gun in the hands of these murderers. Still, I couldn't help being glad Harry wore his.

Just then a half dozen girls clustered out of a saloon called The Jungle. Their ruffled skirts were flouncy and their cheeks full of color. Glittery jewelry adorned their ears, and I realized their ear lobes were pierced right through. They walked toward us on the boardwalk to a door at the Extradition that said Our House Restaurant. They looked me up and down with narrowed eyes, and I felt a hard-edged hostility.

One of the women smiled at Checkela, who blurted, "Hey, Harry, I thought you told Hannah there was a shortage of women in Fort Benton."

"Ah, yes, well, ah . . ." Harry glanced at me from the corner of his eye.

"Didn't you say that, Hannah?" Check persisted.

"So what?" I said.

"Six all in one group looks like quite a few to me."

"Checkela, just because one smiled at you, don't go getting excited. They're probably all engaged."

"Oh, for goodness' sake!" Harry broke in. "What I said is there aren't many *eligible* young ladies in Fort Benton. I assure you, those girls are not eligible in the proper way." He cleared his throat uncomfortably. "Hadn't we best talk about something else?"

Maybe I'm slow, or maybe it's my sheltered upbringing on the colony, but it took that long for it to hit me. My face started to burn, and it wasn't from the heat of the slanting sun. How could I be so naïve?

I was glad my mother could not see me here on this street of sin and corruption. She would faint dead away and think I had gone to the devil just by being here. *Oh, Lord*, I wondered, *why am I here anyway?*

"Checkela, let's go!" I grabbed my brother's arm and dragged him back toward the boat. The least I could do was keep him away from their smiles and fancy looks. "We'll go for a walk by the river, and then get some sleep. Harry, you will come with us tomorrow, won't you?"

Harry spread his arms and gave me his angel wing smile. "Of course. Where else would I go?"

"I'm afraid to ask."

"Don't worry. Just meet me at The Break of Day."

"That's what I had in mind. Where at?"

"The Break of Day."

"You said that. But where?"

"I told you. There's a place called The Break of Day. It's on Main and Bond."

I glared at him. "Harry, you are an exasperation." But I had to smile—until I had another thought. "Is that a drinking establishment?"

"They have sleeping rooms."

"But I suppose it's a saloon."

"It is a good, clean place to stay. And it's not on the bloodiest block."

I looked at him doubtfully. "Just remember, the break of day is *when* we're leaving, so you be ready."

"Absolutely. The break of day it is."

That night as I lay in my bunk on the *Silver Mist*, I thought about the girls with the hardened eyes. Why did people have to live that way, so far from what God intended? What circumstances drove them to a life that corrupted the sacredness of love? I was thankful to have been born into safety and good teaching.

But still I had doubts. Did I know anything about real love myself? Oh, I had no big sinful desires, but still, where was my peace? Maybe I was too stubborn and proud to know God's true love.

Chapter 28

The Break of Day was not hard to find. It was a fancy establishment on Main, the next street in from Front. But there was no sign of Harry. *Probably locked in jail, if I know him*, I thought sourly. The jail was handy enough, too. It was an old log shack, barely fifteen by twenty feet in size, on the very next lot.

"So what shall we do?" I asked my brother.

"Go in and get him, I guess. After all, he's not used to getting up at 5:30."

"I don't think we should go into this kind of—" But Checkela was already disappearing through the doors. *Looking for Harry, or curious about saloons?* I wondered. I had to follow. The air was stale and reeked, much like Harry had smelled the first time we met him, without the vomit. Or maybe not. I followed Checkela right up to the bar, which was made of some kind of rich reddish wood. Behind it, dozens of glasses graced a counter in front of a huge mirror.

A man approached, carrying a broom. "Looking for work?" he asked, eyeing me up and down.

"*Himble*, no!"

"Well, you don't look like a dance girl anyway. Pretty though."

"I'm . . . well . . ." I stammered, caught off guard at his forthright assessment.

"My sister's looks are none of your concern."

"Checkela, *Holt daina Freisn*."

"Shut your own yap," my brother snapped back. The man was beginning to smile.

"Sir, don't mind my brother. We are looking—"

"I'll handle this, Hannah," Checkela interrupted. "*Mensh to Mensh*."

"Oh, fine," I sighed, giving up. Let him have his man to man talk.

As Checkela described our situation, I couldn't help staring into the mirror. The man had called me pretty. Supposedly mirrors were too worldly and vain for Hutterites. But I stared, and had to wonder: would Paul appreciate my looks? My clothes were certainly plain and my kerchief covered all of my chestnut hair except the tight rolls at my temples. Still, I thought my features were okay, fine-boned with a straight nose and the large eyes that Paul claimed to like. What would he think when he saw me today? *Today*! I caught my breath at the thought. After all this time, I would hold Paul in my. . . . Well, I would say hello to Paul.

The barman was talking. ". . . going nowhere. Dead drunk." I tore away from the mirror, shaking off my reverie. *Good Lord, I hope he didn't see me gawking at myself*!

"Staggered upstairs a couple hours ago."

"Has this place been open all night?" I asked in amazement.

"Yep, and Harry was here for most of it."

"The idiot!" I snorted. "I knew this would happen. He said he was going to quit!"

"Harry quit? Not the Harry I know."

"You know him?"

"Used to be a regular—till he got run out of town."

"Run out of town! Who ran him out of town?"

"Sheriff Healy."

"What ever for?"

"Look, Harry's a friend of mine. He didn't do much, but maybe you oughta let him speak for himself."

"Certainly, I'll ask him next time he's sober—if I live that long."

"About that quitting, when I came in last night one of the girls was laughing about him. I guess he said he was only having one. Had to be bushy-tailed in the morning," he said.

I nodded bitterly. "But for Harry, there's no such thing as one?"

"Right as rain, I'm afraid." He hesitated, then stuck out his hand. "By the way, ma'am, my name is Frank."

I put my hand in his, shrinking inwardly at the intimacy of the ritual. Frank's hand was large, but softer than any Hutterite hand I had known. Apparently, serving drinks was not a job to build calluses. "Well, Frank," I said finally. "Perhaps you can tell us how to get to the Tate ranch on our own. Harry said it isn't far."

Soon, we were walking west from town. Behind us, the sound of a deep-throated steam whistle announced the arrival of another boat at the levee.

$\approx$

"We should have taken Harry's horse," Checkela complained. "I hate these cactus plants."

"We can't just take somebody's horse. Now keep your mouth shut and watch for rattlesnakes." *Lord, don't let us step on a snake.* It was bad enough that the hem of my skirt was torn from the wicked inch-long cactus needles. My calves were burning from the ones that got me above my ankle-high shoes.

I hoped, too, that we wouldn't see any Indians. The barman said they'd had trouble with them coming in from the reservations, especially over the winter when game was scarce. Life was getting hard for them, particularly when whites sometimes killed them for stealing cattle to feed their families. He said it wouldn't do to be caught out alone.

We had come almost five miles northeast from town, an easy walk across the grass of the gently undulating prairie. Now, as we picked our way into a ravine through cactus, sage, and yucca plants into the Teton River valley, I strained for the sight of Carson Tate's ranch. Supposedly, it was in the bottomland just below. It was hard to see around the erosion-cut formations.

In spite of my nervousness, I was glad to be away from the town. After the stink of the saloon, the prairie sage was a refreshing perfume. And here there were no mirrors. I had looked into one and seen my own vanity—worrying about my looks when I had come to help Paul, and tell him the sad news about Sannah.

Finally, we emerged from the ravine onto flat bottomland. Like magic, a rutted wagon trail appeared, crossing in front of us. I followed it with my eyes and spied, through a grove of trees, the ranch buildings, maybe half a mile away.

"Finally!" Checkela shouted, running toward the road. "Wait till I tell Paul all we've seen!"

"Check, slow down and shut up, can't you?"

He turned around, staring at me in amazement. "Hannah, what's with you? This is what we came for."

"Okay, okay, of course. Let's go." I don't know why I was so irritated, why I didn't want to walk to that ranch. Maybe I just didn't know what I was going to say. *Hello, Paul, we came to rescue you. Don't ask what from; I don't know.* Just don't let him think I'm a lovesick loony, chasing him across the continent! Oh, how I hated my pride.

"Hurry up, Hannah. Let's go."

"Just watch out for trouble. Harry said Carson Tate is not a nice man." I followed, and my legs had never felt so stiff and slow.

"There's somebody there," Checkela said, at the edge of the

trees. "I think it's him." Checkela was almost jumping up and down with excitement.

My heart was in my mouth as I stared. There he was, in front of a big log ranch house. He wore a rather un-Hutterite plainsman-style western hat, and he looked heavier in the shoulders—more muscular than the Paul that had left Split Rock Colony fifteen months before. But I could see the wiry quickness that I had so often admired, coiled into his build. It had to be him. I felt a flutter in my chest and blood flashed to my cheeks. Paul, at last!

But there was someone else. Someone with long black hair in ringlets, and a slim-waisted day dress—both fluttering in the breeze. Her hands were at her cheeks as if she were in the throes of some great emotion. And as I watched, they came together, Paul's arms encircling her slender body, her face crushing into his chest. This happened just as Checkela shouted in a voice loud enough to wake the dead, "Paul! My old friend Paul!"

I stood rooted like a cigar store Indian, my heart pounding against my ribs as if seeking a way to escape my foolish body.

Chapter 29

I have had nightmares where something terrible is coming after me, and I am trying to run, except that my legs are caught in molasses and I cannot get away. Slowly, agonizingly, an awful fate closes in on me.

That is how I felt as the whole sticky, black absurdity of this adventure settled over me like the molasses of my dream. I wanted to run all the way back to Split Rock Colony, and then awaken in my attic-room bed with my sisters beside me. But my legs would not turn and take me away, and there was nothing to do but allow myself to be drawn toward Paul and the girl.

At Checkela's cry they turned toward us. The girl cowered and clung more tightly to Paul, who stared in astonishment, his jaw hanging open like an attic trapdoor. A day's growth of flaxen-colored whiskers textured his face. Finally, my eyes met that familiar slate-blue gaze I had pictured so often over the past year. But his look was veiled with confusion, as if he were trying to solve the mystery of the universe.

A smile flitted across his face, then vanished as he unhooked himself from the girl, who I could now see had been crying. "Hannah! Checkela! *Vos?* What . . . what are you doing here?"

What to say? The moment I had dreaded. "We, ah, we came to find, uh—"

Checkela interrupted. "We came to bring you ba—"

I cut him off. "We came to see how you're doing, Paul."

"How I'm doing? Well, I'm fine."

"I can see that. I'm glad."

"I can't believe this. How did you get here?"

"We flew on the back of a rooster! How do you think?" He might at least have said, "Glad to see you."

"We took a steamboat, Paul, all the way up the Missouri!" Checkela bubbled. He was grinning from ear to ear, and he punched Paul happily in the shoulder. "And here you are!"

"Yes, and here you are. But I still don't see . . . Where are the others? Who came with you? Your father? Andreas?"

"We came alone," I said.

"They let you come alone? I don't believe it!"

"They didn't know, Paul. We just left," Checkela added.

"Hannah, you can't do that! With only *e Mandl*!"

"I'm not a little boy," Checkela said indignantly. "I'm fourteen, and I'm looking after Hannah."

Paul looked doubtfully at my brother. "You're fourteen already?"

"Yesterday," I affirmed for him.

"Well, happy birthday. But you're still pretty raw."

"What's the problem, Paul? Don't you remember a twelve-year-old who ran away to work on a steamboat?" I asked, referring to Paul's own escapade when we first arrived in the United States. I couldn't believe I was taking Checkela's side after all my efforts to keep him in his place.

"That's different, Hannah. And you shouldn't have come."

I could see why he thought so. The girl still clung to him, still teary-eyed. The last thing he needed was a complication dropping into the middle of a lover's quarrel.

He must have seen me looking at the girl, because he touched her shoulder solicitously and said, "Hannah, this is Pearl Tate. I told you about her in my letter. It's funny you should come just now. I'm bringing her home to Split Rock."

Now it was my turn to stare slack-jawed. I had imagined

him staying out in the world, but not bringing a girl back home. As for his cryptic letter, he hadn't even mentioned her. "What a wonderful coincidence," I said grumpily.

"This is the Hannah you told me about, Paul?" the girl asked hesitantly.

So, she has a voice, I thought. *How nice for Paul that she can talk.* I was surprised by the nastiness of my thoughts, even as I told myself what a good thing it was that I had not entertained any illusions about romance with Paul. We were good friends and that was all. I tried to be glad he had found someone to make him happy.

But she wasn't Hutterite! And she looked so young. And her hair was so shimmery and black. She was so . . . so lovely.

"This is her," Paul said to Pearl. "I still don't know what she's doing here, but she's very kind and I know you'll like her."

"Hello," I said, with a tight barbed-wire smile that was anything but kind.

The whole time, Paul glanced warily around. I had rarely seen him this distracted. "Okay," he said, suddenly businesslike. "Now that you're here we have to make adjustments. Pearl, you go in and get your things. Hannah, you go with her. If you're hungry, get some food for you and Checkela." The greetings were over, and just like that he was brushing us off as if we were nothing more than a glitch in his carefully planned day!

Pearl turned obediently to the house, and I noticed her right cheek, which had been turned away from me before. Why was she so bruised?

Paul pointed to a log barn on the other side of the yard. "Checkela, there are three horses in the barn. You'll see a tack room next to the stalls. Saddle the roan and the black. Can you do that?"

"Of course," Checkela said. "Who can't saddle a horse? But what's the hurry?"

"Just do it." Then he walked off toward a shed, leaving me standing in the yard like some cast off dirty bandage. I stared at his back and felt my anger grow. I had run away from the colony, traveled 2,000 miles working like a slave on a steamboat, put up with Harry and a buckskin-wearing brute of a buffalo-hide hunter, tried to keep Checkela out of trouble, and had to be strong and level-headed the whole trip, not sharing any of my fears—I did all that only to get to this ranch, where I find Paul, not in any danger, but with his arms around this Pearl girl, and so eager to take her back home to the colony that he can't even take the time to say, "Hello, nice to see you!" I kicked a tuft of grass, ripping it from the ground, then booted it across the yard. It was a weak and pathetic excuse for violence, but it kept me from collapsing in a fit of tears. Who did he think he was to walk off and leave me standing alone in this place?

He came out of the shed carrying a shovel, and rounded the corner of a corral. I was glad he liked Pearl. If this was what being a runaway out in this crazy world did to a Hutterite, Pearl was welcome to him. But not before I had my say. I stormed after him. "Paul, you come back here this minute! Come back here and talk."

He did not stop. "Hannah, just go back to the house."

"I did not come all this way to be dusted off and turned into a rich girl's handmaid. You come here and talk."

I rounded the corral and had almost caught him when he turned suddenly, blocking my way. I put out a hand to stop from running him over. As if I could have done that. My palm hit his chest. The muscles were hard as ropes, and he did not budge. "Go back."

"What's so mysterious? What are you hiding?"

"Just go back to the house," he said evenly. "I'll explain it all." He moved, as if to stop me from seeing behind him.

"Fine!" I said. "If that's how you are." I pretended to go

back. But I could be as stubborn as Paul. I turned quickly and dodged around him. "Now let's see what—"

I did not scream. I did not run. I did not even breathe until a ragged sob scraped through my throat. Before me, in a hollow of crushed grass, was the crumpled figure of an Indian. There was a round hole in his chest, and dried blood, caked and cracking, where a rivulet had stained the dusty ground red-brown.

"Oh no, Paul, no," I choked. "*Vos host du getoan*? What have you done?"

Chapter 30

"No, Hannah, it's not like that," Paul said quietly. "But you should not have to see such things."

But I did see it. Through a veil of confusion, I stared at the stiff, cold horror. The Indian lay on his side, one knee pulled up, as if he had tried to rise before the life escaped his body. Flesh sagged under high cheekbones, shrunken by death or malnutrition. Beside the skinny body was a half loaf of bread and a woolen trade blanket. He could not have been much older than Checkela, barely entering manhood. But he would enter no farther.

I felt Paul's hands on my shoulders. He tried to turn me, pulling me toward him and away from the crumpled figure. I felt his strength and wanted to melt into it, to let him hold me the way he had held Pearl, to let him carry all the burdens. But I pushed away. There was too much horror. Too much confusion. To cope I had to stay within my own strength, and think. What was Paul mixed up in anyway?

"It's her father," he said. "Pearl's father."

Now the veil drew darker. "Paul, please, do you think I'm an idiot? He's no older than she is! And Pearl is no Native." Or was she? Her hair was black enough.

"*Himble*, Hannah! I mean it's her father who *did* this."

"Oh, oh, I see," I stammered. "Pearl's father killed him? So you didn't . . ." My voice trailed off. Maybe I *was* an idiot.

"Of course not. You think I go around shooting people now, and telling outrageous lies?"

"No, I suppose not. I . . ." The anger bubbled again. "Actually, Paul, what do you want me to think? You're not a Hutterite anymore. You're a rancher with a dead boy in the yard. You explain nothing, but tell me to go in the house with . . . with this Pearl girl. I'm tired and I have no idea what is going on. How am I supposed to know what to think?"

He sighed. "I'm sorry, Hannah. You're right." He took a half step, reaching toward me again, then thought better of it. "I'm upset too, but I have to bury this poor boy, and we have to leave quickly." His eyes were intense, catching the blue brightness of the sky. "And don't you think I'm confused too? Do you think it wasn't a shock to see you coming out of those trees? I still don't know why you are here."

"I . . . What happened to the boy?" It wasn't time yet for my answer.

Paul shrugged. "Carson has been losing cattle to the Indians. Not so much this summer, but last winter while he was away there were quite a few. There's not enough game anymore and they're hungry. He's vowed to kill anyone he catches near them.

"I was out on the range with the cattle when this boy came around last night. Pearl said he stood out here, waving a blanket—in peace." Now I could hear the anger rise in Paul's voice. "Pearl went out to offer him some bread, and Carson put a bullet right past her and killed him. There isn't so much as even a lame calf anywhere near the yard."

I stared at Paul. This was so far beyond my experience, I could hardly believe my ears. "What kind of father does that?"

"He has moods," Paul replied. "Sometimes he seems like the kindest man you could meet. Dotes on his daughter like she was the Queen of Sheba. Next time, he goes after her like the devil has a claw in his heart. It's why I've stayed this long."

"For her?" I held my breath.

Paul nodded. "*Joh*—yes."
Lord, help me accept what it isn't for me to change.
"He hits her."
"Like last night?" I asked.
"You saw the bruise?"
"I saw it."
"She was hysterical, trying to help the boy. Carson said to leave him be. It was too late anyway, but she was calling him a murderer and yelling at him to get a doctor. So he knocked her down and dragged her back to the house. I didn't know much about it until this morning. Right now, most of the hands are out moving cattle. Carson went early with the only other man here to break some horses at the Eagle Ranch back up the Teton. He told me to watch Pearl. So I intend to, all the way back to Split Rock."

While he talked, Paul dragged the boy to a tree away from the corral, and began to dig. "But first, it's only decent to bury this poor soul."

This was the Paul I knew. At least that hadn't changed. I picked up the blanket the Indian had carried and covered the body. "Shouldn't we leave him here so the sheriff can do some kind of investigation?" I asked.

"Hannah, this is Fort Benton, and he's an Indian. Everybody knows there have been cattle stolen. Nobody's going to investigate."

"But isn't that the sheriff's job?"

Paul talked with the rhythm of his shoveling. His face was beginning to glisten. "The sheriff's job . . . is to keep order in town. Sometimes he protects whites . . . from Indians . . . not the other way around."

"Even if it's murder?"

"You don't know . . . how it works. A few years ago . . . some Bentonites murdered forty Indians . . . up in Canada."

"Cypress Hills massacre?"

Surprise momentarily interrupted his rhythm. "You know about that?"

"I didn't get here in a bubble, Paul. And I know those men were arrested."

"Sure, because of pressure from the Canadian government. The sheriff had to arrest them, and the army had to surround the town to keep a riot from breaking out. Nobody's going to arrest Carson Tate for shooting one Indian he'd say was a cattle thief."

"It's not right."

Paul resumed shoveling. "Lot's of things . . . aren't right, Hannah. Welcome to life in the world."

Life in the world. It was the phrase we Hutterites used to refer to all life outside the colony. And what a world it was.

"You have to understand," Paul continued. "Sheriff Healy himself . . . was one of the most famous whiskey traders . . . in Fort Benton. Across the line . . . in Canada . . . he built Fort Whoop-up . . . to trade whiskey . . . bad whiskey . . . to the Indians. You can't imagine how rough . . . how cheap life was . . . especially for the Indians. It might have wiped them out . . . except the Mounties came . . . and shut it down. I don't think he'll worry about this boy."

When Paul had managed a narrow hole about three feet deep, he quit digging. Together we wrapped the boy in the blanket and lowered him in. "This might not be the Indian way of burial," Paul said, filling in the hole, "but it's better than leaving him for the coyotes."

As the body disappeared, I turned away and stifled the tears that burned behind my eyes. Somewhere across the expanse of Montana prairie was a mother who might never know what had become of her son. What Paul said was true. Lots of things were not right in the world. And now it was time to tell Paul about Sannah.

Chapter 31

Paul and I returned to the ranch house to find the two horses saddled. Through the door we could see Checkela at the table drinking coffee and talking to Pearl. I thought it odd that he hadn't come to see what Paul and I were doing. Maybe he wanted to bring Pearl into his circle of protection.

Paul hesitated before going inside. His eyes were dark steel in the shadowy light of the porch. "Now, Hannah," he said, somberly. "I can only think that something serious must have brought you on this crazy journey. Otherwise, why not just write?"

"Write, Paul? I would have, had you let me know where you were."

"But I did—in my letter."

"What? *One last adventure*? It wasn't much of a letter."

"No, the next one, explaining it all."

"You know there was no next one."

"Hannah, why do I get the feeling you're looking for a fight? I said I sent a letter. If you didn't receive it, I don't know why not. Didn't Sannah *Basel* get one either?"

I shook my head.

"I wondered why no one replied. I sent them at the same time. So how are they, anyway—Sannah and Andreas?"

I took a deep breath and started in about all that had happened. About Sannah's illness. About her concern that Paul needed help. About how everyone else simply thought he had chosen to stay away and refused to chase after him.

"But you did, Hannah? You came to bring me back?" He looked at me expectantly, as if I was supposed to throw myself at him and tell him I needed him. Did his vanity really need that, even when he had Pearl under his arm, bringing her home like a prize? Did he want me to feel more foolish than I already did?

"Paul, I came because Sannah was so sure." I did not mention my own premonitions or selfish concern, or the steamboat call in the night. "I thought maybe Sannah knew something. I have to tell you, Paul, she was on the edge, and now . . . well, Sannah *Basel* is gone."

"Gone? Where?" He stopped as it sunk in. "You don't mean . . ."

"I'm sorry, Paul. She died."

I was afraid he'd blame himself for not being there. That it would awaken all the wounds from the loss of his own parents, the wounds that had almost undone him. That it would awaken the old anger, the anger that had made him almost untouchable. That he would blame God, the God he had almost rejected.

"How?"

"*Cholera morbus*, the doctor called it. I think it means her appendix burst."

He stood stiffly for what seemed like an eternity, his jaw held square and rigid, and I could see him wrestling with his emotion. I wanted to comfort him. I remembered how he had put his arm around me on the ship when I told him the story of my father's death, how he had tried to comfort me, when it was him who needed comforting the most. And maybe he would have found some solace then, too, had Old Gray Beard, as Paul had called the German teacher, not taken it all wrong and stirred Paul to rebellion. Now I might have put my arms around Paul in support. But there was Pearl.

Finally, he said simply, "I should have been there. She brought love back into my life. It was she—and you, Hannah—who saved me."

"You saved her too, Paul—from her bitterness. You brought her back to life."

"There's no bringing her back this time, is there?"

"No."

"I should have been there," he said again, but instead of sinking into self-condemnation, he drew a steady breath and said, "But I didn't know. I couldn't know."

I softened, seeing him deal with the pain. "No, Paul, you could not have known."

"Believe it or not," he continued, "I think God has me here for a purpose. For Pearl. I hope Sannah would have understood."

"You know she would have," I said, willing myself to do the same. I dug into my skirt pocket, pulling out the wad of money. "Four hundred of this is yours," I said, thrusting it at Paul. "Sannah gave it to me for the trip. It kind of multiplied in my pocket."

He raised his eyebrows in astonishment. "I always knew this money was saved for some good use. You hang onto it. Sannah sent it with you."

"But it's yours."

He smiled softly. "If I need it, believe me, I'll come begging." He caught my hand, pushing the money back at me. His hand lingered on mine, and I felt the calluses, and the warmth of his touch. I was sure he was about to tell me something important.

Chapter 32

"Hannah." His voice was earnest and soft. "I just want to tell you . . ." I caught my breath, waiting for his words, pinpricks of heat tickling my neck. "It means a lot to me that you came."

"Well, sure Paul. I'm glad to be here. Sort of." *Did this mean—?*

"Sort of?"

"I mean . . . it's just that . . . I had to bring the news about Sannah, and . . . there's the Indian boy, and the girl—well, you know—her father and all—it's not the happiest of days." *Why was I talking about that now?*

He let go of my hand and stood taller, as if he had suddenly remembered his purpose. "I'm sorry it has to be this way, Hannah. I just wanted to say it's been, uh, wonderful speaking *Hutterisch* with an old friend. I've missed our good Hutterite German."

I looked at him stupidly. *Wonderful speaking Hutterisch? Old friend?* Was that all he'd wanted to say? I could have slapped myself for my fool-headed imagination. But I smiled. "Sure. *Hutterisch is guot*—a wonderful language."

"Let's not wear it out here on the porch then," he said, becoming businesslike. "We'd better be going. I don't want Carson coming along and testing my pacifism." He cocked one eyebrow. "You said I'm not a Hutterite anymore, but believe me, Hannah, I haven't left the faith."

"I didn't really mean that, Paul. I was angry when I said it."

146

"Which is a good reason not to be here when Carson gets back. Sometimes anger makes us do things we shouldn't."

"What's he like, Paul?" I couldn't help wondering about this man who seemed to have changed the course of our lives.

"Carson is not an easy man. At first, he treated me like a son. But he's so controlling, it would drive you crazy. If you disagree with him on anything, he gets nasty."

"But you got along?"

He shrugged. "I don't fly off the handle like I used to. But he's strange Hannah. It's like he wants to groom someone for a partnership in both the ranch and Pearl, but he has to be boss in both departments. If he isn't, look out! I'm not even the first one he's tried it with. There was another man here watching over things when I came upriver with Carson and Pearl. I don't think he was much good anyway, but Carson ran him off because he hadn't gone murdering cattle-rustling Indians over the winter."

"I'm glad you're leaving."

"It's time. I'm out of favor since I started standing up for Pearl and speaking my mind. Carson can run the ranch how he wants, but I can't let him punch his daughter every time he flies into a rage. And now this thing with the young Indian." Sadness and anger clouded his eyes.

"Does Pearl want to go with you?"

"Yes."

"Does Carson know she wants to get away?"

"Maybe, but he also knows she's afraid. Carson is used to being obeyed."

"Some father. Has he no shame?"

"That's the odd part. Sometimes a day or so after hurting her, he'll show up all full of remorse with a new dress or something and promises of a wonderful life from now on."

"But it never lasts?"

"Never. Now, come on. We need to go."

In the house, Paul wrote a note to Carson saying he'd leave the horses at the Montana Livery in Fort Benton. He looked critically at the letters of his German Gothic-style script. "I hope he can read it. Speaking isn't so bad, but this is murder."

Pearl was just coming out of a bedroom. She wore a pleated cotton walking skirt, heavy and serviceable, but still more elegant than anything I owned. I stifled my envy. She had probably paid for that skirt with blood and bruises. She hesitated, looking at Paul, her eyes, still damp with tears, now dark and fearful. "What, Paul?" she said. "What's murder?"

"Oh, nothing. Nothing, Pearl. Just *Englisch*. Spelling it is murder."

Her shoulders sagged as she let out her breath and approached Paul. "Why don't you carry this?" In her hand was a neat stack of bills. "Two hundred and fifty dollars," she said.

"Where did that come from?" Paul asked.

"It's mine. From Father, believe it or not. It's been hidden inside my bedpost. Papa is a great believer in having money on hand if you need it."

"Well, now you need it. You hold it, Pearl. It's yours."

"I'm afraid I'll lose it. Carry it for me. I don't know what to buy anyway."

I felt the presence of Paul's money, which he had refused to accept, still in my pocket, and watched as he took Pearl's offering without so much as batting an eye. "Okay, but I'll keep it separate."

"How much do you have?" she asked. "Did Papa pay you?"

"Not for June. It's okay, I still have about eighty-five dollars." He patted his pocket where he had put Pearl's money. "This is yours. My wages are between your father and me—it's not for you to worry about."

Then Paul picked up two carpetbags that I assumed were Pearl's, and a duffel bag, and said, "Let's go see if Checkela tightened those cinches well enough to keep the saddles on top of the horses."

Pearl was crying again when we left, which was pretty much all I had seen her do. Some people are ugly when they cry, but the way the little dimples on her cheeks puckered up, even crying made Pearl look lovely. I knew I couldn't blame her for being pretty, any more than I could blame her for crying over what she was going through. She was leaving her home and her father—even if Carson wasn't worthy of the title.

I also knew I should feel charitable toward this girl who could probably use a little friendly female companionship. But she irritated me like a thorn in the side. For all my denials about Paul, I realized that inside I had been hoping he would throw his arms around me and whisper how desperately he had missed me. Now, it was plain to me that Pearl had what I wanted. I could try to be gracious, but could not imagine being even remotely intimate with her.

That, however, was before I sat in the cactus patch.

Chapter 33

The horse, my skirt, and the ladder-steep Teton River valley conspired against me. It is difficult for a woman in a skirt to straddle a horse without exposing her legs; so I found myself sitting sideways on slippery horse hair, with nothing to cling to but a younger brother who complained nonstop about having the life choked out of him.

"*Himble*, Hannah, I can hardly breathe you're squeezing so hard. I'm gonna pass out and we'll both fall off," Checkela grumbled.

"I thought you were my mighty protector. Quit yipping and get the horse up this stupid hill." I couldn't help glancing at Pearl. I wondered how she managed to look so cool and confident. With one hand holding the saddle ties and the other around Paul, she looked as if she did this every day. For all I knew, maybe she and Paul went riding like this all the time. Whatever the case, she was better at sitting on the back of a horse than I was.

My big mistake was deciding to get off and walk up the hill, which wouldn't have been so bad except for the wind. Horses are skittish about things fluttering behind them, and just as I let go of Checkela to ease myself off the horse, a wind gust lifted my apron. The stupid horse saw it flapping behind him, and reared up, shying to the side. Just like that, I zipped down his back like a child on a slide and found myself sitting on nothing but thin air. And that was okay, except for the landing. My slide ended up right in the middle of a forest of needle-pointed prickly pear cactuses.

I have never sat down in a fire, but I cannot imagine it being any worse than sitting on all those cactus spines. Suddenly, my backside was alive with the blistering and burning of all the pokers and pitchforks of Hades. I shrieked and tried to get up, but only plunged my hand among the needles. I couldn't move without more spines sticking into me. In the end, I could only sit where I was and cry.

One thing about Paul—he responds well to tears, which was maybe why Pearl shed so many. In a heartbeat he was there beside me. I looked at him helplessly. "*Dos tut veia*," I whined, the self-pity dripping from my voice.

"Yes," he said, "I'm sure it hurts terribly." He held my forearms to avoid pushing on the needles in my hands, and lifted. And, oh, how it hurt when I moved! Stepping gingerly away, I barely noticed the ones that pricked my ankles, but felt as if half the cactus plants in the patch were dangling from my hind end. There is a little bit of poison on each of those spines, and my posterior felt so hot and inflamed I was sure it must have swelled to double its size. But when I twisted around to look, it was normal, with no plants hanging from it. Just a profusion of needles sticking through my skirt.

To my horror, Paul peered intently at the problem area and said, "We're going to have to pull them, Hannah, or they'll end up infected."

I stifled another cry at a vision of Paul kneeling behind me pulling spines from my bottom. I would rather take the infection and die. "Don't you dare come near me," I hissed, desperation overruling my pain.

"I didn't mean me," Paul protested, holding his hands in front of himself defensively.

That is how I found myself behind a bush, with my skirts hoisted up around my waist, suffering the intimate ministrations of Pearl Tate.

In my humiliation, it occurred to me that the Lord must have a sense of humor. Was this his way of correcting my attitude toward Pearl? I had seen her as a thorn in my side; now I needed her to pull them out of my backside. Oh, how deep they go when you fly at them all the way from the top of a horse.

When Pearl finally finished and we emerged from the bushes, I glared at the two men and said, "If anybody says anything or so much as smiles, I don't care what the Bible says, I am going to kill somebody!" Neither said a word.

Sitting on the horse was out of the question, so while the others rode I hobbled along beside them like an arthritic old woman—all the way to Fort Benton.

Yes, I was quite the rescuer! What in the world had I been thinking? I remembered the time I fell off a bridge in Russia and cut my head. I had insisted on going after Paul that time too, and had ended up needing his help. Why did these things have to happen to me when I was with Paul? Perhaps the Lord was telling me to keep my distance.

Eventually, I gave Paul a sketchy rendition of how we had earned our passage by cooking meals on the steamboat. But I was poor company, and we did not talk much.

The Montana Livery was on Main Street. As we approached, Paul said, "Hannah, I can't get over you making your way out here alone, and—"

"Not alone," Checkela interrupted. "I was watching out for her."

"Oh, that's right," Paul said, letting a small grin light his face. "Her guardian angel. I noticed the way you kept her from falling off the horse."

The walk had cooled my temper, so I ignored his insolent grin and said, "Believe it or not, I almost wondered if the Lord had sent a real angel to me."

"Checkela?" Paul asked doubtfully.

"She means an old drunk," Checkela corrected.

"An old drunk angel?" Paul said. "I think you two had better read your Bibles again."

"First off, he's not that old," I said, "although he is a drunk. But he was there when we needed help. The Lord works in mysterious ways, and I couldn't help but wonder."

"I see," Paul said, but he didn't. His face clouded as if he thought I had lost my mind.

"Don't look so worried," I said. "I'll tell you all about it later. In fact, I hope to find him before we leave."

"Sure, we'll look in the bottom of every empty bottle in town," Checkela added.

～

The livery was a typical unpainted barn-like building with a big door in front. Paul slipped off his horse and helped Pearl down. She walked stiffly for a few steps, but limbered up quickly. I envied her and would have traded backsides in an instant. Mine was still on fire. Paul paid the liveryman, and we left the horses behind. That suited me. I never wanted to see them again.

"Where to now?" Checkela asked.

"To the levee, of course," I answered.

"Let's see if either of those boats are leaving soon," Paul finished.

The Break of Day was on the other side of Main, and as we passed by, I wondered if we should stop to look for Harry, but decided our morning saloon visit had been plenty for one day.

Further down, near the I. G. Baker store, the street was lined with canvas-covered green wagons loaded with supplies. They were hooked together in trains of three, and I counted eight pairs of oxen harnessed to each train.

"Hey, there's a sight!" Checkela said, pointing up the street. "Look at those red-coated soldiers!" About a dozen troops waited nearby with their horses.

"They'll be escorting that bull train on the Whoop-up Trail to Canada," Paul said. "They're North West Mounted Police. They get all their supplies here at the I. G. Baker store."

It would make a grand spectacle when all those red coats and green wagons and big oxen paraded out of town. I could hardly tear my eyes away. At least not until I heard a crash across the street, and turned just in time to see a figure tumble through the batwing doors of The Break of Day.

It's funny how several people will sometimes say exactly the same thing at once. "Oh, my goodness," Pearl cried, staring across the street. And Paul, Checkela, and I all joined her in a surprised chorus of "It's Harry!"

"You know Harry?" I asked, staring at Pearl as she and Paul stared back at me.

"Know him?" Pearl said. "He's the man I was supposed to marry."

Chapter 34

I once heard that the events of life go around in a circle. If so, we had just completed one full loop with Harry. This saloon door routine was all too familiar.

"He's the one who wouldn't kill Indians?" I said in surprise.

"*Joh*, but I thought he left town," Paul replied. "How do *you* know him?"

"You were going to marry Harry?" I said to Pearl.

"He said he was going to marry *me*. I never said I agreed."

"But how do *you* know him?" Paul repeated.

"He's Hannah's angel," Checkela cut in.

"And he's as drunk as he was when we first met," I muttered disdainfully. Still, I had to smile, remembering that first meeting. "You should have seen Checkela. He thought he was in a fight for his life. He thought Harry—"

"Hannah! *Shtila*—quiet!" Checkela said. "No wonder you sat in the cactus. You're a pain in the hinder yourself."

"Now, now, little brother. I was just going to say how brave you were."

"Uh, oh," he said, forgetting my teasing, "I think Harry has big trouble this time."

I followed his gaze to a figure emerging from the saloon. "The buckskin man!"

"You know that *Mensh* too?" Paul said.

"Call him a *man* if you want. I will not. I call him a brute. He was on the steamboat—until Harry put him ashore in the

155

middle of nowhere."

"Paul, you have to help him," Pearl said.

"Somehow, so do I," I added. "The brute came after me in the middle of the night. Thankfully, Harry came along."

Paul bristled. "You mean he was going to . . .?" He started across the street. I followed, as fast as I could. The muscles in my buttocks were stiffening painfully.

"Don't worry, Hannah. I'm with you," said the familiar voice of my protector. One thing about Checkela—there were no cowardly bones in his body. I just hoped those bones wouldn't soon be broken.

Harry was on his knees, and I could hear Buckskin snarl as he kicked him viciously in the ribs. There was an awful cracking noise and Harry flopped onto his back. The buckskin man lined himself up for a kick to Harry's head. Paul broke into a run. Buckskin's foot was in the air when Paul hit him, and he went over like a rotten tree in a windstorm. But rotten trees stay down; the buckskin man rolled and gained his feet in one motion, but not as quickly as Paul, who was standing between him and Harry when he came up.

"What in thunder do you think you're doin'?" he shouted.

"I think you were in danger of killing a defenseless man," Paul replied. "You don't want that on your conscience."

"Don't fret about my conscience. This poxy varmint is going to get a dose of medicine, and you'd best stay out of it or you'll get a few swallows yourself." He lunged at Paul, swinging his fist like a hammer. I gasped as Paul ducked and the punch sailed overhead. He swung so hard, the momentum twisted his body sideways right in front of Paul, and even I could see how easily Paul could punch him or maybe push him while he was off balance. I felt my own fists tighten, rooting for Paul. But Paul only stood there and waited for him to come again. Which he did, still swinging. Paul ducked and sidestepped him twice more. The buckskin man's face twisted angrily under his scruffy growth of beard.

"Come on, you mangy coward," he said. "Stand and fight." He beckoned with his fingers. "Come on, let's see what you got." He charged at Paul again, and this time clipped him on the chin. Paul stumbled back, and just managed to dive sideways and roll out of the way of the next onslaught. He got up just in time to avoid a wicked kick.

"Paul!" I yelled. "Do something!"

"Can you get Harry out of here?" he said.

"And leave you to get beat up? Knock him down or something!"

"You!" the buckskin man exclaimed, pointing a dirty finger at me. "I mighta knowed you'd show up again. I got unfinished business with you."

"You will keep your business to yourself," Paul said.

"You got the stomach to back up them words, boy? You're a slippery little dickens, but I got all day, and I'm gonna take you apart. Then I'm gonna deal with the little drunk here— then you." He pointed at me again.

"Paul!" I cried again. "Fight."

"Just go." Paul said.

"But you've got to—"

"Hannah, I'm trying to give you a chance. Either you believe what you believe or you don't. I—"

Buckskin smashed a fist into the side of Paul's head, and Paul went down. He rolled and tried to get up, but fell sideways again. I knew a kick would come next. What a time to be a pacifist! Even if Paul was right, I didn't care. I would fight the man myself if—

Then I heard my thoughts spoken aloud. "I don't care if I am a pacifist. That's my friend!" It was Checkela, rushing in. He hit the man on the run, and the two of them staggered back two steps before the buckskin man caught his balance and pitched Checkela through the air. He laughed. "I am going to enjoy this, squirt! If you wanna be first, it's fine with me."

Checkela jumped up and charged at him again, arms flailing. I thought Buckskin would whallop him with one of those wicked fists, but he grabbed Checkela's face, scrunching his cheeks and mouth in his hand as if he were squeezing an orange. Check's face puckered and stretched, and I was afraid his lips would peel off like a rind. Then he popped free and landed a punch in Buckskin's stomach. The big man spun him around and cuffed him on the back of the head, sending him face first into the dirt. By now Paul was on his feet again. Checkela got up unsteadily beside him. I couldn't help thinking of the irony as the two of them faced the buckskin man: Paul would not raise a hand to fight; Checkela flailed away like a windmill. Yet the result would be the same. Both would be pummeled.

I glanced around, looking for help. People were coming out of the saloon to watch, and I saw a bearded old man under an even older-looking beat-up Stetson. But more important was the whiskey bottle he carried. I was on the boardwalk in two steps and a jump. I had the whiskey bottle in my hand almost before the old man knew I was there.

"What in blazes?" he cried in bewilderment.

"I'll pay you for it," I said. "But I need it now!" He let go. I had forgotten about Hutterite pacifism, too. If that buckskin man went after Paul and my brother again, he was going to get a shot of whiskey. And that shot was going to hit him harder than it had ever hit Harry—right on the back of the noggin'.

"I'm not here to fight you," Paul said evenly. "But you need to leave Harry alone."

"I don't care whether you fight or not. Neither one of you are worth a fig. I'm gonna . . ." His words tailed off, and his face contracted as if he were suddenly in pain. "I'm gonna . . ."

He seemed to be having trouble concentrating. "I'm gonna . . ." He put his hand on his stomach, hunching over, and I saw his mouth open as he caught his breath. "It ain't over. It ain't over," he gasped. Then he turned and bolted like the devil was after him, around the side of the saloon toward the back alley. In dumbfounded amazement, the four of us watched him run. I looked up and down the street, but saw nothing that could have scared him off.

"I hit him in the stomach," Checkela offered doubtfully. "Maybe that's it."

"Must have been some hit," I said. "Almost as hard as the hit you put on Harry that time."

"Hannah, leave it alone," Checkela grumbled. "Go look after Harry."

Pearl was already beside Harry, helping him to his knees. "I hit him with a little prayer," she said. "Could that have helped?"

"You prayed?" I said in disbelief. What could this unchurched rancher girl possibly know about prayer?

"Pearl and I have been studying the Bible," Paul explained.

I should have rejoiced for Pearl, but the only thought that came was, *I'll just bet you have*. I bit my tongue.

"And I gave your buffalo hunter friend a liberal dose of this," came another voice. It was Frank, the saloonkeeper we had spoken with in the morning. On his face was a smile. In his hand was a green glass jar.

Chapter 35

I stared at the man, and then the jar, which his body hid from the onlookers outside the saloon. "Now, don't you go saying anything about this to anyone," he cautioned.

I made out the words Mercuric Chloride on the bottle. In a flash, it all came clear. No wonder the buckskin man had run away so quickly! We had that stuff on the colony, and I knew the crystals in the jar were one of the most wildly effective laxatives you could buy. He had run, not to the back alley, but to the back *house* behind the saloon. Frank slipped the jar into his trousers pocket.

"So you . . ." I stammered.

"Colorless and tasteless," he said. "A perfect little whiskey mixer. That buffalo hunter showed up this morning, snarly as a cornered badger. Said he was looking for an English feller named Harry Orman who was in need of a thrashing. Well, I'm kind of partial to ole Harry, and I figured he could use a little help, considering his present condition. So while that buffalo hunter was fortifying himself at the bar, I fortified his drinks a mite." The saloonkeeper chuckled merrily. "I'd say he's having trouble holding his liquor."

I had to laugh, until I looked at Harry, who was now on his knees, vomiting in the street. "So is he," I said with disgust. It amazed me to see how alcohol could make a talented and otherwise admirable man so pathetic. Couldn't he see what he was doing to himself? I turned back to the saloonkeeper.

"I thought he was sleeping off last night's mistake. How did he get like this already."

"Oh, he stumbled into the bar a few hours after you left this morning with eyes about as red as two bites from a raw beef steak, and says, 'You better give me some hair of the mangy dog that bit me, Frank. Just one, mind, to level me out.' So I set him up a drink. But, of course, for Harry—"

I helped him finish his sentence, "—there's no such thing as one."

"Right as rain, ma'am. Now, you listen—that hunter has a room here, and I believe I can keep him busy hitching his suspenders up and down for a bit, but if you can get Harry accommodated elsewhere you'd be doing him a favor. Sober, he'll whip his weight in wild cats and shoot the pips off the ace of spades, but like this . . ."

"We'll put him up somewhere, Frank. But how did he get here?" I asked.

"Harry?"

"No, the bucksk . . . the buffalo hunter. Harry put him ashore three weeks ago, at gunpoint."

Frank rolled his eyes and nodded. "I wondered why the feller was so riled. The steamboat *Key West* must have picked him up. It put in first thing this morning."

I nodded. "We heard the whistle."

As Frank went back to the saloon, Paul said, "*Himble*, you two are right! Angels do come in the strangest form around here. I think the bartender saved us all from a beating."

I looked darkly at Paul. "I think you should have tried to hit back."

"Well, Hannah, I wanted to, but I guess you either live by your beliefs or you don't."

"*Joh*, Paul. But don't you think . . .? *Ach*, never mind!" I looked at him closely. "Are you the same Paul I used to know?"

He only stared back, his expression appraising, puzzled. It made me nervous. *"Vos?"* I finally asked. "What are you looking at?"

"I don't know Hannah. You've been in town less than one day, and already you're on a first name basis with the saloon-keepers. Now here you are, staggering around the streets with a bottle of whiskey in your hand looking for a fight! Is this the same girl I used to know at Split Rock Colony?"

The bottle! I had forgotten. I stared at my hand. Sure enough, I was holding the bottle as tightly as any desperate old alcoholic in the street. Then I noticed the old man I had taken it from. Evidently he had not forgotten, for he was staring at the amber bottle as if it as if were liquid gold.

A smile cracked Paul's stern features, and I realized he was teasing. He said, "Wouldn't this be a nice picture for your mother to see!"

Dear Mueter. *"Ach,* Paul, it would put three nails in her coffin for sure!" I smiled, but stopped when Paul's face blanched. *Sannah.* "I'm sorry, Paul. I didn't think." I thrust the bottle back at the old man. "I'm sorry to you, too. I didn't need it after all."

"Thankee," he croaked, eagerly taking the bottle. He tipped it to his lips for a drink, then offered it back. "Have a swallow to settle your nerves?"

"No," I said, "but it's kind of you to offer." He followed the other onlookers back to the dark saloon.

∾

I checked the bandage around Harry's ribs. Bruised, possibly cracked, had been the pronouncement. Either way it was going to hurt for a while—not that he had felt much pain at the time, and he certainly wasn't feeling any now. I wondered if the doctor had been wise to give laudanum to Harry. The opium-medicine was freely available in drug stores across the country—and highly addictive. I remembered a Mennonite preacher who once came to the colony, telling how there were people all over America, from Civil War vets to housewives, with life-long addictions to the drug. The last thing Harry needed was to develop a liking for opium. But I couldn't blame the doctor. Harry had sobered up just enough to revive his fighting spirit, and the doctor took the first punch. Alcohol does such strange things to a man.

"Do you think the doctor overdid it?" I asked Paul and the others.

"I don't know," Pearl replied, putting her hand to his forehead. "He's peaceful as a baby now."

"More like a dead man," Checkela added. He and Paul were still breathing hard. "I don't see how a little guy like that can be so heavy."

"Well," Paul said as we prepared to leave. "I've never seen either a baby or a dead man wearing handcuffs to bed.

Chapter 36

Poor Harry. I hadn't known what else to do with him. I could not bring myself to dump him off at the murderer's house—The Extradition. Nor did I want to leave him at The Jungle, where we had seen the troupe of frilly women. There were other hotels, but as far as I was concerned they were all houses of temptation. However, the staterooms on the *Silver Mist* would not be needed until the steamer left Fort Benton the next day, and when I explained the situation, Captain Anders was kind enough to accommodate him in a private room, handcuffed—once again—to a bed. It may have helped that I agreed to cook on the return trip as far as Split Rock Colony.

I had been to the Turner Drug Store on Front Street. Finally, I felt some relief as the camphor penetrated the skin of my burning hind end. And, finally, I found relief from the pace of a crisis-filled day. Things were beginning to work out. We had found Paul, even if he came with an attachment named Pearl. We had survived the buckskin man. We had rescued Harry, safe and sound, if not sober. Now there was nothing to do but wait until the *Silver Mist* started downriver. Yet it still made no sense for me to have come. Paul was perfectly fine, and had been leaving anyway. In fact, rather than being his rescuer, I had done little more than get in the way. And now I had words to regret.

I stood alone on the hurricane deck, leaning on the yawl, which was suspended by great hangers in the shape of upside-down L's. The setting sun washed over the eastern bluffs, spilling reflected gold into the muddy water below. Upriver, the Benton Ferry, with a cargo of two horses and a wagon, nosed a lazy path through richness of the river scene.

In spite of the beauty, my bones ached with weariness. I remembered the conversation I'd had with Paul after getting Harry settled in. I should not have needled him all over again.

"You could have got yourself killed," I chided. "What were you doing, standing there like a punching bag?"

"What was *I* doing?" he answered indignantly. "If you had got Check and Pearl to help drag Harry away like I asked, everything would have been fine. But no, you had to distract me with your arguing until he nearly knocked me silly."

My anger flashed so quickly I hadn't even seen it ignite. "So it's my fault? You want to dance with this man instead of lifting a finger to protect yourself, and it's my fault you missed a step and almost got us all killed! Well, let me remind you Paul, dancing is against the Hutterite religion, too!" I knew it was ridiculous even as I said it, but for a reason I couldn't explain, I felt like hurting the man I cared for most.

"Well, aren't you just the little Hutterite hypocrite!" he shot back. "You . . ." Then he stopped and took a deep breath. "Look, Hannah, what do you want? You accused me earlier of not being a Hutterite. Well, I am a Hutterite, so that's what you get. Nonviolence."

I was already ashamed of my outburst, but said nothing.

He went on. "Who are the fighters you know, Hannah? That buffalo hunter? Harry? Carson Tate? Where does it lead? Where do you draw the line before it comes to killing?" He did not wait for me to answer. "I've thought about it, you know. In the hand of God a clenched fist is not an easy fit.

"Do you remember when we first came to America, and I ran away on the *Astrid Wilhemina*?"

"Of course," I replied.

"Well, there was a man on the boat—a gunfighter. He wore a red sash on his waist, with pearl-handled revolvers tucked inside."

"Bill Hickok. I know, Paul."

"Yes, and he was handsome and confident, and I thought I had never seen such a glorious man. But, Hannah, he was a killer. I finally realized he was dead inside, almost as dead as the men he had killed. And do you know what? I knew I wanted to be a better man than that. I found out I wanted to be the kind of man my father had been. And you, Hannah, you helped me see it. Your peace, your faith, helped turn me in the right direction. And now, here you are sniping at me for not carrying a big stick or gun. It's not like you, Hannah. I don't understand what's come over you."

The Bible says the truth will set you free. And I believe it will. But sometimes the truth is painful. Paul's gentle, but pointed talk jabbed like a cactus spine into my pride. He was right, oh, so right. Maybe I had just been trying to carry too much of a load myself, and somehow I had let it blind me to the presence of the One who could carry it for me, and it was making me into someone I didn't want to be. Silently, so only the Lord could hear, I mouthed a quick prayer. *Lord, help me have the attitude you want.* And then, silently, incomprehensibly, so only Paul could hear, I hissed, "Maybe you should worry more about understanding Pearl."

I had shocked even myself with that uncharitable comment. And no doubt disgusted Paul. He walked away, and we had hardly spoken since. I was sure he would avoid me for the rest of the trip home.

Now, standing on the deck, footsteps made me turn—to one more surprise. It was Paul.

"It's a beautiful evening, isn't it?" he said leaning an elbow on the yawl beside me.

I fidgeted. "Yes, uh, the cliffs are dazzling."

"We haven't had a peaceful moment since you arrived," he said.

"I'm just a natural agitator, I guess."

He backtracked quickly. "No, no, I just mean it's been too hectic to talk. But I thought now might be a good time. Checkela is giving Pearl a tour of your kitchen space."

I had to smile. "Probably talking her into taking over as head potato peeler, if I know my brother."

"I have no doubt." Paul smiled too, a hesitant smile, and I knew it was time to swallow some pride.

"Paul, I think I owe you . . . No, I *do* owe you an apology. I'm sorry for being so difficult. I have been nothing but a grump since I arrived."

"Well," he replied, "I'd say you've had a difficult time."

"It's no excuse."

"It reminds me of old times," he said with a teasing smile. "Besides, I'm glad to see you, though I'm still amazed you came so far alone."

"Well . . ." I grinned back. "I had my protector."

"Sure, and now I'm here to help Checkela look after you." His eyes lit up in merriment, catching the lustrous gold from the eastern bank. "Quite a team, don't you think? A fighting terrier and a street dancer."

"I shouldn't have said that. You were right when you said we have to live what we believe. I'm sorry."

"It's okay, Hannah. You know, I just wanted to give you time to get Harry out of harm's way, but in case you think I'm holier than thou, I wasn't going to stand by and let him hurt you. The saloonkeeper's remedy took effect just in time, but if it came down to it I'd have tried to protect you."

"Everybody's somebody's protector." I said with a biting little laugh.

"I didn't mean it as a joke," Paul said defensively.

"I'm not laughing at you. It's just that . . . it's stupid, but maybe that's what's bothering me. I thought I was going to be *your* protector too, or rescuer. When we didn't hear from you, I thought you might be in some kind of trouble. But here you are, perfectly fine. You don't need help, and the most heroic thing I've managed is to sit in a cactus patch."

"Well," Paul laughed, "that is a brave thing to do."

"You should try it sometime," I added sourly. "But really, I thought I had some purpose. Before Sannah died she said, 'I think Paul needs you, Hannah.'" I shrugged, embarrassed. "So much for Sannah's intuition. Maybe it was meant for Harry."

"Sannah, dear Sannah," Paul said sadly. "I will miss her." Then he put his hand on mine, tenderly, reassuringly. I tried to be casual, but the electric tingle of his touch ran all the way from my fingertips through the length of my spine. I felt the rush of blood, and knew my face would be as pink as the sunlit clouds.

"Hannah, there is something I want to say to you."

"Yes, Paul? What is it?" *Do you love me?* I wondered.

He looked at me, and I could see in his eyes it was important. "Don't take up with Harry," he said. "I don't think I could bear seeing you give your love to Harry."

Chapter 37

A few minutes earlier I'd been surprised that Paul would even speak to me. Now I was stunned by his words. I stared dumbly, weighing his intent. Did he see Harry as a rival? Finally, I found my voice. "Paul, I do care for Harry, but—"

"And I know he cares for you, Hannah."

"How would you know that?"

"He told me."

"What? When were you talking to Harry?"

"Just now. I checked in on him before coming up."

Another surprise. Were men no different than the school-girls back home? A ridiculous image popped into my head. Surely drunken Harry and Hutterite Paul were not passing notes and giggling about the girls they liked! "And he thinks he wants to . . .?"

"Court you, yes. Hannah, I know it's not really my business, but please, don't become attached to Harry."

My cheeks felt warm in the last of the sun. "Why, Paul? Do you have a better idea?" I held my breath for his answer.

"Yes, I . . ." He seemed to struggle for the right words. Then he blurted, "If it comes to that, you'd be much better off with Lorenz."

"Lorenz?" I looked stupidly at Paul, the breath escaping me like wind from a torn sail.

Paul rushed ahead. "Lorenz is a good colony man. With Harry you'd have to give up everything. And you can't save a man like that. He's out of control."

I felt like sighing my entire body into thin air, but I squared my shoulders and sucked in a lungful. This was the surprise to top them all. Now he was arranging my marriage! To Lorenz! "Paul, who appointed you matchmaker? Even if I wanted a man—which at this moment I do not—don't you think I could pick for myself?"

He held up his hands defensively. "But I thought you liked him, Hannah."

"You seem to know all about the men in my life, Paul. When did I ever mention an interest in Lorenz?" Then I remembered, and wished I had kept my mouth shut.

"In your last letter, just before I left Joseph Wallman's farm."

I nodded, cringing inside. I remembered too well my pathetic attempt to manipulate Paul's heart.

"You said boring men sometimes make the best husbands." He looked earnestly at me. "You sounded serious. If you really care for him, a quiet life with Lorenz would be better than a ruined life with Harry."

I dropped my head in shame. What could I tell Paul now? That the girl who had been his best friend since childhood was really just a manipulative conniver? I had thought he would try to talk me out of a dreary life with Lorenz. Instead, he was trying to talk me into it.

Maybe he felt sorry for me, since he had Pearl, and was trying to help me see some options. But what options! Harry said he liked me. So what? Between alcohol and laudanum, he didn't know what he liked. Lorenz claimed to want me. So what? I didn't want Lorenz. I wanted Paul. Paul wanted Pearl. End of story.

I was no dog to grovel for tidbits of affection. If Paul wanted to think I was torn between Harry and Lorenz, I guess he would just have to go ahead and think it. I wouldn't have him feeling guilty or sorry for me.

"I'm going to ask Harry to come with us to Split Rock," I said.

"I wish you wouldn't."

"You're taking Pearl."

"That's different."

"Different how?" I asked.

Paul looked up to the purpling sky as if gathering thoughts from the clouds. "She has a sweet and gentle heart. She is seeking the Lord. She needs a place to rest and heal."

"Maybe Harry needs to rest and heal, too."

"Yes, but I don't think he knows it. *Er suft digonsa Tsait.* He won't quit."

"So he drinks all the time. Should I leave him on the trash heap because he isn't perfect?"

He sighed in defeat. "No. Do what you think is right. I just don't want to see you hurt."

If only he knew the irony of his words. "Look, Paul, I know Harry is a hard case, but he's on the boat already and I can't see leaving him to his own devices. Besides, he came back to Fort Benton because of me, which must have been painful after whatever happened with Carson Tate—not to mention his lost dream of a general store."

Paul lifted his head in surprise. "Lost dream of what?"

"His store. He lost everything on the steamboat wreck. It was going to be his big chance."

"Hannah, I don't know what he's been telling you, but I don't think there was ever any store in his plans, or that he was ruined by a steamboat wreck."

"Well, it's what he told me, and I don't see why he would make it up."

"Maybe he wanted you to think the best of him. He. . . ." Paul hesitated, his mouth twitching as if unwilling to form the next words. Finally, he continued. "Hannah, I wasn't going to mention this, but maybe it's a good thing you're getting Harry out of Fort Benton—to save him from being arrested. The fact is, Harry left because Sheriff Healy ran him out of town."

"Ran him out? Why? For drinking too much?"

"Don't take me wrong for saying this, but on charges of molestation. Molestation against Pearl."

Chapter 38

My hands flew to my mouth, stifling a cry. Surely it couldn't be! Not Harry. "Oh, Paul, please say it isn't true."

"It isn't true, Hannah."

That stopped me. Shock can turn quickly to anger, and I felt it surge. "Then what's the idea saying it? Don't you know how horrible that is? You can ruin a person's—"

"I know. I know. I mean he *was* run out on charges, but the charges weren't true. After Carson fired Harry, he wanted him gone completely. So he told the sheriff that Harry had been sneaking around to the ranch, drinking and interfering with his daughter. Said he was afraid he couldn't protect her from Harry forever, so Healy ran him out on threat of arrest if he ever returned."

"And he had done nothing?"

"As far as I know, he'd just been carrying on much like we found him today, not hurting anyone but himself. But it's easy to believe the worst of a drunk."

The sun had finally disappeared beyond the pink-topped valley edge. Thinking about Harry with his weaknesses, Carson Tate with his ruthless need to control, even if it meant ruining others, Fort Benton with its false-fronted buildings catering to so many lustful appetites, it seemed that the beauty of the evening served only to gloss over a world of corruption. "Whatever possessed you to work for a despicable man like Carson Tate anyway?" I asked.

Paul cocked his head whimsically in the growing shadows. "I don't know, really, unless it was the Lord's leading. It was all in my letter—"

"Which I didn't get."

"Yes, well, I was in Yankton, on my way home. I had bought bread and cheese and decided to have lunch on the levee and watch the steamboats. I kind of half wondered if I might even see the old *Astrid Wilhemina* come along, though that isn't her part of the river, and she may be sunk by now, anyway."

"*Joh, joh*, Paul, just get on with it," I chided.

"Well, the *Far West* steamboat was tied up at the levee, almost ready to get underway. There was a man in a sack suit and Montana-peaked hat yelling at a young fellow about Checkela's age. The man was on crutches and he used one to smack the youngster on the knees, then banged him over the head. He stood over him, and I thought he was going to beat him to a pulp, when a girl in a beautiful white dress sailed down from the boiler deck and stepped in between.

"There were a few roosters there, and they just watched as he raised the crutch at the girl. The boat was right up against the levee, and next thing I knew I jumped across and found myself standing by the girl. I hardly knew what I was doing, but I said, 'Sir, you will have to beat me down too, before you touch this girl.'

"For a moment I thought he was going to go after me with that crutch, but just then the boy shouts, 'I quit! Somebody else can look after your stupid horses,' and he jumped up and scurried away like an alley dog with its tail between its legs.

"The man stuck the crutch back under his arm and laughed. He said he had no intention of hitting his daughter, and was only after the boy because he had tried to steal a bottle of port from him.

"I didn't know what to make of that, but he looks me up

and down, puts out his hand and says, 'Young man, I'm Carson Tate, and this is my daughter Pearl. How would you like a job?'"

"Just like that, he offered you a job? Doing what?"

Paul shrugged. "Not much. Running errands and feeding a string of six horses he had on the boat."

"And you just said yes."

"Hannah, it happened so fast, I don't even know why I did it, but something inside me said, *take this job.* The boat was leaving, so I scribbled that note to you, grabbed my bag, and jumped aboard. It was supposed to be just for the trip up. He said he'd pay me and then buy me a ticket back. But when we arrived he got rid of Harry and asked me to stay. Believe it or not, Hannah, I can't help but believe it was meant to be."

I thought about Paul's story, trying to take it all in. It sounded like what I sometimes called a divine appointment. I remembered trying to convince Paul, years earlier, that the Lord might have put him with us on the ship to America so he could save Checkela from being swept overboard. Back then, Paul had stubbornly refused to believe God had any purpose for his life. How he had changed!

"Well, Paul," I said at last, "you are crazier than I am. My river trip was nowhere near as impulsive as yours."

I don't know if there was something funny about it or if we were just tired, but I giggled and he snickered and we found ourselves laughing in the darkness like two children in mischief. Then Paul caught my hand and said, "Well, you shouldn't have come, but I'm glad you're here."

Then we were quiet again, and it occurred to me that something still bothered me about Paul's story. "Paul, how could you just walk in and let Carson abuse poor Harry the way he did, and then take his job? It doesn't seem right."

Paul let go of my hand. "It wasn't like that, Hannah. When we arrived at the ranch, Harry had been drinking, and rustlers had been getting away with cattle all winter. Carson seemed justified in letting him go. I knew nothing about it. I only found out later that Carson had hired Harry because of his skill with a gun. He expected a tally of dead Indians when he got back, but Harry disappointed him. I guess he thought Carson could afford to feed a few hungry Natives."

"Well, I agree with Harry."

"Except that he was hired to protect the cattle."

"Don't tell me he should have gone shooting Indians."

"Of course not. I'm just saying there are two sides. Harry was right not to murder, but when he couldn't do what was expected, he did nothing at all, except go back to the bottle."

"Always the bottle. Why would Carson have hired him in the first place, the way he is?"

"Apparently, Carson showed up at a livery when two wolf hunters were roughing up a stable hand for not brushing their horses properly. Then Harry strolled in, stepped between the two wolfers, snatched the gun out of the first one's holster and used it to clonk the other one on the side of the head. Harry drew his own gun and told the first wolfer to haul his partner out of there quick unless he wanted his back pockets full of lead. Carson was impressed."

"He's an impressive man when he's sober," I said, remembering how he had helped Checkela and me. "Scary, but impressive."

We stopped talking then, and the murmuring stillness of the night closed around us. Stars now twinkled overhead, and lamplight cast a yellow glow through Fort Benton's nightlife windows. Trickling water lapped against the hull of the *Silver Mist*. From somewhere behind a set of saloon doors, a quiet tinkling of piano notes escaped, and the occasional shout and muffled clip of horse hooves on dirt streets broke through the muttering darkness. It could have been threatening or romantic, depending on your frame of mind. Paul made it analytical.

"You know, your mention of Harry and that steamboat wreck has got me thinking," he said. "I mailed my letters on May 17, a few days after I got here. I think that's about when the *Sundown* sank. I never thought of it, but I'd guess my letters were on that boat."

"How could that be?" I asked. "The *Sundown* was going upstream. It's the one that was bringing Harry's supplies."

"I don't think so," Paul said. "It was in Benton before it sank."

"I saw it in the river myself," I insisted. And then I remembered. I could see the boat, half submerged in the river, the paddle wheel facing into the current. Why hadn't I thought of that before? "Paul, you're right. That boat was going downstream." It hurt to think that Harry was a liar on top of everything else.

～

I knelt, uttered my prayers, and climbed into bed. My peace was shadowed by the pain of cactus spines, the contamination of lies, and the corruption of death. The image of the young Indian especially haunted me. I had seen bodies before, lying peaceful in the coffin in the dignity of the funeral rite. But there was no dignity in this. Violent death was a mix of pallid decrepitude and bubbling gore when what is inside is forced out where it should not be. I had seen death from old age, from sickness, and from accidents. Awful memories. But murder had an ugliness all its own.

The day had been too much. Silently, I cried myself to sleep. I wept for the Indian boy, for Sannah, for my long-dead father, maybe even for Harry and what he had become. And for Paul—my own private, selfish sorrow—for the part of him that I could not have.

Chapter 39

They say that our little lives are rounded by a sleep, and it must be true. I had gone to bed miserable, but felt better in the morning. I dressed in the cleaner of my two skirts, wincing at its rumpled appearance. It promised to be an uneventful day of waiting for the *Silver Mist* to be loaded and to leave. Maybe there would be time to visit the International Laundry, which I had noticed on Front Street.

I brushed the hair back from my temples, then twisted it into rolls and wrapped it and my braids into a bun. I tied my *Tiechl* over my head and was ready to meet the others. We had decided to get breakfast at a place called the Chop House. But first, there was Harry. I hated people lying to me.

"So what was all that nonsense about starting a store?" I began, thrusting open the shutters to air out the morning stink of a drunkard.

"Ooh, Hannah," he said, covering his eyes. "I slept very well. Thank you for asking. But do you think we need this much light?"

"You need a lot more than sunlight in your life, Harry. Why didn't you tell the truth about leaving Fort Benton? I know the sheriff ran you out. And I know why."

He groaned. "Carson made that up to get rid of me. I liked Pearl—and he knew it—but I did nothing improper, I assure you."

"I know, Harry. But why feed me those lies about a store?"

Harry sat up, just as he had done the first time he had been handcuffed to the bed. He put his head in hands, rubbing his temples as if to wipe away the pain and fuzz. Then he leveled what would have to pass for a steady gaze. "Hannah, after the way we first met, would you have believed me if I said I had been falsely accused of something like that?"

I thought for a minute. "No, Harry, I suppose not. But you could simply have said you worked on a ranch and then quit. It would have been closer to the truth."

He snorted, a laugh without humor. "Maybe I don't like the bitter memories. Besides, I told you, you are special. Perhaps I wanted to impress you."

"I thought you were fond of Pearl?"

"I was."

Now *I* snorted. "Me? Pearl? The bottle? Straight and true as a willow stick, aren't you, Harry?" But I couldn't berate him too much. Hadn't I found him attractive—when he was the other Harry, the one that was trying to change?

He shifted uncomfortably. "Look, did you come for a reason —other than to humiliate me?"

"I'm not trying to humiliate you. I just want to sort things out, like why you followed me to Fort Benton."

"How many times do I have to say it? I know it's stupid, but after meeting you I wanted to hold my head higher. I got the idea to go back and make Carson admit he was lying, then maybe start over with Pearl. I even thought I might win some of your affection."

"Alcohol has muddled your head. You can't have two, Harry."

"I didn't mean romantically—well, not at first, anyway. I just found you an inspiration—setting off upriver so clear-eyed and innocent, unlike myself running away in disgrace."

"Was there really something between you and Pearl?"

"I thought so. I was undergoing a sober interlude when I met her, and Carson even considered me good son-in-law material. I believe Pearl and I were actually developing an attraction. She was young, but I thought when she reached sixteen I might have the confidence to ask for her hand." He shrugged despondently. "Things have a way of blowing up."

"You traded everything important for the bottle."

"Yeah, well, some demons are difficult to keep down."

"You had the courage to try once. You can try again."

"I did—when I saw you and the boy board the steamboat." He laughed. "You found your boyfriend, and I found another hangover."

"I'm afraid he's not my boyfriend," I said. That was the irony. Instead of Harry winning Pearl and me winning Paul, Paul and Pearl had won each other. Harry hunched his shoulders and began to cough. I thought he would be sick, but he only hacked up a wad of phlegm. He fumbled under the bed for the chamber pot. I leaned down and pulled it out so he could spit.

"Look what you're doing to yourself," I scolded. "Why can't you try again, and quit drinking once and for all?"

"Hannah, you need to go away and leave me. I've told you how I tried. Stop probing the wound."

"But why? What are these demons that have such a hold on you?"

"Do you know what it is to kill a man?" he asked flatly.

I thought about what had happened to my father because of me, how it had been my fault. But I doubted he was talking about that kind of killing. "No, I suppose I don't."

"Then leave me in peace and quiet." He lay back down on the bed with his back toward me.

I waited, but he was obviously not going to explain. "I'll bring you some breakfast," I said, putting my hand on the door handle. "Harry, I want you to come with us to Split Rock Colony." I waited, but he said nothing. "Give yourself another chance." Still no reply. "Besides, we leave today, and I am not removing your handcuffs."

Paul, Pearl, and Checkela were waiting in the main cabin. "It's about time," Checkela said, as we went outside. "I thought you must have fallen overboard and drowned."

I shoved my worries aside and jabbed Checkela playfully in the ribs. "Well, you are the expert on going overboard, aren't you, little brother?"

"Try this for little brother," he laughed, grabbing me around the waist. I struggled as he threatened to throw me into the water, but couldn't break his grip. When had he become so strong? "Okay, okay," I panted. "You win. Put me down."

He set me on the deck, and I couldn't help but notice the swagger that crept into his gait. "Being a kitchen rooster must be good for you," I teased. "Just think what a man you'll be by the time we get home."

A wide smile lit up his face. "Actually, Hannah, Pearl said she would like to help you with the cooking on the way back."

I looked at Paul, who nodded Checkela's way and rolled his eyes. Then I looked at Pearl, who said, "I thought it was the least I could do after all you're doing for me."

As far as I could see we hadn't done much for her yet, but I said, "Well, I would appreciate that very much. And as for you, brother, you are too predictable for words."

"What?" he asked, his hands held open in innocence.

We piled down the stairway to the main deck, jostling and enjoying the moment. The sun and the clean optimism of a new day made it possible to believe that everything might just work out well. I grinned happily, thinking of the breakfast we would find at the Chop House, a breakfast I didn't have to prepare myself.

I wonder why it is that trouble so often hits just when you're enjoying yourself the most. We were piling across the gangplank when I saw them. Two men were striding straight toward us, one with a silver badge on the breast of his black vest. My first thought was, *It's Sheriff Healy coming to lock up Harry*. My second thought was, *Pearl can explain his innocence*. But Pearl was frozen, her face white with fear. The other man, grim-faced with thin lips and fierce eyebrows, had her pinned with his gaze. Pearl's one-word response was a choking whisper. "Papa."

Then came the surprise. The sheriff looked directly at Paul and said, "You Paul Wipf?" Paul nodded warily, and the sheriff continued, "I'm taking you into custody for kidnapping and robbery. You'd best not make a fuss."

Chapter 40

I dogged the steps of Sheriff Healy and Paul to the old log jailhouse on the corner of Front and Bond next to The Break of Day. Though I pleaded Paul's innocence to the sheriff at every step, he paid no attention. It was easy to understand why.

Apparently, Carson Tate had come home at first light and found Paul's note. He also discovered that Pearl had taken her money, so he went straight to the sheriff and accused Paul of kidnapping his daughter and stealing two hundred fifty dollars. The sheriff checked Paul's pockets and, sure enough, found the roll containing that exact amount of money. I cried out for Pearl to tell the sheriff the truth, but her father held her arm, and she stood like a white stone statue, either unable or unwilling to speak. When Carson dragged Pearl away, I sent Checkela to watch where they went.

For a moment, I wondered if Pearl and her father had set the whole thing up to hurt Paul, but I dismissed the idea. The fear in her eyes had been all too real.

Sheriff Healy blocked my way at the jailhouse door. "You don't need to come in," he said. "You're like to wear me out with your yippin'." Then he shut the door in my face. I stood in bewilderment with nothing to do but stare at the eight-inch squared logs of the building.

An hour ago, everything had been falling into place. Now it was all falling apart, and I had no idea what to do. But I could not just stand outside like an old porch pillar. I pushed the door open just in time to see the sheriff turn the key in an iron-barred cell door. Before I could get a step inside, Sheriff Healy was in my face. "Ma'am, I asked you to stay out."

"I have things to say."

"You said 'em all the way here. Aren't you talked out yet?"

"You didn't listen. Paul did nothing wrong."

"You can say your piece at a hearing. Right now, I got papers to fill out."

"It wasn't Paul's doing. She wanted to leave," I insisted.

"That's not how Carson sees it, and I didn't hear her disagreeing with him."

"She was afraid to speak. She was trying to get away from him."

Sheriff Healy furrowed his brow. "Why would a girl be afraid of her father?"

"For one thing he's a murderer. He shot an Indian two nights ago."

He looked at me patiently. "I don't think you understand this country. There's a cattle rustling problem, and that wouldn't be the first Indian to get shot in the middle of it."

"He was just a boy," I said, "and Pearl was with him, trying to give him some bread. Carson killed him right in front of her."

That, at least, deepened the sheriff's frown, but he only shrugged and nodded toward Paul, who I glimpsed in the shadows of the jail cell. "That has little enough to do with him."

I gaped in disbelief. Paul was right. The Indian didn't matter. But Pearl's bruise might. "Did you see her face?" I asked.

He nodded. "She had a run-in with something."

"Her father punched her for crying about the Indian. He's like that all the time."

Sheriff Healy sighed. "Look, it's a gutless man who hits his daughter, but even if it's true—and that's only your say so—

there's no law to stop it. It's a family matter outside of my doing."

"But don't you see what kind of man he is?" I cried.

"What I got is a girl abducted from her father. I got stolen money that your friend here had in his pocket. And the girl hasn't said a word in his defense. What am I supposed to think? Now, like I said, you'll have a chance to say your piece again at a hearing which ought to be in Helena later in the month."

"Helena! Later this month! But our steamboat leaves this evening!"

∼

The steamboat departure made no difference to the sheriff. He told me I would have to leave Paul behind or let the steamer go without me. Either way, Paul would go to Helena. I wanted to talk to Paul, but he said I would have to come back later.

As I walked back toward the steamboat, Paul's parting call echoed in my head. "Don't worry about me, Hannah. See if Pearl is okay. Then go back to Split Rock."

Go back to Split Rock. And abandon Paul? Pearl might do that, but I would not, though I had no idea what I could do by staying. Unless I could find Pearl and convince her to tell Sheriff Healy the truth.

By the time I got back to the *Silver Mist*, it was after ten in the morning. Roustabouts were loading buffalo robes from a row of mule-drawn freight wagons. I crossed the gangplank, trying to stay out of the way of the bustling workers who stared at me as if I were the prize pig in an agricultural exhibit.

There was no sign of Checkela, and I wandered aimlessly up the stairs to the boiler deck, unable to think of a single plan of action. Eventually I found myself heading toward

Harry's room. Hungry and still in handcuffs, he might be getting owlish, but at least he would be sober and he might have an idea to help. I would get the captain to release him immediately.

Ready with an apology for failing to bring breakfast, I knocked on the door and waited. Lord forbid that I should barge in if he happened to be making use of the chamber pot. No answer. Knocking more loudly to wake him, I pushed the door open slowly. The apology never left my lips. Harry was nowhere to be seen.

Chapter 41

Harry was gone, but I heard voices outside and knew Checkela was back. He was talking to Captain Anders.

"Ah, my cook," the captain greeted me warmly as I joined them on the deck.

"Good morning, Captain. But I don't know if I can be your cook after all. We have trouble."

His brow wrinkled with what might have been fatherly concern. "So your brother has said. Tell me more."

Maybe it was the way he always seemed so unruffled, or simply that I trusted him, that got me talking. As the words poured out, I realized how much I needed to confide in someone, to express my own helplessness.

My brother fidgeted impatiently until, finally, I said, "Check, did you see where they went?"

He nodded eagerly. "The Chouteau Hotel. He got a room—took her upstairs."

From the steamboat, we could see the white, clapboarded Chouteau Hotel just down on Front Street. It was where the captain had said the soldiers stayed.

"There was some thumping," Checkela continued, "and I heard her cry. Then Carson went down to the bar."

"He probably wants to stay in town to see that we leave and Paul remains in jail," I commented bitterly.

Captain Anders tapped a palm against the back of his other hand. It was the first time I had seen him show the least sign of agitation. "Did the girl stay in the room?" he asked Checkela.

"She had to. He locked her in. I listened at the doors and heard her crying."

"Did you speak with her?"

"Through the door, yes. I said Paul needed her to tell what happened, but when she finally quit crying all she said was, 'Go away before he comes.' I don't think she'd speak up for Paul if her life depended on it."

"She probably thinks her life depends on not telling," I suggested. "She's terrified of her father."

Captain Anders's face was impassive again, as usual. "This is very unfortunate. He is a mean-spirited man."

"He did almost the same thing to Harry." I sighed miserably, and explained the lies Carson had used to ruin Harry. "By the way," I added, "did you or one of the officers release Harry this morning? He's gone."

"Yes, I uncuffed him myself."

"Too bad," I sighed. "I told him I was going to keep him locked up and take him home."

Captain Anders wagged a finger at me. "Now that really would have been kidnapping. I did not mind locking him up for his own protection, but he seemed to be himself again so I felt I must release him."

"Well, if he's himself again, I can guess what he's up to." I didn't even feel disgusted anymore. Just resigned to the way he was. It was all too tiring. "Do you know where he went?"

"I'm afraid not."

We talked a few moments longer. Captain Anders remained placid and non-committal. I began to wonder if he really cared after all. "I must think about this a moment," he said, turning to the main stairway. "I hope to be underway by four o'clock. I hate to lose my cook again, but I must also oversee the work of these roosters. I do not want the *Silver Mist* listing because of an unbalanced load."

Checkela and I went to our cabin, and I flopped down on the bunk. Checkela sat at my feet. "What are we going to do?" he asked.

"I don't know," I said, "but it looks bad."

"Bad?" Checkela said fiercely. "It's *Dumhait!*"

"*Joh*, stupidity to us, but serious for Paul. Doesn't robbery mean prison?"

"*Dumhait*," Chekela repeated.

"Don't they hang people for kidnapping?"

"You're not making things better," Checkela said in annoyance.

"Well, you're no help either. At least I'm trying to think of something," I snapped.

Checkela stood up, pacing back and forth. "I hope you think faster than Captain Anders," he said, looking through the shutter. "I think he's forgotten about it already." He raised his hands in frustration. "Go ahead and think. I'm going out on deck."

So while he was gone, I thought. I thought of all the problems. The sheriff would not let me talk to Paul. Pearl was afraid to defy her father. Harry was gone, probably not even aware of what had happened, and well on his way to oblivion. Captain Anders was preoccupied with his freight.

So where would my help come from? I was tired. Nothing I had thought to achieve was working out. I had lost Paul doubly. First to Pearl. Now to Sheriff Healy. Worse, I had not helped him one bit. I felt like giving up and falling asleep. Soon the boat would leave, and I would awaken to find myself going home. That was what Paul had told me to do. Go home. He had also asked me to help Pearl. But where would *my* help come from?

It came over me like a slow rising of the sun. I felt it shiver up my spine and neck, the words coming to life in my mind. *Where does my help come from? My help comes from the*

Lord. Then a slow rise of red, my own blush of shame. Had I forgotten it already—again—the verse that had come when the buckskin man threatened me on the steamboat?

I remembered Pearl's words when the buckskin man had run for the outhouse. *I hit him with a little prayer. Could that have helped?* I covered my face with my hands. Pearl had prayed. I, on the other hand, had been jealous because Paul had taught her how. Pearl had prayed. I had been angry because Paul would not fight. Pearl had prayed.

But hadn't I prayed, too? Night prayers, meal prayers, morning prayers? Yes. All uttered from memory, but not from the heart. Had I let my faith come to that? A recitation of prayers, automatic as the multiplication tables in school? How had I grown so cold, so independent?

Perhaps in my pursuit of Paul I had forgotten my first love, the One who had sustained me through the trial of losing my father, the One who had helped me through the trials of the journey to America, the One who had helped me show Paul the way to peace.

Come to me all you who are weary and burdened, and I will give you rest . . . for I am gentle and humble in heart. Jesus' words. Had I become so unlike my Lord? Had I humbled myself recently? Or had I been so full of my own self-importance since talking to Sannah *Basel*, since going where no one else from the colony would go, that I thought I needed only myself? I had hardly even noticed myself slipping away.

I wondered if Paul was praying in jail even now. I wondered if Pearl, in her fear, was praying in her locked hotel room. It was time for me to relearn humility. If I really believed the Lord had brought me here, for whatever purpose, it was time for me to let go of my pride, to submit myself to him.

I knelt beside the bed and prayed. I prayed for forgiveness for my selfish desires, my jealousy, my self-reliance. I thanked God for the strength he had given me, and asked for his guidance. I prayed for wisdom and for peace. I prayed a long time, not just asking, but waiting, too. Waiting on the Lord.

There was no blaze of light, no sudden conviction to go and pull apart the bars of the jail, no surge of Samson-like power with which to do it. Just a gentle infilling of peace. I wept as I felt the weight lift away from my shoulders. I was not alone.

Finally, I stood up. It occurred to me that Fort Benton would have a telegraph office. Mueter and Fater. How had I forgotten? It was time to relieve their worry. Besides, there was little doubt now that Paul could use some help from the elders.

It is strange how the peace of God is never long in being tested. Outside, I called to my brother, but got no answer. One by one, everyone who had been with me in the morning had disappeared. I searched, but Checkela was nowhere to be found.

Chapter 42

At eighty-five cents for ten words or less, my telegram was brief. *Am safe Fort Benton. Paul in jail. Send elder. Hannah.* I knew those few facts would now be more persuasive than all the pleading I had done at home.

The telegraph was a marvel of communication. Even as the operator tapped his telegraph key in Fort Benton, another operator a thousand miles across the land would be deciphering the Morse code and writing words that would take weeks to arrive by mail. Of course, the message still had to be delivered to the colony, which might take a few days.

I thought with longing of an invention even more amazing than the telegraph. Only four years ago, a man named Alexander Bell had come up with a thing called the telephone. With a telephone you could actually talk to another person from miles away. Apparently, there were already thousands of the things in the larger cities. I wished I had one now so I could ask my father what to do.

As I watched the operator's delicate, almost ladylike fingers tap the telegraph key, my stomach made a very indelicate, unladylike growl. It was past noon and I still had not eaten. I blushed as the operator looked up. He had heard it over his tapping. He grinned. "If you need a bite, the Our House Restaurant, has the best food in town, ma'am."

I recognized the name. "You mean the one at the Extradition?"

"One and the same."

"Murder House," I muttered.

"Beg your pardon?"

"Nothing." I left the telegraph office and went to the Chop House. The Extradition would have to get by without my business. A thick beef stew helped revive my spirits while I decided what to do. I wanted to go to Paul, but after murmuring a quiet, personal prayer, I decided on The Chouteau Hotel. I needed to see Pearl. Besides, what better place to look for my brother?

I finished off the stew and paid my fifty cents. Outside, I ducked up Baker Street to the alley behind the Front Street buildings, skirting the Chouteau Hotel's big four-door outhouse. I climbed the outside stairs, feeling exposed as a fly on a whitewashed wall, and it occurred to me that this was how the adventure had begun—sneaking down the outside stairway of our big chalkstone housing unit at Split Rock. In almost four weeks I felt as if I had experienced four lifetimes of adventure for a Hutterite woman.

The hallway inside was only dimly lit from the windowed door. It was quiet, and there was no sign of Checkela. A tingle of fear for his safety pricked my heart, but I suppressed it and mouthed a prayer. I crept up the hallway, listening at all the doors, wishing I had asked Checkela which room Pearl was in.

In early afternoon most of the rooms would be empty, so I started knocking on doors. I hoped only that Pearl's father would not be there to answer.

I rapped quietly, and there was no answer at the first door. Or at the second. At the third, a snore like a blowing horse ripped the silence, and a voice said, "Wha . . . Who zat? Yer snrgggg." Then silence. Whoever it was, it certainly wasn't Pearl.

Finally, at the fourth door, a timid voice answered. "Who is it?"

Pearl! Thank goodness. "It's Hannah. Are you alone?"

I heard the squeak of bedsprings. She was lying down. "Hannah. What are you doing here?"

"Are you alone?"

"Yes. Father has gone—downstairs I think. Don't let him see you."

"Can you let me in?"

"No. I . . . It's locked."

I knelt down by the keyhole. "Come closer, so I can whisper."

The bed squeaked again, then her footsteps approached the door. "Hannah, you had better go."

"Pearl, do you want to get out of here? To get away, I mean, if you can?"

There was silence. Then she answered, her voice strained. "He would stop me."

"What if you knew he wouldn't?"

"He would."

"But what if. Just tell me that."

"I . . . Yes, but you don't know him."

"Pearl, I think you need to tell the truth about Paul. Tell Sheriff Healy."

Again there was silence. "I can't."

"But Paul is in trouble, for lies. You need to tell the truth."

"He won't let me. Father . . . he'll forgive me if I don't make trouble."

I heard her breath catch and knew she was crying. *Her father would forgive her? The very idea*! "He is the one who needs forgiveness, Pearl, not you."

"Please leave, Hannah, in case he comes back. I wish I could help Paul. I want to. But he would stop me. The sheriff wouldn't believe me anyway."

"Pearl, just listen. If you knew you were safe—would you do it then?" I knew that I could not ask her to speak up in her father's presence. Yet, maybe when the elders came, something could be worked out to protect her. Maybe when Paul went to court in Helena, something could be arranged.

Pearl took a long time to answer. "Yes, if I could be safe from him. But how could I be?"

I had no sure answer—for her or for me—but I did have one question. "Pearl, have you been praying, up here in your room?"

"Yes."

"Good. Don't quit. Where there is God, there is hope." Why had it taken me so long to remember such a simple truth? I did not have to bear the burden alone.

"I am praying for Paul," she said, and I could hear the huskiness of her emotion. "I'm trying to."

I bit my tongue, willing my own acceptance of God's plan for Paul—and Pearl. "Stay with it," I said, trying to be reassuring. "Something good will come. I sent a tele—" The *thump-stump* of boots on the wooden stairs stopped me. Someone was coming. Several people, in fact.

I got up off my knees, trying to decide whether to stay or run. I stayed. There were more than one, which probably meant soldiers. If it were Carson, he would be alone.

I was wrong. The first man entered the hallway. Carson Tate's thin lips and craggy brows were a mask of seething anger. And his eyes bore straight into mine.

Chapter 43

This was not what I had in mind when I told Pearl something good would come. "You!" Carson growled. "Meddling with my daughter!"

For a second I was so afraid I nearly wet my skirts, but something about the way he spoke of his daughter, locked in that room, raised my anger. Frightening or not, he was a lying bully and I would not run. I faced him squarely. "Your daughter or your property?" I spat. "What kind of father terrorizes his daughter and locks her up like a dog?"

"You mind your mouth, or—"

"Ease up, Carson," came a voice from behind. "She's a talker, but I won't have you threaten a lady." *Sheriff Healy!* Then a third man entered the hall. He carried himself with a confidence that said he was used to being in charge. I hoped he was not some rich rancher crony of Carson's. But when the fourth man appeared, my worries departed like a cast out spirit. "Captain Anders," I gasped.

"Ah, Hannah." He smiled graciously. "I wondered if we would find you here. You have already met Carson Tate and Sheriff Healy. And this is Judge John Tattan, a friend of mine and hero of the Cow Island skirmish. Judge, this is my cook, of whom I have spoken."

Judge Tattan bowed slightly and said, "It's a pleasure, to be sure, ma'am. The captain thinks highly of you."

He spoke with what I took to be an Irish accent. I was still reeling from surprise, and mumbled, "I . . . well, thank you, sir. Are you the man with the dented belt buckle?"

"So, my friend has been telling stories, has he?" he said, winking at the captain.

"Nothing but the truth, so help me," Captain Anders replied.

"Well then, I am he. And I can tell you, acquiring that dent gave me quite a belly ache—as welcome a belly ache as a man ever had, considering the alternative." Then he clapped his hands and grew serious. "But we must keep to business."

"The judge," Captain Anders explained, "would like to learn the truth about a recent arrest."

In confirmation, the judge added briskly, "Mr. Tate, I'll be asking you to unlock the door. Straight away, if you please."

Carson dug a key from his vest pocket and reluctantly placed it in the lock. I whispered to the Captain, "She'll never speak up. She's too frightened."

The captain patted my shoulder. "We shall see. I have had a rather detailed conversation with the judge." He bent closer to my ear. "By the way, would you happen to be missing a brother?"

I started. "Yes! He disappeared this morning. Do you know where he is?"

He smiled. "I didn't think you were involved. Don't worry. Mr. Healy is keeping him from further trouble."

"Further trouble?" I hissed. "What trouble?"

But just then, Carson opened the door. Judge Tattan stopped him from entering. "Johnny," he said to the sheriff, "would you mind visiting with Mr. Tate down the hall for a bit. I'd like to see what the girl has to say on her own."

Carson protested. "This is my daughter. I ought to be present when—" He took a step forward, but Sheriff Healy pulled him back.

"Good Lord!" the judge exclaimed, stepping into the room. "What's happened to you, lass?" Pearl stood in the middle of the room, hands clasped in front of her bosom, staring at her father. Her right cheek still showed its yellow-black bruising. While her right eye was puffy from crying, the left was swollen and raw, the deep purplish black of an over-ripe plum.

All my own worries and petty concerns vanished. I forgot about Checkela. I forgot about Paul. I forgot my lingering resentment of Pearl, and rushed to her. Putting my arms around her shoulders and through the black hair cascading across her back, I pulled her close. "Pearl, it's okay," I soothed. "These men won't let him hurt you." She put her chin on my shoulder and held me tightly. I turned my head so I could see Carson Tate. "She was not like this when she left with you this morning," I accused.

The other men looked at him too, their eyes hard. "She fell on the stair," Carson sputtered. I felt Pearl stiffen, and knew he was lying. "That's why I had to leave her in the room. She needs rest." He was squirming.

Like most bullies, Carson Tate was a frightening man when the odds were stacked in his favor. In the presence of men that could not be bluffed or intimidated, he became weak and contemptuous.

"Johnny, get him out of here!" Judge Tattan growled. "If what happened to this girl is from your fist, I've a mind to . . ." He hesitated and started again, "If you've been punching your own daughter, what I'm liable to do to you doesn't bear voicing in the presence of these ladies."

The sheriff walked Carson down the hall. The judge and the captain entered the room and closed the door.

"Now, young lady," Judge Tattan said, more tenderly than he had been fierce a moment before. "Your friend here"—he nodded at me—"has expressed some concern for you, and I've a mind to help, if you've the courage to speak freely.

"There is a young man over in our jail who may or may not

deserve to be there. Again, if you have the courage to speak plainly, we want to listen to what you have to say. I believe you may be afraid to speak up, but I want you to know that we will keep you safe." His gaze, deep and piercing, fed her courage from the well of his own strength.

He continued. "Did you know that my wife presented me with a beautiful baby daughter just last December? I love that little girl and I would not see her hurt for anything. A man's daughter should be as precious a thing as his heart can hold. If she isn't, he doesn't deserve her. That applies to you, too. Do you know that? I am not your father, but you are a lovely young lady, and I will not stand by and see you hurt. Now, do you believe me if I say you can safely tell the truth?" Pearl thought for moment. Fresh tears ran in rivulets down her cheeks, this time not from fear, but drawn out by Judge Tattan's tenderness. Finally, she nodded in agreement.

The judge gestured toward Captain Anders. "This man believes you might have something important to tell me. I think so, too. But I want to know the truth. I want to know if what your father has said about the young man in our jail is true. If it is not true, I want to know that, too. I want only the truth, and nothing else. Are you prepared to tell me the truth?" Again, Pearl nodded.

"Good, very good," the judge said, looking pleased. "Then this is as good a time and place as any to hear it."

Chapter 44

The steam whistle echoed through the bowl-shaped valley as the *Silver Mist* powered into the rippling highway of water. Looking back from the Hurricane deck, I wondered if my life would ever be the same after experiencing the wild Western town of Fort Benton.

I put my arm around Pearl, and reviewed the whirlwind of events just gone by. Extricating Pearl, Paul and Checkela from their separate troubles had taken so long that we should have missed our departure. A steamboat, however, does not leave without its Captain.

Captain Anders claimed he had helped just so he wouldn't lose his cook. I knew better. He was just that good a man.

Another good man was Judge Tattan. He had practically held court right in Pearl's hotel room, though I found out later he was a probate judge and did not even handle criminal cases.

In the end, Sheriff Healy seemed all right too, though after the treatment he gave Checkela, I doubted my brother would agree. If he delivered my hasty message to the telegraph office as he had promised, that would be enough for me. *Coming home. No help needed. Hannah.* I hoped it would save the colony elders an unnecessary journey.

Pearl and I did not linger long on the deck. We had meals to prepare, and soon settled into a routine of slaving in the galley—but a pleasant slavery. Pearl was a much better partner than Checkela had been. She was cheerful and enjoyed cooking.

The time passed quickly, as did the downstream miles. We met several other steamboats laboring upriver, but the nimble fingers of the current drew us quickly along. By the eighth day we were already nearing Bismarck.

With home just days away, Pearl and I worked a batch of dough for *Zwieback*, the small, buttery Hutterite buns. In spite of what I had felt at first, I looked at my hard-working partner with sisterly affection. "Pearl," I said, "I'm glad you came with us."

"Me too," she replied, wiping a flour-dusted forearm across her sweaty brow. "It still amazes me how you brought help at just the right time. You'll always be my hero."

"I told you before, all I did was cry on Captain Anders' shoulder."

"But just think if you hadn't. Paul would still be in jail, and I would be . . . well, I would be home, with Father, alone." She faltered, and paled momentarily.

It occurred to me that maybe being a hero just meant giving your troubles to God and doing ordinary things. After all my self-important striving, I had finally given up and humbled myself before my Lord. *Where had my help come from?* Not from anything I had planned. "When Captain Anders showed up with the judge, I was more surprised than anyone," I said.

"I'm so grateful to that judge. I hated myself for not telling the truth."

"Maybe fear sometimes makes us what we don't want to be," I mused.

Pearl stopped punching dough, and looked at me. "You know what I think, Hannah? I think God sent Paul to me. I think he saved my life. Not from dying, but from what I might have become. Paul is the reason I pray."

It's funny, but you never know God's plans completely. "It's the story of Paul's life," I said. "When he lost his parents, and came to live on our Hutterite colony, I knew God had sent him for a purpose. In fact, we became friends, and I thought God had sent him just for. . . ." *me*, I almost said. "Well, it doesn't matter," I continued. "That's just how it is with Paul."

In spite of my new attitude of acceptance, talking about Paul this way made me weary. Thankfully, Checkela stumped into the room and dumped an armload of wood I had not even asked for into the wood box by the stove. It seemed to me that he was looking for excuses to spend time near Pearl. I tried not to wish she would fall for him. "Well, how is our golden wood retriever?" I asked with a grin.

Checkela glared at me from under his *Katus*. I should probably have gone easy on his bruised pride, but I had been teasing him with dog puns ever since finding him tied to the front step of the Fort Benton jailhouse. Squatting on his haunches, he looked like a pathetic excuse for a chained up guard dog. I was smiling now, but I had been horrified before.

"Checkela! *Bist du narish?*" I had cried when Sheriff Healy and I arrived at the jail.

Checkela had looked at me with beseeching puppy dog eyes that begged for mercy. I couldn't help softening a little. "*Ach Himble*, you *are* crazy, Check. You cannot just break someone out of jail!"

"Hannah, I . . . I'm sorry. I didn't want Paul to go to prison when he didn't do anything." His head had sagged dejectedly. "The sheriff says he's going to hang me."

"I ain't going to hang anybody, you pesky whippersnapper," Sheriff Healy had said. "I was just making a point—which I hope will find its way into that hot little head of yours."

Apparently, a deckhand on the *Silver Mist* had told Checkela the jail was so old and rickety that staying inside was practically optional. In fact, escape was so easy the town was taking contract bids for a new jail.

So Checkela had taken a rope and borrowed Harry Orman's horse from the livery, planning to break out the window bars to Paul's cell, then escape with Paul to the *Silver Mist* for its four o'clock departure.

All of this, which I told Checkela several times, was a completely stupid idea that might have made him a genuine criminal. Fortunately for him, his plan had a major flaw. He had ridden behind the jail only to discover there were no cell windows. He was standing back there trying to decide what to do when Sheriff Healy came around the corner.

The sheriff had read Checkela's guilty look like a statement of confession. Technically, he had not succeeded in doing anything wrong, but the sheriff had leashed him to the front of the jail to keep him out of further trouble.

Now I was making Checkela pay for his crime with a little more embarrassment. "You must have been barking up the right tree to find all that wood," I said. "Thank you for bringing it."

"Hannah, leave it alone," he grumbled. "I'm sick of listening to you amuse yourself."

"Oh, oh, watch out," I laughed. "He's getting growly."

"Hannah, if you don't quit, I'm telling you, I will throw you into the river." He made a grab at me, but I scrambled behind our dough-mixing table. "You don't scare me," I said. "You're bark is worse than your bite." Then Pearl joined the game. She grabbed a handful of flour, tossed it at Checkela's head, and ducked for cover with me on the other side of the table.

"What's wrong, Check?" Pearl laughed. "You look pale all of a sudden."

Checkela sputtered and spit flour. He was so surprised he couldn't stay mad. He started laughing, too, and raised his arms. "Whooooo, Hannah, look out! It's the ghost of the colony graveyard come to get you."

"Hey, not fair," I complained. "That's ancient history."

"Watch out, Pearl," he laughed. "She'll trample you trying

to run away!" Then he threw a handful of flour at Pearl. "Whooo, Hannah! Two ghosts now. We're going to get you!" He lunged at me, and I spun to get away but my feet slipped on the floury floor and he caught my arm.

For the second time in the past few days, I was surprised how much his strength and quickness had increased. Even as he caught me with one hand, his other hand had snatched the big circle of dough Pearl and I had rolled, and before I knew it the whole sticky mass of it was over my head. I scrambled to get away. He let go, and I stumbled blindly across the room—smack into something upright and solid. I tried to catch my balance and found myself clinging to a man, dough from my face sticking all over the breast of his jacket.

Chapter 45

I recognized the lean hardness of his chest immediately. As the dough parted, I lifted my gaze and found myself staring directly into Paul's bewildered soft gray eyes. Except for the slabs of goo sagging and dripping from my face like melted skin, it might have been a romantic moment.

I don't know why my dignity and resolve had to evaporate so quickly. Staring into the pools of his eyes, I felt the beating of Paul's heart against my chest, and melted like the dough on my face, deeper into his arms. He leaned toward me and the puff of his breath was on my eyes. My own breathing quickened, and my lips were suddenly dry as flour. His lips came closer, my own parting slightly, and I wondered—absurdly—*Can he kiss me through this dough*? I must have been losing my mind.

His hand touched my face, tenderly parting the dough, and then he was pushing us apart. I blinked, and my eyelids stuck shut. "My goodness, Hannah," Paul said, his voice sliding from quiet confusion to a chuckle, then to a roaring laugh. "You are the funniest looking thing I have seen since leaving Split Rock Colony!"

When a dream disintegrates privately, it is disappointing. In front of an audience, it is humiliating. Had they noticed what an idiot I was—thinking Paul wanted to kiss my dough-streaked face? How could I have been so stupid—so selfish, with Pearl right there in the room? My face burned in shame.

"'*Gea vecch*," I scolded, jumping back from Paul as if I had hugged a hot stove.

I grabbed at the dough, yanking it in elastic handfuls from my face. I had to get out of there. "Checkela, help Pearl make more dough." Then I was scolding. "I am sick of making buns and I am sick of your games!" Paul's laughter died, and everyone stared as if I were a creature from another planet. I walked stiff-backed and dough-faced from the room, willing myself not to run. Behind me, I heard Checkela wonder aloud, "What's bothering her? It's only a bit of bread dough."

To avoid meeting the captain, I took the aft stairway to the boiler deck, ignoring the confused and amused looks of deck passengers along the way. I ran down the promenade to the door of the room I shared with Pearl and closed it gratefully behind me. I sagged to the bed, "Oh, Lord, I prayed. Forgive me again for wanting everything my own way, and for being so foolish."

I have noticed that one emotion has a way of feeding another. I felt as if I had been on a runaway horse, galloping from hilarity to love struck-idiocy to anger. Now I was stuck with humiliation. I sighed, knowing I would have to overcome it and help Pearl prepare supper. But first, I would pick this wretched dough from my hair and clothes, and maybe escape with a nap. Being human was enough to wear a person out.

∽

The clothing snapped in the wind, fluttering to avoid my grasp. I caught Pearl's skirt, and removed a clothes peg. Then I passed the skirt through the cabin door to Pearl and reach for my blouse. We had washed our sweaty and flour-dusted clothing right after supper and hung it to dry outside our stateroom.

Now a storm was building, blustering its way up the river

to meet us. Captain Anders had drawn the boat close to shore to prevent the wind from smashing it into the bank. More than one paddle wheeler had been destroyed that way. A hawser ran from a bow capstan, anchoring the boat to a single large cottonwood that grew near the bank and towered overhead. The rest of the trees were farther back, and the crew and deck passengers, including Paul and Checkela, were out there cutting wood for the boiler fires.

With the last of the clothing safely inside, I shut the cabin door and draped an apron over a bed rail to dry. I retied my *Tiechl* and watched as Pearl sat on the little room's only chair, trying to run a brush through her tangled hair. I knew she must be tired. She and Checkela had made a fresh batch of dough and baked buns. Then she had gone straight to preparing supper with me when I made my sheepish return. Paul and Checkela had hung around, trying to help. When Paul offered an apology for telling me how funny I looked, I'd had to confess, "Paul, what you said was nothing. I need to apologize to everyone for being so childish. I hope you'll forgive me." Then Pearl and I had sent the men out so we would have room to move in the kitchen.

Pearl made another pull on the brush. "Ooh, I should have been smart enough to wear a bonnet in that wind," she lamented.

"Here," I said, "let me brush it for you." I took the brush and stood behind her, freeing the knots from the bottom, then working carefully up the length of her lustrous thick hair.

"That feels heavenly," she sighed as a smooth brush stroke caressed her mane. "I haven't had my hair brushed since Mama ran off to escape my father."

So that was what had happened to her mother. As a Hutterite it was hard for me to imagine. No mother I knew of had ever left a child, except through death. But, then again, I didn't think any Hutterite woman had ever had an abuser like Carson Tate for a husband. "Where is your mother now?" I asked gently.

"I don't know. Just gone. I haven't heard from her for over a year."

"I'm sorry, Pearl. It must have been hard for her to leave you."

"I guess she thought I would be well-looked-after. Before she left, Father was only bad to her." She sighed. "It's sad not to have someone you love."

The wind was picking up, rocking the boat and jerking it against the hawser. I had to brace my feet, but stroked Pearl's hair all the more tenderly. "I will love you, Pearl," I said close to her ear. "Always, as a friend, I will love you." And I meant it with all my heart. Regardless of Paul and whatever the future held, I knew that the Lord would have me love this girl. And I was willing.

She reached back to touch my hand. "Thank you, Hannah. It means a lot, hearing you say that." Then she took a breath, and said the last thing I expected. "I'm not sure if I should be saying this, but I think . . . well, you're in love with Paul, aren't you, Hannah?"

Chapter 46

"Ouch!" Pearl cried in protest.

"Oh, I'm sorry." The brush was caught in a tangle. I quit yanking.

"Does that mean it is off limits?" she asked innocently.

"No, no, of course not," I stammered. "You surprised me, that's all. I . . . I thought we were talking about your mother."

"We were talking about love," she replied simply.

She must have been waiting for a chance to bring this up. *It's sad not to have someone you love.* Had she meant Paul and not just her mother? Did she think I might try to take him away from her? "You don't have to worry about my feelings for Paul," I said. "We've been friends a long time. I expect we always will be." I hoped I could keep my deeper feelings buried.

"I'm sorry, Hannah, but I can't believe that." She said it matter-of-factly, not challenging.

"All I can tell you, is that it isn't my intention to offer competition." I ran the brush through her hair again, carefully.

"Hannah, don't you think I've seen you struggle? What do you think is between Paul and me?" She spoke softly, like a mother trying to draw out a daughter's secret feelings. I felt foolish, as if we were playing the wrong roles. I was supposed to be the elder sister, helping Pearl, who had gone through so much. And here she was coaxing me to open up.

"What a question, Pearl," I said. "It's not for me to answer. What do *you* think is between Paul and you? That is more important."

"Everything." *A simple answer.* "And nothing." *Not so simple.* "I told you, he came to me like a savior. But it was about faith—and discovering that maybe God loves me. It's not about Paul and me—not like you're thinking."

I brushed faster. Could I have been wrong about everything I thought I had seen? Could I have jumped to conclusions so easily? "Are you saying you have no romantic interest in Paul?"

"I love Paul, but not that way."

"But he said even your father had ideas for the two of you."

At the mention of her father a cloud flitted across the darkness of her eyes. "You may have noticed how much my feelings affect my father's plans for me. Did Paul actually say we were going along with that?"

I tried to remember. "I don't know. I—"

"He didn't. And if you knew how much Paul talked about you, you wouldn't be worrying about what he feels for me."

The wind continued to buffet the boat as clouds darkened the sky and the air cooled. For once, the heat from the boiler below felt good in the little room. I recognized the blood rush in my neck and knew I was coloring again. If what Pearl said was true, how ridiculous I had been. I had thought I was being noble by trying to push him away. No, that wasn't true either. I was pushing him away to protect my pride. I tried to think of a time when Paul had actually declared any romantic feeling for Pearl. I couldn't. Was it all my own assumption? I didn't know whether to laugh or cry. I wanted to hug Pearl for her honesty. An honesty that put me to shame. "Okay," I said. "Okay." I hated talking about Paul this way. I felt as if we were bartering over him, dividing him up and bidding on the different parts of his affection. But, still, I couldn't stop. I had carried so many confused feelings inside for so long. I had to make one more point. "All this may be true, but he hasn't made the slightest effort to capture my affection."

"Of course not," Pearl replied. "You told him you're interested in Lorenz. And, honestly, the way you act around Paul, I cannot understand it."

My mouth dropped open. "Not you, too! Does the whole world know about Lorenz?"

"Paul told me about your letter."

"What did he say?"

"He thought you could do better."

It is true that the shameful things you do in life have a way of finding you out. "That letter was a disgusting ploy." I looked at her apologetically. "It's a long story, but I wish to goodness I had never sent it. The thing has haunted me at every turn." I smiled ruefully, feeling as if I had been cranked through a clothes wringer. "Now you know all my faults. You must think me a poor excuse for a Christian woman."

She took my hands in hers. "Hannah, I barely know you, but you have helped me when I needed it most. I just felt you had some ideas about me that weren't true. If they'll accept me at your Hutterite colony, I want to learn everything I can about the Christian life—from you."

I thought it more likely that I would learn from her, but I grinned and said, "Sure, I'll teach you all kinds of things, like—let's see—how to fall off a horse and become a human pin cushion."

She grimaced. "Ooh, if it's all the same, I'll stick with my own way of riding. I felt so sorry for you when I picked those spines out of your . . . ah, skin." She could not suppress a big grin and tried to apologize. "I'm sorry. I know it wasn't funny."

"It's okay. Pain and humiliation have a way of being funnier in hindsight."

"Did you say, 'hindsight?'" she giggled. "I must say, all those prickles sticking out of you was the most painful *hind sight* I have ever seen."

And then we were both laughing. "Ohhh, that was awful,"

I said. "Most humiliating moment of my life."

I looked at my giggling companion, and wondered if the Lord would ever be through teaching me humility. There was so much more to this girl than I had thought. And here she was, three years my junior, telling me to wake up about my feelings. Was it that I had not allowed myself to see her before, or was she already blossoming in the absence of her father?

Just then a howling wind bucked up against the boat, tilting it sideways. For a moment, I was afraid it might tip us over or maybe blow the top off the boat. Rain slashed against the cabin wall. We gave one another a worried look. Missouri River storms were nothing new to me, but riding one out in a steamboat cabin was a far cry from snuggling behind the thick chalkstone walls of the High House at home. Still, the cabin was dry.

I hoped Paul and Checkela were comfortable down on the deck. Maybe they would shelter in the kitchen, especially since Paul had promised to get up early and light the stove for us.

Above the noise of the storm, the bell began to clang. By now I knew all the signals. "What's that one mean?" Pearl asked.

"The captain wants a crew on deck," I said. "I wonder if something is wrong."

Pearl opened the door to the main salon, where only a few hours earlier our cooking had graced the big table in the middle. A group of gentlemen now tried to concentrate on a game of cards. They were nursing a bottle of whiskey. Always whiskey. I shook my head. It wouldn't be a riverboat without whiskey and cards. A gust of wind blew in as someone entered through an outside door. It was Henry, the young pilot trainee.

"Henry, what's going on?" I yelled as he wrestled the door shut behind him. "Is there trouble?"

"No, no. We'll be all right. But the captain wants to bury a deadman."

Chapter 47

"Bury a dead man!" Pearl exclaimed, her hand flying to her mouth. "In a storm like this?"

"Don't worry," Henry said, "two shakes of a rooster's shovel, and it'll be as good as done."

The two of us stared in amazement. How could he be so casual? "But who . . . who died?" Pearl asked.

I had been wondering the exact same thing, but when the men started laughing I was glad Pearl had asked and not me. A man with muttonchop whiskers leaned back in his chair and said, "He's stiff with *rigor mortis*, that one is."

"Stiff as a board, you might say," another man chuckled.

Unlike the others, Henry did not laugh, though he couldn't help grinning like a cat. "Now, fellows, how would the ladies know?" He turned to Pearl and me. "A deadman is a log. When we're short of big trees, we tie a hawser to a log and bury it crosswise—about six feet down—to anchor the boat."

"It's a right fine funeral," the muttonchops man added, "and all without the aid of a preacher."

"Oh, for Pete's sake," Pearl said, relaxing. I noticed she was smiling.

"And I suppose you dig the poor fellow up in the morning," I quipped, turning back toward the stateroom.

"That they do," the man agreed. "Can't keep a good man down, you know." He pulled an extra chair back from the table. "Say, how would you ladies like to join us for a bit? Let us buy the cooks a drink."

That was the last thing I wanted. Pearl was already backing away toward the stateroom. "Thank you," I said, "but we need to get our rest. We'll be up early in the kitchen."

We undressed, prayed together, and lay down. Pearl had volunteered to take the upper berth, so I had the same bed I'd had before. For some reason—maybe the storm or the drinkers outside—I felt uneasy, and wished I could talk to Paul and Checkela, but the rain was coming down hard now and I could see no sense in getting soaked. I would see them in the morning. I buried my head in the pillow. The boat was rocking like a cradle, but I doubted I would sleep.

∼

I was awakened by a rooster—a rooster on night watch—pounding on the door. I barely heard it over the roar of the wind, and I marveled that I had actually been asleep. Time to get up and cook. At 4:30, we were usually greeted by a sunrise of roses and violets, but this morning the light was gray-hooded and blurry. We fumbled clumsily into cold clothing. I hoped Paul had been true to his word about lighting the stove.

I had heard stories about storms destroying riverboats, and I began to understand them better. It was all we could do to shove the front salon door open against the weather. Outside, the wind was thick with ozone, rain, and wood smoke. Captain Anders had kept a low fire on the boiler, and the hot smoke-stack steamed in the rain like a brooding dragon.

Holding hands, Pearl and I took the stairs to the main deck. The wind clawed like an animal at my *Tiechl*, and the hawser was a gigantic cat's tail, snapping and jerking against the capstan. Yet, as scary as it was, there was something exhilarating about the storm. I grinned wildly at Pearl. She looked at me as if I were crazy, and pointed to the landward edge of the deck. It was covered with dirt. "Is that bad?" she shouted.

I raised my eyes to the bank. Great twisted tentacles thrashed above the deck as if a giant octopus was fighting its way out of the muddy bank. Tree roots! From the cottonwood that moored the *Silver Mist*. I yelled at Pearl, "The bank is washing out!" We were standing under the tree.

I have wondered about the timing that creates what we call coincidence. Why should one person be saved by going to the barn just moments before a tornado destroys his house, yet another die for deciding to check the fire just as the stove blows up? I had often thought of the timing that killed Paul's parents, when they grasped a gate just as lightning ripped through the iron fence rail. Were these things haphazard chances, or did they serve some greater purpose?

Whatever the case, it was at that moment that a great gust roared over the riverbank and grabbed the boat, shaking it like bundled wheat in a threshing machine. The rope thrashed against the deck, and I had a sensation of sliding weightlessly sideways. An overshadowing darkness seemed to settle from above, like owl wings over a mouse, diminishing the dirty morning light.

Together, Pearl and I looked up to see the huge cottonwood tree, a mass of branches and leaves, giving way to the wind. The crack of splintering wood was in our ears and the musty reek of earth in our nostrils. I heard a shriek and didn't know whether it was Pearl or me, but I felt her hand squeeze mine more tightly. We ran.

I pulled at Pearl's arm and we leaped across the deck—but, oh, so slowly, as in a dream, free arm flailing, legs pumping in the wind and rain as if we were swimming in a vat of molasses. Then suddenly, Pearl yanked free of my grips and I was stumbling forward alone. A crunching shudder rocked the deck and something slashed at me from behind, knocking me to my knees. It ripped the *Tiechl* from my head. Then my face was scrunched against the deck.

Panic thrashed like bird wings in my breast, and this time when I heard the cry I knew it was my own. I fought against the suffocating weight on top of me. In my fear, the tree was alive and evil, grabbing and holding me down. I scrabbled and wriggled like a snake and finally came free just under the edge of the boiler deck. In front of me the huge cottonwood lay like a slain giant across the bow. Part of the deck was crushed, and the portside spar and derrick poles were gone. I caught my breath. The lips of death had brushed my cheek. But where was Pearl? I shouted her name, peering through the rain and early light. She was nowhere to be seen. *Lord, don't let her be crushed*, I prayed.

I ran back and forth across the width of the deck, fighting branches. I could not find her under the tree. *The water*! Could she have been knocked overboard? The current would carry her away. I ran to the edge—which was when I saw the skirt, Pearl's skirt, submerged. And then her ankle pinned between the tree and the lip of the deck. Hanging straight down from the knee, her body was under water.

Chapter 48

Pearl's hand broke the surface, flailing to catch hold of something to pull herself up. Hanging backwards, she could not lift her face out of the water. She needed help, and quickly. I tried to lift the branch that held her, but it was too solid, too heavy. My hair had come untied, and the wind whipped it into my face. I leaned down and tried to pull her foot free. It was pinned too tightly. I tried again to shift the tree, gripping the branch and pushing up with all the power of my legs. Still useless. I would have to think of something else. But what? I crawled onto another branch that extended just over the surface by Pearl's hand. I caught her wrist and pulled, felt her body rise. She pulled against my arm, trying to come up faster, and I almost tumbled in with her. I leaned back, pulling harder. If I could just get her head out, everything would be all right. But she would not come up all the way. In the growing light, I could just see the shadow of her face, scrunched and panicked under the water as she fought. But something would not let go. Then I saw it. Another branch dipped under the surface and across her ribs, holding her down.

How long could a person live without air? I thought I remembered someone saying four minutes. It had to be almost two already. She was going to drown, unless I did something —and fast.

"Help! Help!" With all the lung power I could gather, I screamed into the wind. And I remembered. *Where does my*

217

help come from? Help me Lord. Help me, God, to help my friend! The silent prayer behind my cries for help. Still screaming into the wind, I let go of her hand and lowered myself into the water. She thrashed again, grasping at the air as if her hands could pull it down to her in the water.

With one hand gripping the branch that held her, I reached under, got my arm behind her head, gripped her shoulder, and strained to get her face to the surface. She clawed at my arm, trying wildly to pull herself up. The incredible strength of panic was in her grip, and I had to fight to keep her from pulling me down with her. But still I could not get her to the surface.

I peered into the water. Only six inches under, her eyes stared through the murky Missouri, pleadingly, into my own. Only six inches of water, six inches separating life from death. And I could not bring her up into the air. "Please, Lord," I prayed, "give us a miracle. Please move that tree."

Pearl's fight became weaker as her air gave out. The light in her dark eyes was dimming. I shouted for help, and pulled at her again. My miracle had not come. The tree still held her body. I stared down at her lips, still clamped shut, just starting to relax. She must breathe now, or die.

It was then that the Bible verse popped into my head: *Da machte Gott der HERR den Menschen . . . und blies ihm den. Odem des Lebens in seine Nase.*

The answer took root in my heart.

Gulping a lungful of air, I thrust my head under the water. I cradled her head in the crook of my arm. Pearl was not my creation, and I certainly was not God, but maybe the words from that memory verse—*Then God made man and blew the breath of life into his nose*—were just the miracle I needed. If I could do it. I found Pearl's mouth, made a seal between her lips and mine, and pulled at her jaw with my thumb, coaxing her to open. Still she pulled at my shoulders, trying to rise.

Then gradually she relaxed. Her mouth opened slightly and I knew she understood. Carefully, slowly, I exhaled, filling her with the air from my lungs.

Thank God for last-second inspiration. Another few moments and it might have been too late. I thrust my head above the water for more air, then went under quickly to give it to Pearl. Without pausing, I gave her two more quick breaths. It was something I shall never forget. Almost as if the power of God were alive in that air, I breathed life back into Pearl. At first, she thrashed wildly again, but I cradled her head and squeezed her to me, willing her to be calm. To panic now, might be to choke and drown. When she was settled, I gave her more air, and entered a pattern—breathe and shout for help, then breathe and duck under to Pearl. I dared not make a mistake. I dared not let myself panic. I dared not let water get into her mouth. It took so much concentration that I hardly even noticed the storm, except that the wind tore my voice away as I shouted. I kept praying, silently, in my mind. I was getting cold and tired. It could not have been long, but it seemed like forever before the roosters appeared, hazy, on the rain-swept deck. Three of them ran toward me, peering down at me in the water. I went down again, with more air. When I came up, I heard one of them shout, "Hannah, *vos tuost du*?" Paul. Thank God.

"I'm breathing for Pearl," I yelled. "She's stuck. You've got to move the tree!" I went under again. When I came up the three men had their backs braced, heaving at the tree. Still, it would not budge. One of the roosters yelled something about dragging it off with the steam capstan.

"No," I heard Paul shout. "It could rip her foot off."

"Better than drowning," the rooster said.

"It'll take too long anyway," Paul said. But the two roosters were running for the capstans. I ducked under with more air. When I came up, Paul was gone. I breathed for Pearl again.

And again. And then Paul was back, one of the splitting mauls for firewood in his hands.

The wind lashed at his shirt as he stretched himself over the water, examining the tree. His face went grim, and I knew he could see Pearl's face under the water. "I've got to chop this branch away," he yelled, pointing to the one I clung to. "You've got to get out of the way."

"I can't let go of her, Paul."

"Your hand is too close. I could cut it off!"

I tried to slide my arm farther down the branch, but it changed my position, and I could not cradle Pearl's head to give her air. I stayed where I was and gave her another breath. "Just do it, Paul," I said when I came up. "You never miss with an axe." It occurred to me that chopping a branch over the side of a storm-tossed boat, slippery with rain, and with nowhere to plant his feet, presented a greater challenge than chopping in a tidy wood yard. I put the thought from my mind.

Stormy waves lunged at the boat, rocking it and shaking the tree. "I can't do it," he said. "Give her more air. I'll find someone to help hold you while I chop the branch."

"Just hurry, then!" I took another breath, ready to go back under. He turned to go, a shadowy figure disappearing into the rain—just as Pearl's body jerked and convulsed spasmodically in my arm. Her muscles went rigid, then she began to thrash. She reached up, clawing at my neck. I let go the loudest scream of my life. Paul had to hear me. He had to hear me now! "Come back! Paul! Come now!"

Pearl thrashed harder. She must have got water in her windpipe, and her body was trying to cough it out. But how could she cough, under water? She would only take more in. She had get out now. Paul appeared again, hurrying, another man right behind him. He must have been coming anyway, it was so fast. I heard Paul shout for him to get something to reach me with, for me to hang on to.

"Paul!" I yelled. "You have to do it now! She's choking! Paul, she's drowning in my arms!"

He ran to the edge of the boat, getting into position. "Wait for the man," Paul said. "He'll find something to reach you with."

Pearl's body convulsed again. "Now Paul! Now!" I was crying, desperate. "Please, Paul, you have to do it!"

He peered into the water, and his face went white. "*Gott helf mich*," he cried, "God help me, please." He raised the axe high over his head. I saw the muscles in his body bunch as he unleashed his power. The steamboat bucked again, and I clamped my eyes shut tight, the image of the enormous axe head fixed in my mind—coming straight toward my fingers on the branch.

Chapter 49

When cousin George Stahl lost his fingers in the mill, he said at first it didn't hurt. There was just a numbing shock. I felt the shock go right up my arm as Paul's axe struck, and before I could open my eyes I was struggling to lift Pearl and keep myself from going under. The tree branch had suddenly let go. Five inches thick, and Paul had severed it with one blow. But my hand was numb and I was sinking in the water.

Quick as a juggler, Paul flipped the axe around and extended the handle to me. I reached for it, looking fearfully at my extended hand. Thank the Lord: my fingers were still there. Yet, I could barely grip the handle. My fingers must have been numb from hanging on so long in the cold, and from the jarring shock of the axe cleaving the wood.

Pulling with all my strength, I lifted Pearl's shoulders, but was too weak to keep her head above water. Then Checkela was there, leaping in beside me. Somehow, he held her up and shoved me to the edge of the boat. I grabbed Paul's hand. He hauled me out, and I flopped onto the deck like an exhausted fish. Even over the wind, I could hear Pearl panting and coughing.

A deckhand showed up with a crosscut saw and painstakingly cut through the branch next to Pearl's ankle. Sawing was slower than chopping, but there was even less room for error than there had been with my fingers, and with so much weight already pressing on the ankle, the sudden force of an axe blow might have crushed the bone.

Finally, the branch came free. Paul and the rooster lifted Pearl onto the boat. She curled over, coughing and belching until she could finally breathe again. Her ankle was bleeding and when she tried to stand her knee gave out. Paul knelt and cradled her head, caressing it. Then he picked her up and carried her, steady against the wind, toward the stairway. Pearl reached for me, brushing my arm as they passed.

For a few moments I watched them go, feeling unaccountably lonely. Then Checkela was with me, and together we walked toward the kitchen. What I really wanted was to sleep, but there was still breakfast to prepare. The crew would need their food. By now, more passengers had gathered. As we passed, several reached out, lightly touching my arms and shoulders. We all knew the boat was in peril, but we had beaten the storm out of one victory at least.

Checkela stopped me under the overhang of the boiler deck. "Don't you think you'd better go help with Pearl?" he asked, his mouth close to my ear.

"I need to cook. Besides, Paul is there," I answered.

"Somebody needs to get her into dry clothes," Checkela returned. "A woman should do it. I'll start the food."

Younger brother's wisdom. "You're right," I said simply. "Don't burn anything."

≈

It happened later in the morning. Pearl was safe in bed, her ankle bandaged where the tree had cut and bruised it. Her knee, too, was wrapped. Otherwise, she seemed none the worse for having almost drowned. I had helped her into dry clothes, and then Paul and I finished what Checkela had begun—while Checkela sat watch with Pearl.

The last of the food had been hauled upstairs by the

stewards. The storm still rocked the boat, and I braced my feet to finish scraping the skillet. The boat had nearly blown free of its moorings, but Captain Anders's crew had managed to bury two more deadmen. The lines held and the storm had begun to ease.

I wiped my brow with a cloth and leaned against the table. Finally, there was time to sit back. Only eight o'clock in the morning and I was exhausted. Paul leaned next to me. "Well," he grinned, "I never realized kitchen duty was so much work."

"You'll fit right in with the women back home," I teased, "now that you've had your training. You and Checkela both."

He grimaced. "I think I'll stick to farm work. But from now on I'll have more respect for what the women do. Of course, most of them don't have a slave driver like you ordering them around."

"When there is a job to do, it's best to knuckle into the dough and get it done, wouldn't you say?"

"I would, and I've never seen anyone who can knuckle into a job the way you can, Hannah." He stepped back and looked at me, appraisingly, as if I was something strange and unfamiliar. There was a look of wonder in his eyes that made me self-conscious. I smoothed my apron with my hands. I must have looked a sight. There had been no time to dry or brush out my hair, so I had simply put my extra *Tiechl* around my head and left the stringy mass of hair hanging down my back. My clothes were rumpled and splashed with bacon grease.

"You look like you're sizing me up for a new set of clothes," I scolded, staring back at him uncomfortably.

"You amaze me, Hannah. You always have. Who would have thought you could save someone by breathing into their lungs under water? Without you, Pearl would be . . ." He flinched at the thought. "She'd be dead."

Was there really nothing between them? "It was not my idea, Paul."

That surprised him. "Then whose?"

"Believe it or not, a verse just popped into my head. I believe the Lord showed me what to do."

"What verse?"

"You know the Bible. Can you guess?"

He thought, looking blank. Then he brightened and said, "*Eine richtige Antwort ist wie ein lieblicher Kuß.*"

"Don't be ridiculous. 'An honest answer is like a lovely kiss?' Believe me, that was anything but a kiss!"

He shrugged disarmingly. "You told me to guess. So I guessed."

He smiled, and I felt myself blush. *An honest answer is like a lovely kiss?* Our eyes met, and the intensity of his gaze took my breath away. "Hannah, there is no one like you, and I doubt there ever will be."

I felt the pulse quicken in my throat.

"I have thought so almost since the moment we met."

I swallowed. He continued. "Hannah, I lied when I said you should go to Lorenz Hofer. He could never love you the way you deserve to be loved."

My throat constricted. He went on in a rush. "But I can. Hannah, I don't care what you said in your letter. I love you, and I don't want to let you get away."

I gasped. They were the words I had longed to hear. He took a step forward, his arms opening before me. And suddenly it was too much. I held him back with my hand. A sob wracked my shoulders and I could not control my crying.

Chapter 50

At first he just hovered helplessly, probably wishing he had kept his feelings to himself. Even I hardly knew why I was crying.

"Hannah, if you don't feel that way about me . . . I'm sorry. But it's how I—"

I cut him off. "No, Paul. Don't say any more. It's not that." I couldn't let him apologize to me when all the confusion came from inside my own muddled head. The tears subsided and I tried to begin. "It's just that I thought that you thought . . . Well, I've never not understood myself this way before." I struggled for a sensible explanation. Then I gave up and just let it all out, a jumble of words and feelings that had been building for weeks. "Paul, it's just that I feel, well, I'm just trying to get by, you see, and you think I'm the strongest person you know. And you think I'm good and honest and perfect. And you don't even know how proud I've been, and how I wanted you and tried to let you go, and how scared I was for you and I had to be strong for Checkela, and how I've had to fight to trust God, and I didn't tell you I'm not interested in Harry though I tried, and how I lied to you, and I don't even like being around Lorenz Hofer . . ."

I took a huge gulp of air and plunged in again. "And this storm is blowing everything crazy and the tree was coming down on top of us and the axe came at my arm and it was so scary with Pearl under the water and only me to help her . . . And here you are, thinking I'm perfect and saying what I've always wanted to hear, and now it's just all mixed up." Finally, I ran out of air and quit talking. Maybe it was being tired that made everything seem hard, but I have noticed that just speaking your troubles can make them smaller. By the time I finished, I wondered if they had been worth so many tears.

Paul wrapped his arms around me and squeezed. "Hannah, *Lieba*. Everything is fine. I don't care if you're strong or weak or proud or afraid. Or if you are sometimes confused. You are who you are, and it's you I love—just that way."

I listened to the soothing sound of his voice, and let myself relax in the comfort of his arms. *Just that way?* It reminded me how the Lord accepted us, too. Just as we are. What more perfect love could there be?

As I had done at the ranch, I marveled at the strength and peace in the man Paul had become; it was such a contrast to the angry and hurting boy he had been in Russia. Then, he had desperately needed my help. Now I leaned on him.

Paul looked into my eyes. "Hannah, I want you to know, so you don't have to worry . . ." He grinned mischievously. "I think you are far from perfect."

I had to smile. "Thank you for the kind words. But be careful. I don't know how much kindness I can stand."

"I also want you to know . . . you are perfect for me." And then we talked, easily, comfortably. And it felt like coming home, home to the friendship I had known for so long and had feared lost when Paul went away over a year ago. Now, after a storm I thought would pull the world apart, I felt my world coming together. It was the perfect morning. Or, it was until Paul said, "There's just one thing I think you need to tell me. Why did you write all that stuff about Lorenz Hofer?"

Sometimes men are unbelievable slow, or maybe he knew and just wanted me to come clean. Whatever the case, I knew Paul deserved to hear my confession. I explained my shameful attempt at manipulation and admitted to being a fool. The lessons in humility just seemed to keep coming.

Paul listened patiently, and said at last, "I was the fool. I know you well enough that I should never have believed it could be you and Lorenz." He shrugged. "But maybe knowing you so well is why I believed it. I would never have suspected you'd play that kind of game." There was no recrimination in his voice. He was just stating the obvious.

"I'm sorry," I mumbled. "I've hated myself for it ever since. I can only ask your forgiveness."

"I forgive you a thousand times over—on one condition. Tell me who you really love."

His eyes were alight with either mischief or hope, I wasn't sure. But I took his hand and said, "I love you, Paul. It has taken me too long to be open about it, but I love you like . . . I don't know. I love you like morning loves the sunrise."

He raised his brow. "I like the sound of that."

I blushed. "Without you, it doesn't happen for me."

For once I saw the color rise in Paul's face. "Is that an honest answer?" he asked with a self-conscious grin.

"As honest as a lovely kiss."

And as our lips came together, I found out just how lovely a kiss could be. I felt the boat deck sway, and had no idea whether it was from the storm outside or the one raging in my breast. Nor did I care. I was in the arms of the man I loved.

Chapter 51

The final few days of our journey were disaster-free. The storm had passed on, leaving our boat damaged, but still afloat. Even as we got underway, the crew cut up the huge cottonwood tree for firewood. They patched the deck where it had been crushed on the portside edge and fixed the derrick pole. Pearl was soon up and about, though limping badly. Checkela, who had appointed himself her guardian and helper, carved one of the cottonwood branches into a crutch. Pearl had spirit, and helped in the kitchen as much as possible. Because Paul and Checkela were always on hand, my job was much easier than it had been on the way up.

As we neared Split Rock Colony, I found myself thinking how different the protected communal life was from life in the outside world. Out here, there had been a constant passing of new and different people. On the colony, except for birth and death, the people rarely changed. In the world, there were dangerous people to guard against. On the colony, except for a few squabbles, each person worked for the good of the other. In the world, lost and hurting people could be found on every corner. On the colony, everyone was looked after and the rest of the world was easy to forget. In the world, the challenges were different every day. On the colony, the days were regulated by tradition and routine.

I had seen the outside life on our trip from Russia, but this time I had lived it and been challenged at every turn. Life on the outside demanded a resourcefulness I had seldom needed on the colony. It had forced me to make life-changing decisions almost every day, with no one to rely on but God and myself. It had tested my faith, and I had almost failed. On the colony, it had been easy to think I trusted God without the onus of proof.

And I had seen another great difference. On the colony, life was held in check by rules and accountability. The watchful eye of the brethren and the elders made sure that everyone prayed, went to church, lived a sober life, avoided temptation of every kind. In the world, with temptation all around and no one to say *don't do it*, the strength to resist had to come from the heart and from God, or not at all.

In the old times of persecution, no one had been tested more than Hutterites. It had made us strong. But now, in times of peace, perhaps untested faith was our greatest weakness.

I had to admit that, in a way, I had enjoyed being on my own. And my faith had been tested in a way it had not been since the death of my father. I had traded a reliance on colony routine for self-reliance, and finally for a reliance on God. I'd had to leave home to find a stronger faith, and with it came a sense of fulfillment. Still, there was one thing that worried me.

Paul entered the kitchen, carrying a hindquarter of elk meat, and I said, "Paul, do you think you can be satisfied living on the colony after being away so long?"

"Why not?"

"Do you think you can come back to all the rules—give up your freedom?"

"That's the idea. You're not having second thoughts, are you?"

"Not me. But I was born to it, Paul. The colony will always be home to me. You know it was different for you, how you struggled at first."

He thumped the hindquarter onto the table and took my

hands. "It's home to me now, too, Hannah."

"It's not a perfect life, you know."

"Of course not, but I like it. Okay?"

"Then tell me what you like about it."

He winked. "It's where you live, which is where I want to be."

"Is that all?"

"Isn't that enough?"

"I don't think so, Paul." I had to make him understand. "I don't want you ever to resent me, if you can't stand communal life. There has to be more than just me."

"Look," Paul said, his eyes serious. "I've had a year to think and pray about it. I told you in Fort Benton that I am still a Hutterite. I meant it. I love the Hutterite people, the togetherness, the sharing. I know it falls short—way short sometimes—but the entire reason for having a colony is to live a life devoted to God. I found salvation *at home* on the colony. I believe it's where God wants me to live."

"Okay," I said, relaxing, "I just wanted to be sure."

"So are you?"

"Yes. And Paul?"

"What?"

"I love you."

"I love you, too," he said, "but we'd better get to work." He pulled a knife from the cutting block and began to cut steaks, which I threw onto the grille. I admired the ease with which he handled the knife, glad that in his hands it was a tool and not a weapon. Which reminded me. "You know, Paul, I've been wondering what became of Harry."

"Why, are you still interested in him?" he teased.

"Of course. As a friend."

"Are you sure that's all?"

"With Harry, it's plenty. Mind you, I did find him attractive."

Paul's brow furrowed and he wagged a finger at me. "Ah

ha! I thought so, though I can't understand why you would."

"You didn't see him at his best," I said. "In some ways, he reminds me of you."

"I don't believe it! How?"

I shrugged. "Well, he's built like you—not that big, but quick and wiry."

"That's just physical. It's the inside that makes a man, Hannah."

"Okay, he likes to help others, and he's kind. That's you, too, Paul. Inside, he is a good person."

"Except he carries gun, likes to fight, and drinks like a fish."

"Nobody's perfect."

"*Er is e Laid in Cnac*. From what I saw anyway."

I threw up my hands in exasperation. "Like I said, he reminds me of you. *You're* being a pain in the neck right now."

Paul grinned. "Okay, okay, Hannah. I'm sorry. I'm just trying to understand you."

"Well, you needn't be threatened by Harry, if that's it. You'll always be the only one for me."

Paul nodded. "I guess he can't be all that bad. In spite of what Pearl said, I think she was fond of him, too."

"He has a good heart. We might not have gotten to Fort Benton without him." I sighed. "I wish I could have repaid him."

"At least he doesn't have to worry about Carson Tate's lies any more. You helped sort that out—for Harry and me."

I nodded. "I suppose I wanted to help him change his life."

Paul kissed my cheek. "That's what I love about you, Hannah. You've always had that compassion. Remember the old Jewish man and the juggler back in Russia? I saw a crazy man and a thief; you saw people who needed God's love. You wanted to help."

I turned the meat on the grille. "But did it do any good?"

"I believe there comes a time when a man has to face up to his own frailty and turn to God. You helped me see that. Who knows, maybe something you said to Harry will help him see it too."

"Sure, maybe he'll be fine." I said it, but I had a feeling there were harder times ahead for Harry.

As Hutterites, we are an inward-looking people, maybe too much so. Hutterite prayers rarely extended beyond the concerns of the colony. But from now on, I would have at least one outbound prayer—a prayer for Harry Orman.

Chapter 52

My nerves tingled with excitement as we neared the colony. I had left with so much uncertainty; I was returning with new confidence. I had left to find Paul; I had done so, and discovered myself as well. I had left as a girl; I was returning as a woman.

The only uncertainty was the reception I would get from the elders. There might be a penance to pay for leaving. Paul, of course, would be confined to the colony for a time as well. It was the Hutterite way, and to be expected. I hoped the elders would welcome Pearl.

The only sadness was that Sannah would not be there. I could see it working on Paul's mind as we approached. Years ago in Russia he had thought he hated her, but later a bond had grown between them; a mother and son could not have loved one another more. Paul asked me several times for the details of her death, and everything she had said and done in his absence. I was glad I had been close to Sannah, and could tell him the things he needed to hear. That her last request should have been for me to find Paul gave us a feeling that our coming together had somehow been ordained.

Finally on July 23, Paul, Checkela, Pearl, and I joined Captain Anders in the wheelhouse where he had called us to say good-bye.

"Are you sure you won't change your mind?" the captain asked. "There's plenty of summer ahead, and you'd have a pocketful of money to take home in the fall."

I shook my head. "I can't thank you enough for all your kindness, Captain. But this is not my life."

He sighed, in mock consternation. "Ah, well, I have learned something about determination from watching you, young lady, and I know when I am beaten. With luck I shall make Yankton tonight, and I'll find someone to fill your shoes—if that be possible." He smiled so I couldn't tell if he was making fun of me or not. "There," he said, pointing, "I believe that is your destination just ahead." I peered into the distance, and sure enough, there were the chalkstone buildings of Split Rock Colony on the Missouri's north bank. Rising to the sunlight above the trees, the High House loomed like an enormous brick of shining gold.

"I can put you ashore in the yawl," he said, "almost at your door. But first I'd like to offer you a concluding bonus. Would you like cash for yourself, Miss Stahl, or free passage for one of your friends?"

"Captain, you are a wonderful man! A free passage would be lovely."

"I thought so," he said, pulling an envelope from his pocket and placing it in my hands. "One deck fare refund."

I gave it to Paul, and watched him give it Pearl. "Just in case you ever have need," he said.

Then the captain shook hands with us all, and we went down to the yawl. But not before I had turned back to the captain. Whether it was proper or not, I hugged him and kissed his cheek, much to the delight of the roosters standing nearby.

~

The two men assigned to row the yawl brought us around Bon Homme Island and glided to shore beside the mill. "*Ach*," Paul exclaimed in delight, "I could go straight to work right now. I've spent many good hours in there."

We thanked the oarsmen, and headed up the slope toward the old ranch house, which we called the Big House and used for kitchen and living quarters.

Checkela grabbed Pearl's bags and caught her by the arm. "Here, lean on me. I'll look after y—" His feet slipped out from under him, and the two of them almost landed in the river.

Pearl untangled herself from Checkela and picked up her crutch. "Thank you," she said, "but, please, I can do it."

With 140 people living in one yard, there was no hope of a quiet entry. Someone had spotted the yawl, and a crowd, cautious at first, gathered at the edge of the buildings. Then I heard the cries. "*Himble*—it's Hannah! And Checkela! God be praised, there is Paul!" The crowd poured down toward us, children first, running. Then the women.

Even without the men, most of whom were in the fields and barns, the commotion was nearly enough to scare Pearl back to the steamboat. Everyone was talking and shouting at once in German. The children circled around Pearl, their eyes big with wonder at the sight of this strange girl leaning on a stick, dressed like an *Englischer*. Were she in a mischievous mood, she could have yelled "Boo!" and sent the whole lot of them running for the houses.

And then Mueter was there, weeping and throwing her arms around me first, then Checkela. She had always been demonstrative. "Hannah, *Lieba*, thank God, you are safe from out there in the world." She was a small woman, though now a little rounder than she used to be. She nearly choked the life out of me, and I wondered where someone so tiny got so much strength. Then she was pulling at my clothes and touching my arms as if to make sure I was still in one piece. To Checkela she exclaimed in delight, "*Ach, ma Bua!*" and pinched her boy's cheeks the way we usually did to infants.

To his credit, Checkela swallowed his embarrassment and hugged her back. "I watched over Hannah, Mueter, and brought her back safe." He *would* have to make himself the hero. I wanted to pinch his cheeks myself—hard! Then my sisters were on us. I hugged Maria, and Checkela lifted Barbara into the air.

Several of the older boys gathered around Paul, asking questions and listening as if he were a messenger from heaven. But there was no family to greet him, and I sensed the emptiness that Sannah should have filled. Mueter must have felt it too, for soon she was smothering him with her own welcoming hugs.

Finally, I had the opportunity to introduce Pearl. For now, I said only that she was unable to be with her parents and would be staying a while. As we climbed the hill toward the kitchen, a group of women whisked Pearl away. She looked at me helplessly, as if to say, "What do I do?" I just smiled, raised my hands and shrugged. She might not understand a word they were saying, but she would know she was welcome.

Mueter got beside me and asked anxiously, "Did you not see *dai Fater*?"

I looked at her strangely. "How would I have seen my father? Isn't he out in the fields?"

"Of course not, Hannah," Mueter replied. "With Andreas he has gone. The two went on a steamboat to find you."

Chapter 53

My telegram! Had Sheriff Healy not sent it? "Mueter, didn't the colony get my message? I said not to come."

"*Joh, Lieba*, it came, but Andreas and your father followed only a week after you."

"A week! How did they know where?"

"They were asking everywhere. In Bon Homme a tavern man said you talked to him. A tavern man, Hannah! *Ayi yi*." She threw her hands up in despair. "Such places you go! I have worried ten years of my life away."

I stopped right there to hug her again. "I'm sorry, Mueter. I only did what I thought I had to do. Wait till we talk. You may yet think we've seen the Lord's hand at work."

"Well," she said, "at least you have found our Paul, exactly as you wished."

"*Joh*, Mueter." I smiled contentedly. "Exactly as I wished." I left it at that. Later there would be time to tell her more.

The next few days were an exciting time of acquainting Pearl with the ways of colony life. She was given a place to sleep in the attic room with me. After sharing her father's ranch house, it must have been a shock to stay in such a tiny apartment with so many people, but she did not complain.

Pearl did not have a job because Preacher Michael Waldner was away at one of the other colonies helping sort out a dispute between the elders and the community membership. When he returned, he would speak to Pearl about how she might fit into the colony. He would also decide about penance for Paul and me. Fortunately, we had not yet been baptized, so leaving was not considered so serious as it was for those who had officially dedicated their lives to the community.

Meanwhile, Pearl made friends quickly. Her leg was healing nicely, and with no shortage of tour guides she soon knew her way around the colony as well as anyone. Colony life was busy, and wherever there was work she was willing to pitch in.

She tried to help when Mueter and I sewed a new shirt and vest for my father, but after watching her, I think Mueter was afraid she would sew the buttonholes shut or put the pockets on backwards. So, she asked me to tell her in English that maybe she should start on something easier. I couldn't resist suggesting that she practice by sewing some new pants for Checkela.

When it came to cleaning and cooking, I could see that Pearl would fit right in. She knew how to squeeze a cow for milking, too, and I guessed she could show the younger boys a thing or two about riding old *Homercupf*, the horse. She was even learning some German.

Paul found himself helping put up hay—cut from the long prairie grass above the valley, then piled in rounded stacks like buns at a wedding feast. When that was done they began to cut the ripened wheat.

Paul and I still found time in late evenings to walk hand-in-hand along the river, listening to the ripple of water on its way from Fort Benton. Or sometimes we sat together up on the big hill between the vastness of the starry sky and the cozy glow of lantern-lit windows below. Under God's heaven and a part of God's people. And with Paul home, so much more promise for the future.

The sermon on the second Sunday after our arrival was based on Hebrews 13. Pearl had been permitted to attend. She sat on the women's side in the back pew, which was sometimes called the sinner's pew where those who had gone astray had to sit. But it was also for visitors from outside the faith. Pearl stood up and kneeled at the right times with the rest of us, but I doubt she recognized more than a sprinkling of words.

I sat with her to keep her company. Because Paul had abandoned colony life for such a long time, he could not come to church until Preacher Michael decided on a Sunday for him to be publicly accepted back into the fold.

Other than doing the necessary chores, Sunday was a day of leisure. I looked forward to spending it with Paul, and found him after church at the west end of the colony. He was in the cemetery, not far from where my adventure had begun, sitting by a mound of freshly turned earth. There was no marker, no stone. For Hutterites, it was not important to glorify the resting place of an empty shell. The real person had left it behind and gone on to a heavenly dwelling. There were no ghosts left behind either, and I rolled my eyes, remembering how Checkela had scared me the last time I was here.

I watched Paul sitting by the grave, lost in either thought or prayer. I backed quietly away to let him to come to terms with his loss, but he must have sensed my presence. He turned as if pulling back from somewhere far away, and smiled. "The girl with the big brown eyes," he said softly. "With the eyes I thought could see right into my pain. That was what I thought, Hannah, the first time I saw you at the cemetery in Hutterdorf. Now here we are again, and you still have those comforting eyes."

"I'm sorry, Paul. I know how you loved her." I went to him. "This time I am with you to share the pain."

"You shared it then, too," he said, enfolding my hands in his.

I remembered that day, how I had seen him standing by the grave of his mother and father in Russia. I had never seen anyone so bereft and alone in my life. Maybe because I knew something of what he was going through, I had wanted to help him. I had seen my own father lowered into the ground. But Paul had erected his loneliness and anger around himself like a wall.

That day he had looked up and our eyes had locked. Though I could not have guessed how our lives were to intertwine, I had felt a connection, as if something inside, something deep, had snapped together in that moment. And now, as he said, here we were again, this time at the grave of his mother's sister, who had shared so much healing with Paul, had loved him so dearly.

Then, Paul had been a lost and hurting boy, frail beneath a tough exterior. This time, he was strong clear through. I knew he was okay. But I asked him anyway.

"Yes, *Lieba*," he said, holding my hand. And as if to prove it, he kissed me, right there in the cemetery.

I admit that I kissed him back, but I couldn't help chiding, "*Himble*, Paul! In the cemetery yet!"

He raised an eyebrow in amusement. "What, Hannah, are you superstitious?"

Maybe there was just a hint of old Hutterite superstition lurking in the back of my mind, but I said, "No, of course not. It's just . . . well, it's unseemly, that's all."

"Nobody here is looking," he said. "Besides, I'm sure Sannah *Basel* would approve. After all, isn't she the one who sent you to find me?"

He was right. If anyone from here were looking, it would be Sannah, smiling down from heaven. "*Ach*, Paul, since you put it that way . . ." I threw my arms around him and offered my lips in the playful delight of another kiss.

Leaving the cemetery, holding hands and chatting, Paul asked innocently, "Do you think you might be ready to start studying for baptism?"

I caught my breath. "I have been giving it serious consideration, Paul." I watched him carefully, trying to read his meaning. Baptism meant taking a stand for one's faith, but also only the baptized were eligible for marriage. "And you? Are you ready to start learning all those verses?"

Paul's eyes twinkled. "The sooner the better. I am in the mood for memorization."

Never before had an afternoon that started in a cemetery filled my heart with so much gladness. By the time the supper bell rang, I was sure it could not get any better. About this I was right. I had thought it a perfect day. About *this* I was wrong.

As the evening meal ended, we filed out of the dining hall, men's side first, then the women. Pearl was chatting happily, her face bright against her black hair, when she froze so suddenly that several other women ran into her from behind. I laughed and caught her arm. "Hey silly, get your paddle wheel turning. Come on!" But her face had gone as white as sliced potato. Then I saw the man in the Montana-peaked hat. Standing at the end of the sidewalk was Carson Tate.

Chapter 54

A sense of excitement flashed through the crowd, and the people surged past Pearl, flocking directly toward Carson. Mueter pushed ahead of the others and I heard her happy cry, "God be praised!" With Carson were my father and Andreas, both smiling broadly. A saddled horse, soaking wet, cropped the grass nearby, and I could just make out a yawl rowing back to a steamboat far out in the river channel.

Fater and Andreas strode into the crowd while Carson waited at the corner of the building. For a few moments they tried to answer questions. Then Andreas spied Pearl. "Ah," he said, approaching and speaking in halting English, "you will be Pearl Tate." Pearl nodded. "Your Anson *Vetter*—I mean, your Uncle Anson—has come. I am sure you will be glad." Pearl stared at Andreas as if his words had come out in Portuguese instead of English.

Uncle Anson? What was he talking about? "Andreas, forgive me," I stammered, "but I think you are confused."

"No, *Ich vass*," he said, switching back to German. "I know, I know about the trouble with her father and the jail for Paul and all." I stared at him, too dumbfounded to translate for Pearl. "We spoke with the sheriff in Fort Benton, who told us of all these things—how you helped prove her father a liar, and how you and Paul brought her here. Hannah, it seems you were right about going to find Paul, and I thank you. Had you not listened to your heart—and to my dear

Sannah—Paul might have been lost.

"But the Lord works all things for the best," he continued. "We have even met the girl's uncle on the steamboat coming home. You see, he had learned of her father's evil, and had gone to Fort Benton to help her. But it seems he came late, just as we did. God be praised, he is here now to take her home with him to Wisconsin."

"Andreas *Vetter*," I said, using the word uncle myself as a term of endearment, "This man *is* Carson Tate, her father."

"No, this is the mother's brother Anson from Wisconsin. He has told us so himself."

"*Er lieg.*" It was Paul, appearing by my shoulder. He said it simply. "He's lying."

Andreas's jaw worked up and down in confusion. "But, but—" He turned to Pearl. "Is this not your uncle?" Everyone now stared, silent as January snow, waiting for her answer.

Pearl only swallowed and shook her head. Carson sauntered up the boardwalk. I put my hand on Pearl's arm. My father glared at Carson. "You have lied to us, every day on the boat as we traveled with you in good faith."

"I've come for what's mine," Carson replied casually. "I only said what was needed to make it easier. You come on now, Pearl. We'll be riding over to Bon Homme to wait for a steamer."

At first Pearl did not move. A wall of Hutterite men had slowly begun to materialize in front of her. I prayed without moving my lips, and Andreas said, "You need not obey him."

Carson's tone became harsh. "You didn't think I would let you go, did you girl? Did you think you could run out on me like your good-for-nothing mother? Now you come here." He pointed to the ground by his side. But she still did not move.

"Stay with us," I whispered to Pearl. Then my father said, "You have your horse, Mr. Tate. It would be best for you to leave."

Carson Tate's thin lips tightened to a bloodless slash in his face. He ignored my father. "Pearl, you will come. There's no judge or sheriff this time to hide behind. Don't expect Paul and his band of Hooterites to do anything for you. You know their stomach for fighting. Now, you saw that Indian boy, and you know me. Who else do you want to see die?" He waited, for effect, then said again, "Get over by your father."

Pearl's fists were clenched, but her whole body trembled. Finally, she hung her head and walked stiffly to her father. I caught at her sleeve, but she shook loose.

"You made the right choice," Carson said. "Now you get the horse and we'll go. When we get home, I'll buy you a nice new dress and all the fancy things you could never have with fanatics like these." Pearl shrunk in fear as he put his arm around her and said, "You know how I love you. You'll be happier at home."

I could stand it no longer. I pushed through and faced Carson. "Is this what you call love? To threaten your daughter, to bully her, to punch her, to scare her half to death when she doesn't do exactly as you like? To keep her like a prisoner out there at your ranch? I don't know how you have the nerve to call yourself her father. You have no idea how precious she is."

I took Pearl by the hand. "You don't have to go. He doesn't own you, Pearl. He has no power over you."

I'll say one thing about Carson Tate. He was quick. I barely saw it coming before I was lying on the ground with a pain in my head. I pulled myself to my knees, the flat, sick taste of blood in my mouth. He had backhanded me in the face. My lip was cut.

Then Paul was there, his face a mask of anger. He helped me up, and his hands felt like steel. His voice was low and dark. "Enough is enough! This time, Hannah, there will be no dancing." He turned to face Carson.

"No!" I cried. I caught Paul's arm, and pulled. "You were

right, Paul. I was wrong in Fort Benton. Don't let him win this way! Do we live what we believe or not? Is our faith real?" I gave Paul his own speech, and he hesitated. Pearl, too, was frozen. Carson stood to one side, dominating her by his presence, even as his violent eyes bored into me like a physical violation.

And that is when Mueter rushed forward. I braced myself for her onslaught. This was no time for her hugging and fussing. I could see the tears in her eyes as she came, but to my surprise the usual softness was gone. In its place I saw the heat of anger. She did not come to me, but marched straight to Pearl, caught her by the hand, and whisked her back to the people, out of Carson's reach. I heard her mumbling, "*Er is narish!*" I had to agree. If he wasn't crazy, who was?

Carson's voice roared, "Unhand my daughter! Pearl, get back here!" And suddenly, there was Checkela. Everything was happening so quickly that no one else had a chance to react. It was the problem with the pacifist position. When fighting seemed the natural answer, what else was there to do?

Checkela did not try to figure it out. He faced Carson like one of those bare-knuckled fighters on Captain Anders's steamboat. "You hit my sister. You are yelling at my mother. If you do anything to Pearl, it will be through me. She is staying with us."

"No, Check," I said. "It's not for us to fight. You don't know where it will end."

Carson's lip curled in anger, and I thought he was going to knock the stuffing out of my brother. But I was wrong. Carson merely lowered his hands—all the way to the waistband of his trousers and under his jacket. A woman shrieked as his right hand came up again. In it was a revolver, and it pointed straight at Checkela's chest.

Chapter 55

If the scene had been frozen a moment before, it melted into chaos at the sight of the gun. Had the devil himself jumped out of Carson's pocket, it would not have created a greater furor. Shouts of "*E Flintn!*" "*Er umbringan!*" sparked like lightning through the crowd as the men turned around, yelling to their wives—"A gun! He kills!"—and pushing the women toward the children. Behind the men, a whirlwind of skirts and aprons fluttered and flapped as the women caught their children and rushed them behind the chalkstone walls to the kitchen. I caught sight of the widow Justina Wallman hustling my sisters around the corner. Then the commotion ended as quickly as a prairie dust devil blows itself out. A standoff remained. On one side, Carson and Checkela faced one another. On the other, Pearl and my mother held hands. Between them stood the barricade of Hutterite men.

Carson called his daughter, just as he had before. "Pearl, get the horse. You and I are leaving." Just as before, Pearl did not move. "Pearl, come now, or you will have dead Hutterites on your conscience."

"Don't listen to him, Pearl." It was Checkela, still defiant, but I thought I could see a tremble in his pant legs.

Andreas spoke up. "Do you not know there is a law to answer to? Do you think you can murder and go free?"

"You have stolen my daughter. You are holding her captive. I am in the right."

"Sheriff Healy and Judge Tattan know better," Paul said.

Carson's eyes shifted uncertainly from side to side, his confidence wavering. He should have known he was beaten. Still, he held the gun on Checkela.

"If you are hung for murder, will you have your daughter with you then?" Paul asked. "Leave us in peace."

"No bunch of weak-kneed, Bible thumping home wreckers tells me what to do!" His hand had begun to shake. There was a desperate, irrational look in his eye. "Pearl, get over here, or I am telling you I will start right now by shooting this boy!" Pearl did not move. "I will not be defied," he snarled.

I had no idea what to do. We couldn't ask Pearl to leave with this madman, but somebody had to do something and quickly, or my brother could die. And how many others? Truly, he was *narish*. He seemed to have gone beyond caring whether he could get away with it or not. He wanted to win. I knew he would kill. I had seen the Indian boy. Carson cocked the gun.

My father, his slim face a crisscross of hard angles, stepped forward. "Wait! I wish to stand for my son. If you will shoot, begin with me." He walked toward Carson.

"Get back!" Carson shouted. "Or he'll be dead before you take another step."

That was when Pearl finally broke away from my mother. She pushed through the sheltering line of men. "No father," she said. "Not this way."

He grinned a leering, unbalanced kind of grin, and chuckled. "Good, good. It's about time you did as you were told. Now get the horse."

But there was something different in Pearl this time. Her mouth was firmly set, and she stood straight, not cowering. "No, Papa, I'm not going with you. I will not be locked away to hide the truth of your evil. If you harm anyone here I will go to the law myself. You won't stop me."

If Pearl had expected her father to give up that easily, she was mistaken. He jabbed the gun like a finger three times into Checkela's chest and cursed. "Daughter, get that horse, now, or I swear this boy's death will be your doing!"

Pearl did not get the horse. With some of her father's quickness, she shoved herself between Checkela and the gun. She grabbed the startled man's wrist and pulled the gun barrel against her own breast. "There, father, will you kill? Will you start with me? One way or another, I stay." Then she said one of the German words she had learned, loudly enough for the men to hear. "*Beitn! Beitn!*"

She didn't have to plead. I'm sure everyone was already praying under their breath. I know I was, and I knew the women would be praying in the kitchen.

"What does that mean?" Carson asked angrily.

"That you don't have the power to do this," Pearl said. "That I'm trusting a better father than you."

"What is a father's love?" It was Andreas. He pointed to my father and said to Carson, "Two fathers. This one is willing to die for the love of his child. Does your kind of love allow you to kill yours?"

"Shut up!" Carson's hand was white on the gun, and he stared wildly into his daughter's eyes. It was strange to see how Pearl's courage had shifted the power.

Carson held his daughter's life between his finger and the trigger. But the power of fear over his daughter had been broken. The real power had shifted to Pearl. He could no longer smother her will. As he realized it, staring helplessly into her eyes, something crumbled inside of him. The hard edges of his face sagged almost imperceptibly. "How can you do this to me?" he asked bitterly.

"You have to go now," Pearl replied simply.

Carson pulled the trigger, his thumb holding the hammer and easing it harmlessly back into the body of the gun. Pearl let go of her father's wrist, and his arm dropped to his side.

"After all I have done for you, you side with this band of fools!" He squared his shoulders, trying to salvage his dignity. But he knew he was beaten. I have often thought how strange it is that when someone corrupted by evil can no longer make you afraid, the pathetic emptiness inside becomes so visible. I had seen it in the crazy Russian, ruined by what had happened to his sons, and in Vladya the Great, the juggler, worn down by his unprincipled life. I saw it in Carson now. Something pitiful.

"You will regret this," he said. "These people are not you. When you can't stand it here any longer and are scratching to survive on your own, do not expect me to take you back."

"Please go," Pearl said evenly.

Carson glared at the Hutterite men, still watching quietly, still standing with Pearl. They knew better than to risk setting him off again with more words. Even Checkela stayed quiet. Carson walked stiffly to his horse, picked up the reins, and pulled himself into the saddle. "You are no better than your mother," he said to Pearl. He walked the horse deliberately along the kitchen boardwalk, then made for the roadway past the cemetery toward Bon Homme.

Pearl watched him go. "My mother was better than you," she said, more to herself than anyone else. Her face was streaked with tears.

Paul tried to go to Pearl, but I was gripping his arm, unknowingly holding him back. I looked at Pearl, and thought how I had disliked her, had disliked Paul's nearness to her. *Naidish*, Checkela had accused. He had been right. And it was only in letting go, in surrendering my will to God's, that I had learned how to love them both. I released Paul's arm, and together we went to her, to this incredibly brave, weeping girl with a tiger-like faith growing inside. With us were Checkela and my mother, all of us surrounding our Pearl, enveloping her with caresses, with hugs, with reassurance. Enveloping her with love, the love of family and of home.

∾

"Oww, *dos tut veia*," I smiled, reluctantly pulling back from Paul's lips.

"I'm sorry." Paul said, breathlessly. "I shouldn't have kissed you. I forgot your cut."

"No, never stop kissing me. You'll have to be tender, that's all." I put my hand on his chest, feeling the muscles beneath his shirt. He pulled me to him, and my neck tingled with the warm caress of his breath. "I want always to be with you," I murmured.

His hands roved up my back and down again. Then he pulled me tightly against him, into the strength of his body. My heart shivered and I could hardly breathe. I had never felt so alive.

"Hannah, I will never leave you again," Paul whispered. "This is my home, our home together."

He released me and we stood together on the big hill, holding one another's arms. I sighed contentedly. Below, the heavy chalkstone buildings of Split Rock Colony sat firm and strong in the valley, the cornerstone of our existence.

The light slowly faded, and I watched the glimmering river, a golden thread in the reflected light of the cliffs. It would always be there, the great Missouri, flowing past the circumscription of our lives in Split Rock Colony, a reminder of the beauty and corruption of the outside world.

From somewhere far off came the throaty moan of a steamboat whistle. I felt a shiver in my spine, and the touch of God's guiding hand that we so often do not understand. I smiled and gazed into the beauty of Paul's eyes. Deep gray in the evening light, I saw peace, and the reflection of my love. I felt the depth of Paul's desire, the awesome wonder of our togetherness, and the promise of so much more to come.

His arms opened, and I nestled back into the enfolding perfection of his embrace. I stood on tiptoes, lifting my arms to his neck as he pulled me closer. Our lips came together in a kiss, tenderly, oh, so tenderly in the fullness of our love.

Afterword

Fact or Fiction?

This novel is intended as neither a history book nor a sociological study. However, the details of Hutterite life and beliefs, riverboat travel, and life in Fort Benton are accurate to the best of my understanding. For those instances where I have missed the mark, I apologize.

Though Split Rock Colony is fictional, readers familiar with the colonies of South Dakota may note a similarity to Bon Homme Colony on the Missouri River near Yankton. Bon Homme is the oldest continuously occupied colony in North America. Remarkably, Bon Homme's present minister is a direct descendant of Michael Waldner, one of the Hutterite's founding fathers in America.

The adventures of Hannah, Checkela and Paul are fictional, yet certainly within the realm of possibility. The early years in America were a time of adjustment for the Hutterites, with an ebb and flow of people joining and leaving the colonies. Hutterites were occasionally involved in extraordinary adventure or tragic misadventure. For instance, one man disappeared mysteriously in New York City while returning from a trip to Russia. His luggage was found, but he was presumed by many to have been murdered.

When the River Calls is set during the last days of the great Missouri River steamboat trade, just before the railroad pushed west to Fort Benton, ending the era. The rugged mountain sternwheelers plying the river's changeable waters would have been a familiar sight to the Hutterites of Bon Homme Colony. Except for the *Silver Mist* and the *Sundown*, all the boats named were real and on the water during the summer of 1880.

Fort Benton was a thriving western town, wild and woolly in 1880, though less so than in the 1860s when it had been one of the most violent towns in the American West.

Fort Benton's I. G. Baker company was the major supplier to Canada's North West Mounted Police; Mounties, and bull trains loaded with supplies bound for Canada were common sights in Fort Benton.

The Cypress Hill Massacre in Canada, and its connection to Fort Benton and *The Extradition* hotel, is well documented, as is the casual murder of Indians in and around Fort Benton. The reference to the problem of opiate addiction is also accurate. Opiate drugs were legal and widely available in America at the time.

Sheriff John Healy and Judge John Tattan are historical. John Healy was, indeed, a multi-faceted man, involved in the whiskey trade so damaging to the Indians, yet much admired for his skill as an enforcer of the law. Judge Tattan's dented belt buckle is on display in Fort Benton's *Museum of the Upper Missouri*. However, the words and actions of John Healy and Judge Tattan in the present story are purely fictional.

Most other characters found in the pages of this book are fictional, bearing no relation to anyone living or dead.

While the fictional Hannah Stahl does not entirely approve of the historical Fort Benton, this in no way reflects poorly on the town of today. It is a friendly and fascinating place, alive with history and character.

Who Are the Hutterites?

In one sense, they are a people locked in time. Named after Jakob Hutter, an early leader, they are the oldest group of communal-living religious people in the Western world. Because the Bible (in Acts 2 and 4) records that early Christians shared their possessions, the Hutterites adopted a communal lifestyle, living together in colonies and sharing all of their resources. They continue to live that way today.

Like the Amish and Mennonites, the Hutterites began as Anabaptists. They believed in adult baptism, pacifism, and in living by a direct interpretation of the Bible rather than the rules of the Catholic Church. Because of these beliefs, Jakob Hutter was burned at the stake, and many others were imprisoned, tortured, or executed.

To escape persecution in Germany, Switzerland, and Austria, many Anabaptists sought safety in Moravia, where the Hutterite lifestyle began. They lived there for almost a hundred years before being savagely driven out. Escaping to Hungary, they lived in peace for a time. Then persecution began again, and the Hutterite beliefs were almost completely stamped out. They survived only because several wagonloads of Hutterites had been kidnapped earlier and taken to live in Romanian Transylvania where they were safe for a while. Eventually more trouble forced them to escape to Wallachia, where the Hutterites once more built colonies—in the middle of an area soon to be fought over by the Turks and Russians. The colonies were repeatedly robbed, and most were eventually burned to the ground by bandits and Turks, who killed many of the men and abused the women.

A Russian general finally saved the Hutterites by giving them a letter of safe passage to Russia, where they settled and lived peacefully for a hundred years. In 1874, with worrisome changes in the air, the Hutterites once more looked for a land of promise. At first, not all were willing to move. However, within five years all but about a dozen had settled in America, where three colonies were established. The first, on the Missouri River, near Yankton, South Dakota, was named

Bon Homme Colony. The other two (*Wolf Creek* and *Old Elmspring*) were built along the James River to the north. The three colonies tried, but failed, to work together under a single authority. Though they maintained the ties of faith, they gradually broke into three distinct groups, now known as the *Schmiedeleut, Dariusleut* and *Lehrerleut.*

Of the approximately 1,265 Hutterites who settled in America, only about 425 joined the colonies. Today, that number has multiplied by a hundred times, and there are colonies in five states and four Canadian provinces.

Modern Hutterites

Hutterites live according to traditions that are nearly 500 years old. With up to 150 people living on a colony, everyone shares duties of farming and daily living. They even eat together in a large, communal dining hall. Like the Amish, Hutterites do not believe in using devices like computers, televisions, radios, or musical instruments for entertainment. Unlike the Amish, however, they use the most up-to-date technology available for their farm work.

The Hutterite lifestyle—from furniture and types of clothing worn, to the age when a couple may marry, to the time when a man must grow a beard—is strictly controlled by the rules of Hutterite tradition. To outsiders, the rule-bound Hutterian lifestyle may seem restrictive and harsh, yet the people are contented, fun-loving, and generous. While some Hutterites may have fallen into the trap of living more for colony rules than for God, most have an abiding faith in Jesus Christ that brings contentment and peace. This faith has given the Hutterites the strength to survive centuries of trouble, to become the prosperous and growing society they are today.

Glossary of Hutterisch Words and Phrases

Note: Hutterite German, or *Hutterisch*, is not a written language. Hutterites read the High German Luther Bible, but speak Hutterisch for everyday communication. In the glossary of *When Lightning Strikes* I reported that because there was no Hutterite dictionary I had found it necessary to invent spellings for most of the words I used. Since that time, I have discovered the *Hutterian-English Dictionary* and a grammar and lexicon called *The Hutterian Language*. These resources, which have proven invaluable to me, were written and published by Dr. Walter B. Hoover of Saskatchewan, Canada, in an effort to preserve the Hutterian language.

In the interest of preserving the continuity between *When Lightning Strikes* and *When the River Calls*, I have strayed somewhat from Dr. Hoover's spellings, and have kept with the usual German practice of capitalizing nouns. Any mistakes in my rendering of the language are my own, and not Dr. Hoover's.

Basel: aunt
beitn: to pray
Bist du narish?: Are you crazy?
Bua: boy
Cum Bruder: Come, brother.
dai: your
Der Jüngste Tag: the judgment day; literally, doomsday

Dos tut veia: It hurts.

Doss is recht: That is right.

Du bist e Engala: You are an angel.

Du Nookela Cupf: You dumpling head.

Dumhait: stupidity

Flintn: a gun

e Mandle: a boy

Englischer: An English person. Term generally used to refer to any non-Hutterite person.

Er is e Laid in Cnac: He is a pain in the neck.

Er is narish: He is crazy.

Er lieg: He is lying.

Er sauft di gonsa Tsait: He drinks all the time.

Er umbringen: He kills.

Fater: father

Gea hinter: Get back.

Gea vecch: Get away.

Gemein: the Hutterite community, or colony

Gott helf mich: God help me.

guot: good

Himble: heaven

Holt daina Freisn: Hold (or shut) your (big fat) mouth.

Homercupf: Hammerhead

Hutterisch: Hutterite language

Ich vass: I know.

joh: yes, pronounced *Yo*

Katus: Hutterite boy's cap

Lieba: Love, used as a term of endearment

Mensh: man

Mueter: mother

naidish: jealous

Prairieleut: prairie people. The name given to Hutterites who opted to live independently in North America (often homesteading) instead of joining a colony.

Sholch: scoundrel
shtila: (be) quiet
Shvainhok: pigpen
Tiechl: a shawl or kerchief to cover the head
Tsucer: sugar. Tsucer pie is a traditional, very sweet pie
Vecchclufner: a runaway from the colony
Vos host du getoan: What have you done?
Vos tuost du?: What are you doing?
Vos: what

The Author

An award-winning author and teacher, Hugh Smith lives in rural Alberta, where he has taught in a Hutterite colony school. Smith's extensive research and firsthand knowledge of Hutterites and rural life give authenticity to this novel and to the first book in the series, *When Lightning Strikes*. In addition to his novels, he has written numerous articles and  co-authored a history resource book and several collections of comedy skits for schools and community theaters.

Nicola Ford